PISCES HOOKS TAURUS

Signs of Love #4

ANYTA SUNDAY

First published in 2018 by Anyta Sunday,
Contact at Bürogemeinschaft ATP24, Am Treptower Park 24, 12435 Berlin,
Germany

An Anyta Sunday publication
http://www.anytasunday.com

ISBN 978-3-947909-02-5

Cover Design: Natasha Snow
Pisces and Taurus Art Design: Maria Gandolfo (Renflowergrapx)

Content Editor: Olivia Ventura at Hot Tree Editing
Line Editor: HJ's Editing
Proof Editor: Labyrinth Bound Edits

Warning: This book contains sexual content and a main character who takes
bromance to a new level entirely.

For Julien and Ryan.
You are a beautiful couple.

We are all fools in love.

—Jane Austen

Chapter One

Zane Penn was horny for three things in life: his art, pecan nuts, and romance.

He strode through the suburbs with a fake bearskin rug draped over his back, its terrifying head nestled over his shoulder. The back of his T-shirt was damp with sweat—it had been an uncomfortable sixteen-block walk from the secondhand store.

Or in more optimistic words: the ultimate Prince Charming workout.

Late afternoon sun streamed into his eyes. He winced and hooked the bear's head over his own, its long polyester-covered plastic jaw shielding him. He hunched to keep the heavy rug from slipping.

A skater in a baggy T-shirt passed him with a snicker. "Halloween's six months away, man."

True, but he had a date tonight.

All he had to do was ask SmoothSinger to meet in person.

They hadn't shared their real names yet, but they'd already been chatting for two days. Their chats were pleasant with a small serving of must-have cheek.

This morning, Zane woke with a funny flutter in his gut. He was close to the holy grail of romance: love at first sight. He just knew it.

The bear head slipped, and sunshine warmed his smile.

Mark his words. By the end of the month, he would be happily married and making love in the twist of fresh sheets, his hard body intimately tormenting hers into spiraling arousal.

It'd be *perfect.*

It'd happen before his visa ran out.

He unlatched a chain-link gate and hoofed up the path toward a brick bungalow. He'd spent almost two years traveling Europe, Canada, and the States and had settled in Redwood, one of the quaintest cities he'd visited, three weeks ago. His flatmates had been far less welcoming. But oh well. Couldn't have it all.

A cloud of weed-laced smoke hit him as he entered. His flatmate Rex slouched on a threadbare couch, tracking him with his eyes.

"What the—" Rex's joint fell out of his mouth and he chased it to the floor. He plucked it up. "You know what today is?"

"Saturday."

"Jane will be back from Minnesota any minute. So, you know . . . ." Rex sucked on his joint and frowned as Zane shook off the bear rug. The frown grew as he spotted Zane's jandals. "Flip-flops? It's spring out there. Aren't your feet cold?"

Said the buck-naked guy swathed in smoke.

Zane backed into his bedroom with a shrug. "Can take the Kiwi out of the country, can't take the country out of the Kiwi."

He shut his door on a billowing cloud of approaching smoke, flung the bear on the bed, and jumped next to it. He grabbed his phone and stared at the bear's beady eyes. "She's online, shall we?"

Zane typed and excitedly flicked the bear's large bared teeth.

"*You said you liked taking the bear by the tooth. Want to take it tonight?* My message sounds good, right?" Later, he'd rock up to his date with the bear draped over him, she'd laugh, and fifty years later they'd be telling their Meet Cute to their great-grandchildren.

His phone vibrated and he eagerly read.

SmoothSinger: Yes, but I like NSA

He'd gone to such lengths to get the bear, but sure, they could watch the stars, too.

PrinceAbroad: Space is awesome. One of my brothers studies astronomy.

SmoothSinger: Wtf? NSA not NASA.

Zane blinked and slammed the end of his cell phone against his forehead with a groan. He flashed a meek smile at the bear and typed.

PrinceAbroad: LOL. I'm an idiot. :P So, NSA . . . Gonna be a spy or something?

SmoothSinger: What college did you say you went to?

PrinceAbroad: I didn't say. I, uh, didn't go to college.

SmoothSinger: FYI: NSA = No Strings Attached.

No strings. Oh. Of course.

He glared at the low ceiling, his hollow laugh echoing in the bare room.

PrinceAbroad: I like strings. A lot of them.

His dream? To be a tangled heap of nose-bumping spaghetti Bolognese and meatballs with someone.

No response yet.

He rolled off the bed and sank into the creaking chair at a small table he'd turned into a desk. He strapped on his headphones and blasted The Smiths' "Please, Please, Please Let Me Get What I Want."

Hyped on the music, he sent another message.

PrinceAbroad: Do you want to meet tonight?

He'd failed relationships at the Meet Cute stage before. Multiple times. Most times, to be honest, although not usually *before* the Meet Cute.

PrinceAbroad: Hello?

His scalp prickled with a cringe. He shouldn't have added that last hello. It pushed idiocy to its limits.

Sighing, he tossed his phone next to his beloved drawing tablet, picked up a stylus, and swiped through the illustration panels he'd been hired to craft for *Scarlet Sentinel vs. Fire Falcon*.

The panels were due to the author tonight. He'd slaved over them all week, staying up past midnight every day. They were done. Why couldn't he bring himself to send them off?

He'd followed Rollo's instructions down to the letter, except . . . the second-to-last half-page panel didn't convey enough emotion. If Fire Falcon were half-hidden in the shadows and smiling wryly, a deeper level of meaning could surface in the story. Rollo didn't ask for it, but . . . .

Crafting a second version couldn't hurt, right? If Rollo didn't want it, Zane would give him the first version.

Besides, starting a new sketch would keep his mind off his failure with SmoothSinger and his one-hundred-dollar splurge on a faux bearskin rug.

He tapped his stylus against his chin in time to the music. Never mind. He'd find true love; he felt it in his chinny-chin-chin.

He was nothing if not a glass-half-full kind of guy.

A pounding knock sounded at his door and his flatmate Jane barged in with a burst of weed air. She scanned the room with a growing frown.

Zane pulled his earphones to his neck.

"You know what day it is?" she snapped.

"Funny, you're the second person to ask me that."

"You were supposed to move out. I told you my sister's coming. I need the room."

She'd mentioned her sister, but he didn't understand that she wanted him to leave. Had he misunderstood? Wouldn't be a first.

Jane gave him an exasperated look. A look he knew well.

The hazards of being a dreamer meant eliciting that pinched look on a weekly basis. Daily basis. *Bi-hourly* basis.

Zane gathered his tablet, phone, and stylus. "Your sister needs the room. Sure, yeah. I've scheduled an Uber. Should be here any minute now."

"I need to make the bed fresh."

Zane needed to schedule an Uber.

"You have ten minutes," she said, twisting on her heel.

Zane packed his unfinished panel. He stuffed hoodies, jeans, and mismatched socks into a dusty cardboard box and laid his comics, electronics, and a secret stash of pecans in his suitcase.

He side-eyed the bear. "You scare the freak out of me. But I couldn't bear to leave you here with them."

He squished the rug on top of the box, its head flopping over the cardboard flap. Hefting the box and dragging his suitcase, he rushed a goodbye to his flatmates and headed out into the darkening evening.

Under a streetlamp, he set down his belongings and zipped up his hoodie against a biting May breeze.

His ride—a yellow Subaru—would arrive in ten minutes.

He stared at his fast-numbing toes. It was a bit chillier now than it had been two hours ago.

He rummaged through his clothes to his sneakers. Eureka! He pulled out a pair of mohair ankle socks and slipped them on under the jandals.

Ready to hike the Himalayas, Zane searched for a hotel.

He called one that looked promising and was met with a laughing snort. "You know what day it is, right?"

He was sick of that question.

The concierge continued, "It's the day before Redwood's annual marathon. The weekend's booked solid. Not just this hotel, all of them. Hostels and anything via Airbnb. Dude, you are under the bridge tonight."

"Surely there'll be a couch somewhere."

The concierge laughed and hung up.

Didn't hurt to double check.

Triple check.

Quadruple check?

Crap. No one offered so much as a bathtub anywhere.

He rubbed his phone against his forehead and laughed. How did he always get himself tangled in these situations? The frustration almost had him scrolling through Tinder for an NSA hookup.

He groaned and called his oldest brother, Jacob.

His brother answered, "Sorry, Zane. Gotta be quick. What's up?"

Zane settled his ass on the lip of his box. "I don't have a place to sleep for a few days. Could I bus to your farmhouse? Or maybe you know someone in town I could crash with?"

A muffled exchange, and then a shriek.

"Okay, um . . . a bit tricky . . . um . . . ."

"Are you okay?" Zane asked.

"Haha, yes, no. I mean, Anne's having contractions, and I'm beside myself being useless."

"Oh, oh! Contractions. So, the baby's . . . . Yeah, you're a bit busy, then. Totally don't worry about me. I'll figure things out."

"You need somewhere to stay, I'll think of something—"

Anne's ragged voice surfaced from the background. "My brother's, of course. No, wait, his place leaks and he's crashing with his boyfriend. Fuck!"

"Hold on, sweetheart," Jacob said. "We're headed to the hospital."

Anne gasped something about the stars and "birthday." Jacob must have been carrying her because her voice sharpened down the line. "Becky lives near the university. Send Zane there."

"Professor Fisher?" Jacob sounded doubtful. "You two are good again?"

"Water under the—motherfucker."

Sounded promising.

Jacob hurriedly spoke to Zane. "I'll text you Becky's number. I have to drive my wife to someone qualified. The baby isn't supposed to arrive for another two weeks. Holy shit, I'm gonna be a dad."

Zane was going to be an uncle! "I'm thinking of you. Call me as soon as she's in your arms."

Jacob laughed, swore, and disconnected. Zane grinned like a loon. An uncle! Jacob, a dad. Crazy shit.

The cardboard under his ass gave in, and his feet whipped into the air. Polyester fur cushioned him, and the bear's head bobbed with the jerking flap like it was laughing.

In the belly of the beast was how the Uber driver found him.

Zane struggled out of the box, introduced himself, and made quick work of piling his things into the back seat. His phone buzzed with Becky's number, and Zane slung himself in the front seat.

His driver tipped his baseball cap. "You were unclear where you're going."

He still was. In the physical sense. Not in life. In life, Zane was 100 percent sure he would settle down and marry. He would spend his weekends visiting Jacob and his almost-niece and be the best uncle ever.

The driver cleared his throat.

"I don't have an exact address," Zane said. "Could you head toward Treble?"

A short nod. "You got ten minutes to find a street name and number, or I'm leaving you at the campus."

Zane copied Becky's number and messaged her.

Zane: Hi, Becky.

His finger slipped, and he sent the message.
Becky replied before he could explain.

Becky: Sorry, who is this?

Zane: Sent that too fast. I'm Zane. Anne gave me your number. Sorry to bother you, but I wondered if you'd let an out-of-luck guy crash with you a couple of

nights? Long story. Stupid marathon. Kinda desperate.

Becky: I'm not in the habit of letting strangers sleep in my house.

Zane: Random guy in your safe space. I get that. But maybe I can convince you?

Zane sweated three minutes for a response.

Becky: Go on then, twist my arm.

Zane: I'm certifiable for romance and comics and I love eating babies and cats.

Becky: What kind of monster are you?

It took Zane a second to realize his mistake.

Zane: A coma monster!

Becky: Comma?

Zane: The little things used for pauses?

Becky: I just snorted my wine. You don't know me, but I *never* snort my wine.

Zane: Snorting? That's a good sign. So can I crash with you? You can lock me in a room until morning if that makes you more comfortable.

Becky: That would make me the monster.

Zane: I'm a regular guy, promise. Bit cheeky. Big dreamer. Bigger idiot.

Another couple of minutes passed. His driver was nearing Treble.

His phone dinged. It wasn't Becky but a woman he had chatted with over LoveBugsDating.

FireAndNice: We messaged a few weeks ago? Good connection, bad timing? The guy I was dating turned out to be a dud. You up for meeting?

Zane spun off a message, suggesting they hook up for drinks tomorrow night.

His driver cleared his throat. "You have no idea where you're headed, do you?"

Zane tapped his phone, praying for a message.

Ding!

Becky: I'm in the middle of hosting a small get-together tonight. Why don't you come around and convince me in person?

He grinned at the driver. "I'm headed for Becky."

Becky sent her address, and his driver tapped it into the navigation. She was two streets off. Estimated time of arrival: one minute.

Zane paid the driver, adding a hefty tip.

Zane: Be there soon, Becky.

Becky: Only very, very close friends call me that.

Zane: Sorry, Rebecca. How presumptuous!

~

ALSO PRESUMPTUOUS: TOTING HIS BELONGINGS UP THE PATH TO Rebecca's half of the duplex.

Zane hugged his box, gripped the handle of his suitcase, and trundled down a brick path.

On the neighboring side of the tidy duplex, an elderly woman sat on a porch swing and watched him over the low picket fence.

He drummed his fingers over the box in an awkward wave.

"Moving in?" she croaked, hand flexing on her walking stick.

"If I can convince Becky to let me." Rebecca, damn. Better remember that! "I'm nervous."

She squinted, pointing her walking stick at him with a delighted squeal. "You're a fish."

Zane paused. He smelled like a fish? Or did she mean he was a dish—as in, good-looking?

He ducked his chin and sniffed. No fish, only the woodsy deodorant he'd put on this morning.

"You have a watery glow about you," she said. "Friendly, aren't ya? Wear emotion where everyone can see it." She took him in from head to toe. "Quite the catch, too."

He set down his belongings, tucked the bear into the box, and offered a warm smile. "Catch? Are you trying to reel me in . . . ?"

"Darla. But _you_ can call me darling."

Zane chuckled and pressed the metal doorbell. "Wish me luck, darling."

"Sounds like they disabled it for the party," she said. "Just give me your name and go in."

The door swung open and three primly dressed women

sauntered outside. "Thomas Pynchon? I've read one of his works. *Gravity's Rainbow*, it's . . . well, take it from my shelf and experience it yourself."

Zane pressed himself against the cool fence pickets, letting the women pass. He bounced his palms over the rounded spikes and grinned at Darla. "I'm Zane," he said over drowning chatter. "I hope you'll need to remember that."

"I'll commit it to memory, Zane." Darla studied him like a full-page comic panel. "Yes. You're just what a broken bull needs."

Broken bull? What was the colorful old darling talking about?

"The professor loves literature," she said through a bout of coughing. "My advice? Talk books. Talk Dostoyevsky and *Toy Story*."

Dostoy-what's-it-called or *Toy Story*. He hadn't known *Toy Story* was a book first. Good thing he'd seen the movie. "Thanks for the tip. Think you could keep an eye on my things?"

"Sure," she said. He stepped over the threshold, and her voice trailed after him. "If anyone tries to steal it, I'll whip out the Krav Maga."

Who ever loved that loved not at first sight?

—Shakespeare

Chapter Two

Zane followed the highbrow hum of classical music to the living room. Rebecca's home cocooned him with its plum-colored walls and soft carpet, framed paintings of galloping horses, and book-swollen shelves.

A handful of people milled about, slurring words that even a sober Zane couldn't pronounce.

He clammed up in the doorway. Each breath tasted like library. Ice tinkled in glass—interrupting fervent debate—and he hoped that the fruity scent of wine overpowered his nervous sweat and desperation.

He cast an eye over the room for a possible Rebecca. Three suited men circled a kitchen island, hands cradling whiskey tumblers. Two younger women sat on a windowsill deep in conversation, neither old enough to be the professor.

Which left the middle-aged woman in front of the stone fireplace, standing beside an overstuffed armchair. Gray streaked her wavy hair and she wore a green-knotted silk scarf. Rebecca.

She spoke to a man with dark locks lounging on the cushions. One leg hung over the arm of his chair as he stared at the light playing through his wineglass. Murmuring something, he raised his drink.

Rebecca took the glass and sipped.

Zane squared his shoulders and tripped into the room toward them. He caught himself and then Rebecca's gaze. Nothing a grin couldn't cure.

She tentatively returned the smile, dropping her gaze to her much younger . . . boyfriend? Lover? Muse?

The boyfriend-lover-muse tensed, his piercing gaze rolling over Zane.

Zane had that effect on people. A lucky mix of genes gave him good height and a solid build—but it also made him appear far more intimidating than he was.

Hopefully his dimpling smile put them at ease.

Smooth as possible, he winked at Rebecca and dove right in to twisting her arm. "I'm Zane. So, this *Toy Story*. Pretty imaginative stuff, huh?"

Rebecca held the wine glass against the breast of her woolen dress and nodded politely. "I, yes, I enjoyed it."

"I loved the friendship between Woody and Buzz. Great characterization."

The boyfriend-lover-muse coughed, mouth hidden by a fist, eyes glittering. He swung his leg off the chair and sat upright, homing in on Zane. An electrical ripple pulsed down Zane's side.

Did the boyfriend-lover-muse misunderstand? Did he think Zane was flirting with Rebecca?

Zane backed up and flashed him an easy smile. *We're all good here. No need to worry.*

Not that there would have been any competition.

Not against this man's sharp cheekbones and deep gaze. Not against the air of intelligence that framed him as well as his brass-buttoned jacket.

"Fun friendship, yes," Rebecca said, sounding like she

wanted to finish the conversation and continue whispering sweet literary nothings to her man.

A curl of panic shot up Zane's throat. His belongings waited on the porch. He was *one* conversation on literature away from earning a couch for a couple of nights. He could do this.

He had to do this.

"How much of an effect has *Toy Story* had on modern literature, do you think?"

Rebecca's gaze pinged back to him. "Excuse me?"

Zane repeated the question, distracted by the boyfriend-lover-muse pushing to his feet. Their gazes snagged, triggering a nervous tickle in Zane's stomach.

The boyfriend-lover-muse paused, a copper streak in his dark locks glowing in the light of the glass chandelier. So much younger than Rebecca, he had a smooth perfection that Zane had always admired in models. Dark brows framed sea-blue eyes that seemed overwhelmingly sad, despite how composed the rest of him appeared.

He pivoted, breaking the connection. With graceful steps he moved to the fireplace mantel, lifted an opened wine bottle, and poured himself a large glass.

"You mean Tolstoy?"

He jerked his head back to Rebecca. "Sorry?"

"No need to apologize. If you'll excuse me, I need to visit the bathroom." Rebecca whisked past him with a quick smile to her boyfriend-lover-muse.

Was the key to Rebecca's heart in convincing her prince?

Wait. Did Rebecca say *Tolstoy*?

As in peace and war and all that?

He swallowed a groan and fought back a blush. Nothing to do but recompose before she returned. He moved toward the fireplace, leaned against the back of the armchair, and rubbed his palm against the tight weave of the fabric.

The boyfriend-lover-muse followed the motion.

Did Rebecca draw still lifes? Was this guy a model? They seemed the types.

Art could be something they had in common. He could twist her arm into letting him stay through a discussion on comic book artists that had shaped popular culture.

Zane met the boyfriend-lover-muse-model's gaze. "You're looking at me like I'm trying to steal her away."

Rebecca's man halved the distance between them. His voice, soft and nuanced, hit Zane with a curious shiver. "You've been looking at me like you think I'm intimate with *my mother*."

Mother?

He straightened. That put a new spin on their dynamic. "Rebecca has a son?"

The barest glimpse of amusement tinged his eyes. "Natalie Fisher has a son." He lifted his wineglass and swirled the contents. "Zane, right? Here because you desperately need me?"

"I need—" Zane noticed a splotch of red wine on the breast of the guy's jacket. "*Becky?*"

"Beckett."

"You're a man."

His lips played on a smile. "You're an observational wizard."

So much for convincing *the professor*. He winced. "Any chance you could pour some wine and we could start over?"

"I don't know," Beckett said, a touch of humor in his tone. "Are you planning to engage me in more discussions on *Toy Story?*"

Palming the back of his neck, he rang out a boyish laugh, loud and rough to Beckett's quiet and collected one. "Remind me never to use literature to impress a stranger again."

Beckett poured a second glass. "How do you know Anne? I tried to message, but I haven't heard back yet."

Zane accepted the offered glass and took a merciful oak-spiced gulp. "She's kinda busy tonight. She married my brother Jacob."

Beckett stopped swirling his wine. "You should have said that from the start."

Zane carded his hand through his dirty-blond hair. "Yeah."

Beckett's gaze slid down Zane's length, lingering at his socks and jandals. "You don't look anything like Jacob. Which brother are you? The dentist?"

"You don't want me drilling your teeth. Or drilling anything, honestly."

Beckett's lips twitched, followed by a doubling of caution in his eyes. "The astrophysicist?"

Zane gulped the smooth wine. "The high school dropout." The lesser of his brothers. Loud, dramatic, and scornfully romantic.

Beckett drummed his fingers over his wineglass, making a tinkling sound. "I don't recall anything about a dropout. Which leaves the youngest brother. Jacob's favorite."

Youngest brother. A nicer descriptor than *dropout*, which the rest of his family used. And Jacob's favorite? His chest tickled. Exactly why Zane needed to marry and shift his roots here for good. He needed more nice in his life.

"Beckett!" The abrupt call had Zane swinging around. Three Suits were hailing Beckett toward the kitchen.

The Suit loomed as big as Zane and smiled widely. His tight, muscular body and intelligent air made it seem as if he consumed books for breakfast.

Beckett heeled his way toward Books for Breakfast, angling his head for Zane to follow. Zane mustered a lethargic gait. He'd embarrassed himself already tonight—he didn't care to continue revealing his ignorance about bookish stuff. Any stuff, really.

"How long do you think you'll be here, Zane?" Beckett asked.

"Oh, um, I hope to marry and stay forever."

Beckett's step stuttered, but he smoothly recovered. "I meant with me. In my home."

Right. "Does that mean you'll let me stay?"

Books for Breakfast raised his whiskey tumbler with a secret nod to Beckett, then drank the last dredge. "We're all heading to Chiffon," Books for Breakfast said to Beckett. "You'll join us, I hope. I'll buy you the best wine come the stroke of midnight."

Beckett sank both thumbs into the pockets of remarkably tight black jeans. "As much as I'd love to take you down in a synonym standoff, it will have to wait."

"You're postponing the fun?"

"Putting it off to next week."

"Why do you need to raincheck me?"

Beckett side-eyed Zane. Curiosity edged his otherwise guarded blue gaze. He looked at Books for Breakfast with a head nod toward Zane. "He twisted my arm."

"What is *that*?"

Beckett's mum and guests had left, and Beckett had brought Zane and his worldly belongings into an exposed-beam attic with a chain-pull light.

Zane set his box and suitcase against a slanted wall. The small, empty space contained a tiny window, a chest of drawers, and a low futon. Dust spokes glittered under the swaying light.

Beckett pointed at Zane's box, one brow arched.

Zane laid the bearskin rug on the floor and straightened

out the kinks. Beckett gaped at the bear poised as if to eat his ankle.

"I thought it was romantic," Zane said with a sigh. He rested back on his heels, soft fur against his knees. "Now I'm kinda stuck with the beast."

"Tough cross to bear."

Zane grinned. "What's with the word-wittage, anyway?"

"Word-wittage. Nice alliteration. I like playing with words." Beckett sidestepped the bear and gestured around the attic. "The wooden slats are creaky, the bathroom is back down the ladder. My sister is returning from Europe Thursday, staying here until she finds her own place. The couch is too small for you, so . . . ."

"I'm totally cool to bunk with you."

Beckett swept a hand through his hair, gaze darting toward the bed, the window. "There'll be no bunking."

Understood. He had a few days to find another accommodation—or convince Beckett that bunking could be fun.

Zane pulled his drawing tablet and stylus from their cushioned compartment. "Did you want to head to Chiffon with your friends? Whatever Chiffon is."

"It's a bar where we professors drink pinot noir and pontificate on the pleasures of punning."

"Um . . . ."

"It's a pretentious penis party."

Zane turned around, armed with the supplies he needed to finish—or fix—the comic. "Sounds like a . . . picnic?"

The corners of Beckett's mouth pulled up. Zane dropped the electronics to the bed and crossed over to the professor.

He tapped a finger against the wine stain at the side of Beckett's blazer lapel. "Proof that you snorted your wine while we texted? I'll have it dry-cleaned, if you'd like?"

"It's not your fault. I'll sort it out. Use it as an excuse to buy another one."

Zane caught a whiff of Beckett's clean scent with a subtle spicing of aftershave. Blue eyes met his, curious and hesitant.

A fat, black spider bungee-jumped from the beam above them and dangled in Zane's face. He dropped the fingers that had lingered on Beckett's chest and scrambled to the wall.

"Does a big, strapping man like you need me to remove the tiny bastard?"

"That's a big, strapping yes."

A few precise movements later, Beckett trapped the hairy beast in his *hands*. Insane, yet heroic.

The bed squealed as Beckett kneeled on it. Zane crawled next to him, opened the window, and beat a quick retreat as Beckett set the spider free. "The sheets are freshly changed, and you can help yourself to breakfast."

Fresh bed and breakfast? Lovely. But Zane was more concerned about suicidal spiders. He studied the ceiling with a shudder. "Do you think there are more?"

The window clapped shut, sealing off the cool breeze. "Would you feel better sleeping with my cat?"

Zane's attention pivoted to Beckett's hands fitting the lock. Long-fingered, deft, sure. "I'd feel better sleeping with you."

Beckett let out a strangled sound, swung off the bed, and zipped to the ladder. "Good night, Zane," he said and dropped out of sight.

Zane called after him. "Fine, I'll take the cat."

I would always rather be happy than dignified.

—Charlotte Brontë

Chapter Three

Shrugging off sleep, Zane used the bathroom, struggled into jeans, and slunk toward the smell of slightly burned toast.

He'd spent half the night arduously finishing the Fire Falcon panel, music pulsing in his ears. His stomach gurgled for caffeine.

Morning light poured through the living room windows, its edges playing over the table and his host. Sharply dressed Beckett sat sloped over a journal, toast between his lips, pen-wielding hand a flurry across the page. The soft light emphasized the smooth texture of Beckett's jaw, the slender column of his neck.

Paused in the doorway, Zane's stomach made another plea for coffee, but his heart's cry to sketch the scene drowned it.

Zane scouted the room for a makeshift canvas. "Stay as you are." He cleared his raspy voice. "Please."

Beckett looked up. His toast seesawed. "What are you doing?"

There! A cup of pens perched on a block of Post-it notes atop a massive thesaurus.

"Keep doing what you were doing." Pen in hand, Zane straddled a cushioned chair, stuck the paper to the wooden table, and sketched. His forearm shifted over the cool, polished table with each rough stroke until the wood under him warmed.

Comic art was nothing if not snapshots of emotion, and this panel made him imagine a wounded soldier, bleeding his heart out in ink.

His breath caught with emotion. What was Beckett writing?

Beckett closed his journal, gaze darting to Zane's Post-it note.

Zane blurted, "I'll show you mine if you show me yours."

As if contemplating the offer, Beckett finished chewing and swallowed. "We barely know each other. Let's keep our treasures zipped up. Toast?"

Zane snapped up two pieces. "You're funny, Becky."

"Beckett."

Beckett sounded familiar. Like a brand he should know. "Where have I heard your name?"

Beckett offered him the butter. "Samuel."

"It's Zane." He grinned and took it. "Samuel's my brother. The one you want drilling you." At Beckett's dry blink, he clarified. "The dentist?"

"You're lucky you are so easy on the eye."

"I guess I am lucky." Zane studied Beckett. Short, curly hair wet from a shower sat a tidy distance from his jacket collar. His regal posture made Zane want to sit up and pay attention like he'd never done in school. "Nothing quite as lucky as you are."

Beckett lifted the last wedge of toast to his mouth, not quite hiding the gentle quirk of his lips. "Samuel Beckett was an Irish writer famous for the play *Waiting for Godot*."

Zane rocked his chair back on two legs. "Kinda sounds familiar. So. You were named after this Samuel Beckett guy?"

"My mom's sentimental like that."

"I like her. More now that I know she wasn't robbing the cradle."

"Good God." He paused a beat and added, "I'm not that young."

"Pretty young to be a professor though, right?"

Beckett smiled, and Zane sensed an undercurrent of pride. "I don't have much of a life," Beckett said. "I just got tenured and am an associate professor."

This guy intrigued him. "Does the professor have plans today?"

"A couple loads of laundry to fold and a mall sale to stalk."

"You party animal." At his stomach's growl, Zane searched the table. It was suspiciously absent of coffee.

Before he could remark, his phone vibrated in his pocket. The front two chair legs snapped against the floor as Zane breathlessly answered Jacob's call. "Are you a dad?"

"I'm a dad!"

"Holy shit!"

Pride soaked his brother's voice and oozed into Zane's bones. "You're an uncle to the beautiful Cassie Greenwood. Born just past one this morning."

"When can I see our Cassie?"

Anne's laughter tinkled down the line. "Come next weekend. Bring Becky along, too. I can't help but think it *means* something."

Zane frowned. "What means something?"

"Becky and Cassie. They share the same birthday!"

Zane's gaze snapped to Beckett, who was dancing a finger through crumbs on his plate. "That *is* interesting," he murmured.

It shed new light over Beckett's little get-together last night, but it didn't explain why none of his guests had made a fuss. He hadn't seen any shredded wrapping paper or a half-demolished cake . . . although it did explain the drink Books for Breakfast wanted to buy Beckett at midnight.

"I'm sorry I didn't talk more last night," Anne said.

Jacob droned in the background. "You were only giving birth to our firstborn daughter."

"I hope you guys get along, oh, and wish him a happy birthday. If he lets you—he didn't pick up when I called. Swear to God he avoids this day like the plague."

"I'll work on changing that today. What can I get Cassie and her parents?"

Jacob laughed. He'd stolen back the phone. "Anne and I talked about that."

"What do you want? Anything."

"There is something I've wanted from you for a while, and if I can't ask for me, I hope you'll let me ask on behalf of your sweet niece."

Zane's smile faded, a nervous knot forming in his stomach. He sensed what his brother was about to ask, and he couldn't do it.

Not that he didn't *want* to.

He couldn't.

He shoved to his feet and moved into the kitchen. Coffee had never been so necessary.

"You're an amazingly talented artist," Jacob said.

Zane flung cupboards open. Pots and pans. Tinned food and cat treats. Horse-print mugs, dainty teacups, and a spatula wedged under a teapot. "We love the graphic novels you work on."

"But . . . ." Zane's fingers tightened on the phone.

"You need to work on a project you're passionate about. That you're allowed to have an artistic vision for."

He whipped open another cupboard and banged his head against the door. From the table, Beckett quirked his brows.

"You have one month before you have to head back," Jacob said. Zane's stomach twisted at the reminder. Four weeks left to make America his permanent home. "Couldn't you make massive headway on your own comic by then? You've always been so imaginative. It'd be great."

He was as likely to write a good story as he was to find coffee in Beckett's cupboards.

"I draw, not write."

"You started drawing because you couldn't find words. You drew your stories. Now you draw other people's."

A high-pitched wailing down the line saved Zane from replying. Jacob gave a panicked squeak and ended their call.

Zane stuffed his phone deep into his pocket right along with Jacob's wish. He'd figure a way to wrangle out of it later. Give Cassie something else.

"Where's your coffee?" He focused on Beckett. Birthday Beckett. Nicely dressed, yet nowhere to go.

"I don't keep coffee in the house."

This would never do. "You're not a coffee drinker?"

Beckett tapped the last wedge of toast against his lips. "I love coffee. I prefer to buy it from my local café."

"Is this another pretentious thing?"

"Probably."

Zane jerked a thumb toward the street. "Right, then. Let's go have our version of a penis party."

KING'S COFFEE WAS HORSESHOE-SHAPED. WARM, COZY lighting doused cushioned chairs, chunky wooden tables, and lovingly framed Elvis posters. The place called for sinking into comfort, forgetting about crafting stories, and drifting into a daydream or three about his future.

". . . Zane?"

Beckett rested a hip at the counter, pointing at the menu.

Zane scanned the chalkboard. "Best Cap in the world found here? I wouldn't mind one of those."

The barista, who looked like a Japanese movie star, flashed his teeth in a wide smile. "Two large cappuccinos coming up."

Zane swooped in and paid for both drinks before Beckett could protest. It was the least he could do. For putting him up and for it being the man's birthday.

A fact he somehow needed to weasel out of him.

Beckett glided down the café's left flank, and Zane followed, breathing in the nutty smell of roasted coffee. A frantic fiery-haired woman whisked past him and slung herself into an armchair, throwing off her hat and scarf.

Zane draped his jacket over the back of an L-shaped sofa, where Beckett was doing the same.

A flung glove landed on his foot.

Zane picked it up and glanced back at the oblivious woman. Was this a sign? Was the universe telling him that love waited right under his nose?

A polished boot nudged his sneaker as Beckett sat on the short end of the L sofa.

Zane pulled the drawcords of his red hoodie until they were even. "Do I look good?"

Beckett's fingers splayed on the sofa arm. The stuffed blue cushions eerily brightened his eyes. A considering gaze roamed over Zane, lingered on the glove in his hand, then swept to the woman behind him. He sighed. "Of course."

That sigh didn't sound convincing. But Zane would take it.

He slunk a few feet down the aisle until he stood before the woman. "Excuse me, you dropped this."

She looked up, startled, then recognized her glove. "Oh."

Should probably hand it over now.

He continued playing with the stretchy material, casting his best grin. Would it be over the top to slip it on her hand and kiss her fingers? Perhaps tricky to do seamlessly, though.

Gah. He was still smiling at her. Holding her glove hostage. She motioned for it.

One chance to make a romantic impression.

He held the glove next to her face. "Russet is a great color. Almost the same as your eyes—"

The stretchy material slipped from his grip and snapped into her cheek.

She winced in pain and rubbed the spot.

Heat rushed up Zane's neck, and he dropped the glove before her. "So sorry. Um, maybe I should buy you a coffee to apologize?"

She glared at him.

Or not.

He shrank into his hoodie and backed up. "Sorry. Bye."

He pivoted and stole to his seat, wishing the ground would swallow him. It didn't, though the cushions made a good attempt at pulling him into their depths.

"That went well," Beckett said.

"I'm ready to write my vows."

"Not the smoothest approach, but you looked good trying."

Their cappuccinos arrived, and Zane took an eager gulp. "This is my problem. I keep putting myself out there but never make progress, and I only have four weeks left."

"Four weeks?" Beckett dipped his spoon into his cappuccino heart.

"To find the one I want to marry."

Beckett's spoon paused mid-air. "Are you looking for someone to mock you?"

Zane shook his head. "Humiliation isn't my thing. This isn't about sex at all—"

Coffee sloshed over the sides of Beckett's cup. He set it on the saucer before it dripped onto the table. His gaze smacked to Zane's. "M.O.C." He sounded out the letters. "Marriage of convenience. Moc you."

Zane rang out a frustrated laugh. "What's with all these damn letters!"

"Acronyms."

"I wish there were ways to win someone over without having to open my mouth."

"And deprive a pretty girl of your deep, humored voice?"

Deep and humored? A slow smile pulled at Zane's lips. "Becky? I think this is the beginning of a beautiful friendship."

The tip of Beckett's spoon swirled around his cappuccino froth. "*Casablanca*. One love story I can bear."

"Casa-what?" At Beckett's horrified expression, Zane laughed. "Kidding. Of course, I know *Casablanca*. I may not know *literature*. But name any animated film, rom-com, or classic love story, and I've seen it."

"Yet you still haven't perfected the hook."

What dry cheek! Zane loved it. "One of these days, it'll happen right. I'll fall in love—and be in love for the rest of my life."

Beckett hummed.

"Don't you believe me?"

"You're young."

"I'm twenty-three."

"*Very* young."

"You're sounding bitter."

"No one falls in love just like that. I'm sorry to break it to you, but 'happily ever after' is a big, beautiful lie."

"Oh, Becky."

"Beckett."

"Becky—"

Beckett tapped his spoon against his lips. "Why are you chasing after a green card?"

"I'm not."

"Let me rephrase. Why the deadline to marry?"

"A deadline to *fall in love* and marry. If I'm not 100 percent head over heels, I *will* go back to New Zealand and stay back. But I'm just . . . determined to be head over heels."

"Right."

"I mean it. No marriage would survive without love, and I intend to marry only once."

A flash of pain shot over Beckett's face and he jerked his head toward a framed, winking Elvis.

Zane instinctively slid over to the corner of the sofa until their knees knocked. "Becky?"

A chesty laugh. "You're unbelievable."

"I'm sorry if I'm bringing up bad memories of some silly girl who played with your heart and left it broken."

Beckett's lips twitched. "You're sounding very sorry."

Zane took a napkin and soaked up the coffee Beckett had spilled onto his saucer. "I have three brothers and a healthy mum and dad, but Jacob is the one who means everything to me. I want to be there for his kids as he . . ." Zane swallowed the lump in his throat. "As he was for me. That's why I want to stay here."

He knew it wouldn't be as simple as falling in love and marrying and, *voilà*, he could stay. He knew there'd be a whole complicated process of applying for permanent residence after marriage and proving his marriage was real. Knew it would likely involve a period of time flying between here and New Zealand.

If he could just fall in love before the month was out and start the process . . .

It had to be for love, though.

He cleared his throat. "So, this girl that broke your heart . . . ."

Beckett cradled his coffee, staring at the soaked napkin on his saucer. "I'm divorced. Luke left me two months after tying the knot."

Well, this Luke was an idiot. "Wait. Luke?"

Beckett's face showed coolness and patience, but his hands twitched. "Yes, I'm gay. Luke is a man. Is that an issue for you?"

"Not at all." A mischievous grin lit him up and he barely kept his words steady. "I mean, you're born gay. Gay from the day you were born. Gay since your *birth*day . . . ."

Beckett's gaze hesitantly jumped to him. "That's . . . right."

Not nearly enough of an admission. But Zane would get him there. "This shopping you wanted to do. Sounds like the perfect time to buy presents."

"Presents?" Beckett sounded right suspicious now.

"For Cassie, you know. Also, I could do with a new pair of shoes. Something to wear on my date later. Speaking of, what would you do for a date around here?" Zane winked at him. "Let me guess. You'd take him to Chiffon for a synonym standoff."

"I'd do dinner, and if that goes well, a romantic walk." Beckett looked over his coffee cup at him and winked back. "It's not classy to pull out the synonyms until the second date."

There is no charm equal to tenderness of heart.

—Jane Austen

Chapter Four

"Shopping for blazers. Fun."

Zane and Beckett stood in an elegant clothing store eyeing a wall lined with sleek jackets.

"I have an academic dinner party at Chiffon in two weeks," Beckett said distractedly, glancing for the fourth time to the exit, "and I've been looking for something special."

Zane fingered the cuff of a tweed jacket. "Blazers are totally the way to go."

"How about you focus on your task of looking irresistible for your date. We can meet again in an hour."

"And miss out on the gay-guy shopping fun? I'm hoping you'll go crazy."

Beckett shook his head and inspected a gray double-breasted jacket.

Zane pinched the rough fabric, eyed the exaggerated lapels, and hooked it back on the clothes rail. "Totally wrong. It doesn't have elbow patches."

"Elbow patches?" Beckett cast him a quizzical look and shrugged into a navy-blue blazer that fit him like pixies had sewn it just for him. "What about this one?"

Perfect. "I don't know. You could stand to be a little less *Vogue* and a little more professor-like."

"And elbow patches are the way?"

"On everything."

Beckett returned the blazer to its hook. "How about I be professor-like and tirade you on Tolstoy?"

"The *Vogue* look is good. *Vogue* is hot." Zane jerked a finger across the busy store. "I'm heading to the shoe section way over there in the farthest corner of the store where I can't hear any lectures."

Beckett gave a snarky lift of his brow. "And miss out on all the fun?"

Grinning, Zane sidled out of earshot. Two steps into the shoe section, he gravitated toward the perfect boot modeled by a mannequin. Could a plastic model look hot? Because this one did. Tight black pants and crisp white shirt. And the *boots*.

A half-inch heel and turquoise leather that molded tightly up the calves to the knee.

He'd never been so entranced by shoes before. But these. Princely.

Zane wanted to *be* that model.

He knelt and stroked the leather. He needed these boots.

He flagged down an assistant. The boots only got better. They featured a waterproof footbed and elastic lace at the front of the ankle. Easy to slip into. He strutted in front of low-hung mirrors. Elegant yet modern.

Half-off in the today-only sale.

Ten minutes later, he paid for his purchase, threw his sneakers in the shopping bag, and snapped into the snug turquoise leather. His stride produced a confident click of his shiny, new heels. His jeans weren't tight enough for a perfect fit, and he needed a better shirt, but damn. Look at him. He'd purchased a literal step closer to snagging true love.

On a roll, he picked out two blazers Beckett might like.

"What about these?" he said, holding up two woolen variations. "These are very you."

Beckett glanced over a freestanding rail of coats. "Platitudinous tan or psychopathic brown. I see I've impressed you."

"I was thinking bookish tan and hidden-depths brown. You're a *mystery*, Becky."

"Be*ckett*—" Beckett's gaze lifted over Zane's shoulder. His face paled, and he let out a soft, frustrated "Oh God" and sank out of sight.

Straight-laced Beckett wouldn't do anything as crass as *ducking*.

Zane's lips hitched with amusement. "A *real* mystery."

He turned, startled to recognize the man meandering around a table of cashmere vests. Short, chestnut hair. Preppy, yellow-knit cardigan. Glasses he didn't need to wear. And a boyfriend draped over his shoulder.

Anne's brother.

They'd met twice, once at the farm and once at the wedding. Zane wasn't his biggest fan. Not after being laughed at during a word-association game that required Zane to spell "burglar." He still thought "burgerlar" made sense.

On instinct, he called out, "Luke!"

The rail shifted behind him along with Beckett's tired-sounding groan.

It hit him the moment Luke left his beefy boyfriend and hiked toward him.

Luke.

Suddenly it was clear why Beckett and Anne might not have been "good" for a while. Brother and best friend. Exes. Ex-husbands.

He winced. Poor Beckett, seeing his ex-husband wrapped in his young lover's arms.

Hailing him over had been one of his more idiotic moves.

"Zane?" Luke said. "Small world."

Zane shifted to block any hint of Beckett and reluctantly shook Luke's hand. "Even smaller town."

"We're uncles. Jacob and Anne are parents. Can you believe it?"

"There's a lot I have trouble believing." Like imagining Beckett with this pompous cheeseball. "Jacob being a dad is not one of them. He'll be the best."

How could he sneak Beckett out of here unseen?

"What brings you here?" Luke asked.

Zane's boots clicked as he shifted, making Luke pivot with him. "Shopping for my date."

"Still hounding after marriage, eh?"

Zane wished he'd never blabbed about his mission. They'd met the weekend Jacob and Anne had revealed the pregnancy, and he'd blurted it out in enthusiasm. He had the distinct impression Luke thought he hadn't the brains to hook anyone classy. To secure anything long-lasting.

"Hounding after *love*."

Mockery edged Luke's smile. "Good luck."

Zane shrugged through the sting. "Can't all have PhDs like you."

"No, but you could buy yourself a dictionary. Read a book or two."

Ouch. He'd have to question Beckett on his taste in men.

Luke glanced at his boots. "Fun color."

Zane clapped a palm on Luke's shoulder—a little harder than necessary—pulling Luke's gaze upward and away from any glimpse of a crouching Beckett. "Fun is right. Elegant and modern, with elastic lacing." He steered Luke around, raising his voice a notch for Beckett's benefit. "Let me show you. All the way over there in the farthest corner of the store. . . ."

AFTER DISTRACTING LUKE, ZANE MADE ANOTHER QUICK purchase and hoofed out of the store. At the far end of the bustling mall, he spotted a brusquely retreating Beckett.

Zane wended through shoppers, his boots clip-clopping over the shiny floors. Heads turned to take in his purchase. The heels smacked against the stairs leading to the parking lot, and the sound echoed in the underground parking lot. The harsh light exaggerated the brightness of the leather.

A gaggle of kids snickered as they passed him.

Were the boots too much?

No, no. He looked good. He *felt* good.

The heel rubbed a bit, but he'd wear them in.

A car horn tooted, and Zane backpedaled.

Beckett's car, meticulous and tight, reflected Beckett's demeanor. The clean smell of cared-for leather hit his nose. Zane squeezed himself and his purchases into the front. He shouldn't fit in at all, yet there was just enough give to the leather that it hugged him nice and snug. A little time, the seat would warm and all his purchases would perfectly cushion his ridiculous boots.

What on earth had he been thinking?

Beckett lowered his head. A similar thought no doubt simmered on his mind.

Two could lift such a baffled brow. "So Anne's brother broke your heart."

"I'm not heartbroken."

"The lone clothing rail I watched mysteriously trundle to the exit painted a different picture." A picture that would make a great panel for a comic . . . but one panel did not make a story.

He buried the plea of Jacob's voice swirling in his head. He had more pressing things to do than write his own superhero comics. Like falling head over heels.

Like getting Beckett to admit it was his bloody birthday.

Beckett held the back of the seat and looked over his shoulder as he reversed from the spot. Sarcasm was light on his tongue. "I loved how you beckoned Luke over for a chat."

"How was I supposed to know Anne's brother, Luke, was your ex-husband, Luke? Luke is a common name."

Beckett changed the gear into drive, throwing him a look. "Did you think I dropped to my knees for some other reason?"

The softly spoken words triggered a twitch in Zane's gut. A surprised, nervous laugh tickled his chest, and he rearranged the shopping bags on his lap. "How do you know Anne?"

"Our family's homes are close. We got to know each other when we went to college, though—Anne bussed to school here, and I went to the one in Greenville. We took turns driving each other back home to save gas. Somewhere during that mileage, we became friends. Then best friends."

"Then you met her brother and fell for each other?"

"Not immediately, but yes." The tightness of Beckett's voice pleaded him to drop the conversation.

Fine by him. He didn't much care for Luke anyway.

Even less after this afternoon.

The drive back was met with the same roadblocks as their way in, courtesy of Redwood Marathon. Zane didn't mind. It gave him more time to weasel out a birthday admission.

"Let's go to that store." He pointed. "On days like these, I love to bake." And he needed to grab coffee.

Beckett eyed him warily and parked outside the local grocery store.

Once the car was loaded with food and Beckett settled into the driver's seat, Zane bit back a shit-eating grin and kept his eyes on the professor.

He gestured to beefy clouds that played peekaboo with the sun. "Nice day today, huh?"

"All right, all right. What do you want?"

Zane fished for the bag with his earlier purchase and handed it to Beckett. "You know what I want."

With a soft frown, Beckett played with the plastic on his lap.

"Some people like pontifying with puns." Zane leaned over the console conspiratorially and lowered his voice. "Others like pretty presents, Becky."

Beckett peered inside the bag and drew out the navy blazer that had fit him perfectly in the store. He shook his head, smiling. "Anne had to tell you it's my birthday, didn't she?"

"There it is. Hallelujah. An admission." He playfully nudged Beckett's arm. "You share a date with her firstborn. Course she would mention that."

Beckett caressed the smooth material. "You're probably right."

Zane twisted in his seat, angling toward Beckett. "This day. Cassie. Your birthday. Bumping into Luke. The universe is telling us our paths are meant to converge."

Beckett's eyes shot to his. "Converge?"

"Fate, Becky."

"I don't believe in fate. It's not even coincidence."

"What?"

Beckett gave a sad laugh. "Running into Luke at a one-day sale at Equestrian Mode? His favorite outlet? I knew he'd be there."

"But . . . . Do you have self-torture issues?"

Beckett tucked the blazer into the shopping bag. "People are complicated, Zane. Yes, I wanted to run into him today. But when he showed up, I didn't want to see him at all." Beckett looked at him. "Fate had nothing to do with it."

Maybe fate had nothing to do with bumping into Luke. But he wouldn't dismiss it—

"Just a second . . . Equestrian Mode? As in horses and stuff?" He frowned at his boots. Beckett ogled the tight-fitting turquoise beasts too. Zane pushed out a laugh. Riding boots. He'd bought fancy riding boots. "You're right, Becky. People can be complicated. We can also be ridiculously simple."

Beckett studied him, then tentatively reached out and clasped Zane's shoulder. A warm, brief squeeze. "You're not simple, Zane. You're charming."

"Really?"

A soft laugh. "Charming and ridiculously romantic."

"We all need romance in our lives—know what? You and me? We're gonna be two guy friends who are all about the romance."

"Bromance?"

Zane clicked his fingers. "Exactly."

Intelligent blue eyes met his, creased with curiosity, amusement, and detectable wariness. "Should I point out we've just met?"

"Hook 'em from the start, right?"

ON THE DRIVE HOME, A FLASH OF NEON CAUGHT ZANE'S EYE. A string of restaurants sparkled across from Treble's green campus. Brilliant. Restaurants within walking distance to their place.

He typed FireAndNice a message where they should meet for their date.

His fingers stilled before sending. "Becky, what are your plans tonight?"

"Laundry. Plus I have course material to sort through and a bottle of Pinotage to help."

That would never do.

He deleted the message and typed a new one.

INSIDE THE DUPLEX WITH FIVE SHOPPING-BAG HANDLES BORING into his palms, Zane paused at the full-length hallway mirror. "You know what?" He winced at the snug, knee-high turquoise that made his calves seem slim. "These boots are too awesome for wearing outside. They'll be my indoor shoes."

"Not going to wear them on your date?" With nonchalant grace, Beckett toted his bags into the living room.

Zane followed and plunked the groceries on the kitchen. "No date. Canceled it."

"You canceled?"

"I shifted it to tomorrow." His phone buzzed against his thigh, and he read it with a sigh. "Scratch that. She said not to bother."

Beckett stopped pawing through their purchases. "If you're doing this to be nice—"

"Nice? Try romantic, Becky. This dinner is all about your birthday and our burgeoning bromance."

A hesitant smile teased at Beckett's lips, blue eyes boring into Zane like Beckett was trying to find an answer.

"What?" Zane asked.

"Would it matter if I told you a bromance is a bad idea?"

"Bromance is never a bad idea."

But Beckett had a valid question. Would it matter if they didn't have one? The answer was yes, without a doubt, but why?

Butterflies swarmed his gut, each fluttering a different feeling. Filtering them would be difficult. Cooking would help. He reached into one of the bags, pulled out a packet of nuts he'd already opened on the drive home, and popped another in his mouth. "Let's make dinner and bake pecan muffins."

Beckett leaned on the other side of the counter. "Pecan muffins?"

"For Darla."

Surprise glittered in Beckett's eye. "You've met Darla?"

"She called me a fish. Our relationship can only go up from there."

"Tell me you heard the part about my sister coming on Thursday?"

Zane smirked and sorted through the groceries. "The muffins are to thank her for watching my things last night." He set two lemons, a plastic manual juicer, and a mug covered in multi-colored hearts in front of Beckett. "Grate the rind, juice them, and pour the liquid in there."

Had his need for a bromance stemmed from Beckett's sad eyes? He was wounded, and Zane wanted to take his pain away. He'd always been like that. Like the time Jacob had been dumped by a girlfriend after three years. He'd spent a week in bed drowning in rock music, and Zane had slung himself on that double bed and given his misery company.

He frowned as he grabbed a bowl, cutting board, and various utensils.

Beckett stared at the sieve he procured and watched him set the macaroni on the stove. "You sure know your way around my kitchen."

"Thanks to your pretentious coffee habits."

"Tomorrow morning you will sip your own filter coffee and head straight back to King's."

"We'll see." Zane layered a glass tray with cream and cut an onion.

"What is the lemon for?" Beckett asked. "The muffins or dinner?"

"Dinner." Zane picked up a long zucchini. "We're having a zucchini-lemon macaroni bake." Under running water, he glided his hand up and down the length of the vegetable.

Beckett's hand faltered on the lemon he was juicing. He cleared his throat and continued twisting the lemon. "You are very thorough there."

"Don't want the skin to bruise." He pointed the zucchini at Beckett and his lemons. "Wring out every last drop."

Beckett's gaze flickered to his. "I always do."

Zane laughed so hard a few butterflies fluttered to his crotch.

"Would you mind pointing that zucchini elsewhere?" Beckett asked, voice rasping.

Zane leaned over and prodded Beckett's cheek, making Beckett drop his lemon. "Intelligent and cheeky. I brove you already."

"Brove?"

"Bro and romance. Bromance. Bro and love. Brove, right?"

Beckett's playful expression gave way to uncertainty. "You're awfully fast to whip out the 'brove' word."

"I believe in love at first sight, so why not brove at first sight?"

"Because it doesn't exist, and could we please have this conversation without that fat zucchini plundering my cheek?"

He set the vegetable down with a grin. "Love at first sight *is* real. It's the holy grail of romance. Your gazes connect, and you silently share every secret and vulnerability, hope and fear in a few desperately magical seconds."

Beckett focused on pouring lemon into the mug. "No, love is intimate. It takes time and experience to develop. Physical attraction isn't enough; it's about emotional fostering. About trust. Takes time and effort to nurture. It's not something that's entitled."

Beckett slid the cutting board and the zucchini to his side of the counter and sliced like a pro. Zane seamlessly moved to prepare the muffins. Butter, sugar, eggs, flour, rising agent.

He stopped between each addition to eat a few roasted pecans, creamy and sweet under a fine layer of salt.

"Maybe first sight isn't the best wording," Zane said. "Maybe first connection is better. It's the feeling when you meet someone you are instantly comfortable with. You see they're not perfect, but you don't care. You want to know more. You need to."

Beckett rounded into the kitchen, pulled down a pan, and set it on the stove. They stood adjacent to each other, their arms so close Zane could feel Beckett thrumming with energy. Beckett's shoulders deflated, and he stared at the heating pan. "First connection? People can fake their personality, and after time, you see what a jerk they are."

Zane twisted, leaned back against the counter facing Beckett's profile. "Was Luke a jerk?"

"No. He was young."

"How old was he when you married?"

Beckett dropped onions into the pan and they sizzled. "Your age."

"That's why you think I shouldn't marry?"

Beckett finally looked at him. "I understand why you want to marry. Just don't fool yourself that it'll necessarily be for love."

Zane pushed off the counter, coming so close to Beckett that he felt the man's breath stutter over his jaw. "I'm boiling with the need to prove you wrong, Becky."

Beckett added the zucchini to the pan, covered them, and sighed. "I hope you do."

Taking Beckett's pain away, yes, that was why he needed this bromance.

Flutters still nagged at him, and frowning, he ate another handful of pecans and checked his phone for the next step in the recipe.

While he believed in love at first sight, he wasn't a fool to force Beckett into returning any brove-like feelings. Besides, he liked Beckett's idea of fostering emotion. He opened a new tab and did a quick search.

"Zucchini is done," Beckett said. "Shall I dump it into the dish and put it in the oven to bake?"

"With a whole bag of grated cheese." Zane smiled at him over his phone. "'Cause you know I'm all about the cheesiness."

Beckett tried not to smile but Zane saw it twitching his cheek. Once dinner was in the oven, Beckett sidled to the counter. "What next?"

Zane set his phone down. "Cinnamon."

Zane grabbed the container from the bags, tore off the plastic, and turned to find Beckett pulling another container off a spice rack.

They looked at each other's containers and at the muffin mixture on the counter between them.

With his thumb nail, Zane flicked open his lid. "Cinnamon standoff?"

Beckett stepped closer to him and the bowl, gaze steady on his, the air between them crackling. "I told you it's not classy to pull out the cinnamon until the second date."

Zane inched closer. "How about we adapt those rules? Second date *and* birth date."

Zane and Beckett's hands shot out and spice misted the air over the bowl and between their mirrored smiles. A fine layer settled on Zane's boots. Great, his boots smelled good. Probably tasted good. Everything but looked good.

He grabbed a paper towel and wiped his boots clean. "They'd suit you. These boots, I mean."

"It probably helps to have the whole style to go with it."

"I wanted to look like you. I like your look."

Beckett tucked himself against the counter with lazy elegance. "My look?"

"Yes, bookish and intelligent." Zane cocked his head and hummed. "I think I've figured out why this bromance matters."

Beckett raised an eyebrow.

"If I can make a smart man like you laugh with me and not *at* me, it'll give me hope that I can hook true love." He dropped the used paper towel in the bin and moved back to the counter with a satisfied smile. "Now, pass the pecans."

Beckett stared at him, brow creased.

"Are you okay, there, Becky?" Zane asked.

Beckett jerked his gaze to the counter. He dragged the pecan packet over the counter and upturned it into the batter. A lone pecan fell into the mix.

Zane cupped the back of his neck with an embarrassed laugh. "Not the first time that's happened. I have a secret stash in my suitcase . . . ."

"Know what?" Beckett said, picking the pecan out and popping it into his mouth. "Cinnamon muffins are great, too."

~

ONCE THEY'D STIRRED THE BATTER, THEY REORGANIZED THE oven to accommodate the muffin tray. Zane crouched, peering inside the glass window, and Beckett stripped off the oven gloves, stood, and set them on their designated hook under the label: *cooking mittens*.

Zane glanced up at the same time Beckett glanced down, and Beckett froze. His thighs were dusted in cinnamon, and being as close as he was, one dart of Zane's tongue and it'd be a cinnamon feast.

Beckett pivoted and stepped away. "I've got laundry . . ."

Zane ensnared him around the legs, face plastered to the outside of one thigh. The fabric of his jeans was thin, and the warmth of Beckett's leg heated his cheek. He looked up at Beckett's startled face. "We're not done yet."

"What else, exactly, did you have planned?"

"Oh, I don't know, just the burgeoning part of our bromance." Zane let go of Beckett, clambered to his feet, and grabbed his phone from the counter. "Question one: what's the funniest-slash-best text message you've ever received?"

Beckett's gaze zipped from Zane's phone to his face to his phone again. "What are you doing?"

Zane scrolled. "I'm asking you questions. Two, what movie star do you have a crush on?"

"What are you doing asking questions *off your phone*?"

Zane looked up at Beckett's bewildered face and waved his phone screen at him. "I found 'How to Start a Bromance in 13 Steps' on wikiHow, and this other awesome blog is full of questions to deepen our knowledge of each other."

Beckett picked up a half-full bottle of wine and moved out of the kitchen to the dining table. He pulled out a chair, perched on the end of it, and set the bottle in front of him.

"Do you need a glass, Becky?"

Beckett stared at the bottle. "Yes."

Zane brought him a large crystal wine glass from the cabinet in the living room. Beckett pulled out the wine stopper and poured himself a glass.

Zane straddled the chair across from him, forearms digging into the wooden back as he scrolled through the wikiHow page again. *Spend lots of time together. Start casual.*

Beckett finished pouring.

"That's a good amount of wine," Zane said.

Beckett pushed the crystal glass toward him and chugged from the bottle. "I've never needed it more."

"Are you too shy to answer my questions, Becky?"

"No, no. Just too sober. Pass me that phone."

Zane did and watched Beckett read the extensive list of questions. His thumb stilled on the screen. "Why is 'what do you do for a living?' question fifty-two?"

Zane shrugged. "Dunno, but to answer, I draw comics. Mostly for *Scarlet Sentinel vs. Fire Falcon.*"

"Do you like your job?"

"Love it."

"You love a lot of things, don't you?"

"Just the best things. Drawing is one of them."

"Does it pay well?"

Zane laughed. "Hardly."

"How do you fund your travels around the States?"

"When my grandmother passed, me and my brothers were left an inheritance. I have enough to last a good while." Zane stretched his wine glass toward Beckett. Beckett lifted his bottle and toasted to bromance. After they'd taken another sip, Zane's smile widened. "So . . . best text message? Movie star crush?"

"You're tenacious, I'll give you that."

Zane wasn't sure if he knew what tenacious meant. "Is that a good thing?"

A wavering smile played at Beckett's lips. "I don't know yet." He pulled his own phone out, swiped around, then read aloud. "'Sorry, Rebecca. How presumptuous.' Definitely ranks in the top two texts."

Zane ducked his head into another gulp of wine. "Not going to live that one down, am I?"

"But 'I'm certifiable for romance and comics and I love eating babies and cats' is the winner."

"Going to tell me commas are my friends?"

Beckett inclined his head. "They are, but not to worry, looks like I'll be your walking comma."

Zane's smile felt too big for his face. "Which movie star gets you hot and bothered?"

"Did I just hear the oven timer ding?" Beckett swept off his chair and danced into the kitchen.

Zane followed, arms folded. "It didn't ding. Tell me."

"Maybe it's broken. Those muffins look very—"

"*Unbaked* is the word you're searching for, Professor."

Beckett abandoned the oven, turning around with a sigh and a tight shake of his head. "Chris Hemsworth."

"The Australian?"

"His body, his accent . . . ." Beckett bit his bottom lip.

That wouldn't stand at all. "Aussies might be as cool as Kiwis and have beaches you can actually sit on, but their accent?" He exaggerated a wince. "Bit strange on the ears."

Beckett's face was blank. "It sounds exactly like yours."

Zane glared. "Take that back! Our accents are totally different. Bananas and oranges."

Beckett huffed a laugh. "Both sound like fruit to me."

Zane shook his head. "That's it. You're in the bad books until you see the error of your ways."

"Hear the error of my ways, by the sound of it."

Zane grabbed the dish towel and tossed it at Beckett's highly amused face. "Take that, and go do your laundry."

Sounds the same? Outrageous!

Clearly, Zane had to educate Beckett on the important things in life.

Friendship is the inexpressible comfort of feeling safe with a person, having neither to weigh thoughts nor measure words.

—George Eliot

Chapter Five

B eckett disappeared to do laundry and Zane tripped over a slinky ginger cat. They exchanged warbling hellos and a claw snagged the elastic bed of his boot.

Not love at first sight, but Zane knew where the cat treats were.

When the muffins cooled, Zane plated ten and visited Darla.

They sat on rickety wooden chairs with velvet cushions around a small square table.

The room mirrored Beckett's, the kitchen, dining, and living space all connected. Where Beckett had paintings of horses, Darla had framed family pictures.

Zane inhaled incense and grinned at Darla, who watched him with a thoughtful spark in her eye.

"Your family?" Zane asked, flicking a finger toward the photos.

"The lovely girl there is my daughter, Crystal. Most of these were taken before she was twenty. She lives in Minnesota and has a grown family of her own."

She prodded a large portrait of two gap-toothed children

with her walking stick. "Those are my darling grandchildren, Theo and Leone. They're grown now, of course. Theo lives close with his boyfriend, Jamie. They are busy on weekends, visiting the surrogate carrying their twins, but they pop by regularly."

Darla halved a muffin and added butter. "The handsome older fellow was my Timothy. May he rest in peace."

Zane hopped off his chair and investigated the photos. Such tender memories.

His mum and dad had a similar wall at home. He'd been the surprise fourth kid, and they'd already done the photo rodeo. All firsts had already been taken.

They did have a nice picture of him piggybacking on Jacob. And then there was the other photo that his brothers always had a good chuckle over. The one he laughed at too, even though it hollowed his stomach. Him onstage at fifteen for a school production. Gangly and gaping.

He shook off the tender memory. He'd come to Darla's for two reasons, and he'd already thanked Darla for looking after his things.

"Darla?"

"Hmm?"

"On the porch last night, you said something about a broken bull. You meant Beckett, didn't you?"

Darla gave a sad smile.

Zane leaned forward. "Could you tell me?"

Darla spoke softly. "Beckett is reliable, honest, compassionate, and stubborn. He is strong. Downright resilient. He was an out gay kid in a rural high school and faced daily bullying; his horse spooked, and he fell, breaking his collarbone and arm. He learned to write left-handed to ace all his upcoming examinations. His dad left his mom when he was young and never bothered to keep in touch. He picked himself up every time. A true steel bull. But everyone has their weakness, and his is his heart."

Zane perched on the arm of a suede sofa, swallowing a lump in his throat. "How do you know all this?"

"For seven years, we've had dinner together three times a week. He shops for me. Before Theo moved back, he came over every second week to mow my lawn and vacuum my house. Gave me some real insights into his character. Plus, he's always been open about his past, doesn't believe in having secrets." She stretched out of her chair and passed him with a whiff of perfume. She gestured to a picture at the far end of the wall. "Beckett when he moved in. A fine young man."

Zane followed her and studied the picture of the smiling man. He looked regal in his blazer, and his eyes glittered like the whole universe lay before him.

"It takes time to earn the trust and loyalty of a Taurus," Darla said, "but once you do, you're deep friends for life. At least, that should be what happens. Luke came into his life, promised him a world of love and devotion, earned that trust, and smashed it in front of his eyes."

Her sigh fogged the glass of the photo, and Zane slung an arm around her neck and squeezed her shoulder through the cardigan she wore over her floral dress.

"I keep telling him there are more fish in the sea. Better fish." She looked at him. "A perfect fish just waiting for him to catch it."

"But he doesn't believe you?"

"Not yet."

A ginger cat leaped onto the sofa beside them and Zane jerked with surprise. Darla laughed and petted the cat's head. "There's my little lion."

Zane frowned. Either he was going nuts, or . . . . "Didn't I just see this cat at Becky's?"

Darla scratched Leo under the chin. "I'm too old to look

after a cat. But I love the company. Beckett thought sharing a cat was a good idea. Leo comes for cuddles with me, and Beckett takes care of his feeding and vet visits."

What a good person. No wonder he felt a connection.

Zane gave Darla a toothy smile.

She chuckled. "Such a Pisces. Big heart, bigger soul." She moved back to the table and the remainder of her muffin with a pondering expression. "You're thinking up something. What is it?"

Zane stopped fingering the lacy tablecloth and leaned forward. He barely knew Beckett, but he knew this.

"I want to make him whole again."

AFTER A CHEESY DINNER OF BAKED MACARONI WITH BECKETT, Zane snuck back to the kitchen, dirty dishes in hand.

He had finally taken his boots off, but the blister on his heel tightened with every step. He probably should have taken them off earlier, but he'd wanted to convince himself he'd made the right decision buying them.

He pulled out two muffins he'd set aside, fished in the cupboard where he'd stashed the candles he'd bought, and used the stove lighter to flame the wick.

Singing "Happy Birthday," he brought the muffin to Beckett. "Make a wish."

Beckett stared at the muffin, the lone flame glittering in his eyes.

"You had to know there was one for you," Zane said, grabbing his plate and rejoining Beckett at the table.

Beckett turned the plate around. "I *was* expecting a muffin, but not after the Hemsworth incident."

Zane glowered, but the look was impossible to maintain

when Beckett's lips twisted up at the edges. A broken bull got a pass. At least, for now. "Good thing it's your birthday."

"Where did you buy the candle?"

"From the store while you were committing the back of a wine bottle to memory."

"I like nutty tones."

"Two peas in a pot."

Beckett's cheek quivered. "Pod."

"Why would it be a pod? These aren't peas in space." Zane bit into his muffin, pushed the bite to the side of his cheek, and pointed a finger at the wax running down Beckett's candle. "Make a wish and eat up." He swallowed. "I need to scout for good after-date kissing locations, so we're taking a walk."

Beckett blew out the candle in an exasperated whiff. "Only if you wear sneakers."

Zane gave a tired laugh. "Too embarrassed to be seen with me in my awesome, amazing, kick-ass turquoise boots?"

"No."

"Why sneakers then?"

"Or socks and flip-flops if you wish." Beckett polished off a forkful of muffin and set the fork down. "Whatever avoids more blisters."

ZANE WORE JANDALS.

Each step in the fresh outdoors felt lighter than the last. Sure, his blister nagged a little, but the jandals helped, and the sting kept him in the moment. The sky glittered with stars and he loved the way their foggy breaths stretched toward them.

"If we cross the road and cut through that park— What are you doing?" Zane asked.

Beckett stopped and pulled out his phone, his loafer tapping against the rim of a pothole. He wore the navy blazer Zane had given him and a light blue scarf knotted around his neck. Maybe not his usual casual walk attire, but to show appreciation for Zane's gift. Zane had spent a considerable amount of their walk admiring the way it molded to his shoulders and tapered torso.

"I'm doing what I should've done after *jumping a ditch.* Google Maps."

Beckett's voice was professor-like, words perfectly pronounced.

Zane tried to steal the phone, but the professor was as quick with his hands as with his tongue. "We'll get home, Becky."

"Funny."

"What is?"

"You think I'm looking up directions to get us home. I'm looking to keep us alive."

Zane dropped his gaze from the crescent moon and glanced around. Overgrown ivy darkened the dead-end street, and shadows in the park across the road stretched eerily. The heavy fumes of fresh graffiti hit the back of his nose. "I suppose the park is a little creepy."

"That's because it's a cemetery." Beckett shook his phone. A broken ivy vine from a six-foot chain-link fence drooped over Beckett's head, the pointed tip of a leaf teasing one of his locks. "Bastard. No reception. How did we end up here?"

Zane shrugged. "*I* was scouting for romantic places to take a date while *you* explained why it's peas in a pod and not pot, and lectured—in crazy detail—what makes Tolstoy so 'fascinating.'"

"You're joking." Beckett's eyes looked soulful in the dark, but his tone did not match.

"I kind of hoped *you* were. *War and Peace* sounds boring as hell, and *Anna Karenina*? Talk about trust issues."

"Romantic places to take a date? The cemetery should nail it." Beckett's sarcastic reply sounded shaky.

Zane spotted two people emerging into the dead-end corner of Mordor. "Oh, look. We'll get directions from that other couple."

"*Other* couple, Zane?" Beckett strode toward the couple, pausing when they began yelling at each other.

"Whoa," Zane said, sharp disgust prickling his stomach.

"You're breaking up with me?" the guy shouted, shaking that poor—very pretty—girl too hard.

Time to barrel to the rescue.

"Leave it," Beckett warned. Followed by a muttered, "For God's sake," and Beckett's loafers slapping behind him on the cracked pavement.

Zane yelled, and the couple lurched apart. The guy took one glance at him and puffed himself up.

"You wanna piece of this, fucker?" puffed dude said, hitting his chest.

Zane ran faster toward them.

The guy's eyes widened, and his bravado waned. He shifted uncomfortably, tucked his tail, and raced off. The girl hiccupped and scuttled off across the road.

Thank God.

He might look like he could beat up three guys with one hand tied behind his back, but the truth was, one tickle to his flank and he'd be on the ground begging for mercy.

He pivoted on the spot where the couple had stood. A few yards behind, Beckett hopped on one foot, one shoe lost, glaring into the bushes. Had it flipped off as he raced after him? Had the laces loosened after their ditch-jumping shenanigans?

Zane crossed back, searching for a sign of the missing loafer. Beckett displayed cool control over his body as he elegantly shuffled on one foot, hands on hips, searching for his shoe.

Streetlight flickered over the sidewalk, playing over the tip of Beckett's loafer peeking out between flat leaves. With an amused grin, Zane plucked it free.

A disbelieving, somewhat impressed face turned on him. "That," Beckett said pointing toward the vanished couple, "is not the way we do things here."

Zane widened the laces of Beckett's shoe. "How do you do them?"

"We gather all our manly strength and run away."

Zane was generally not opposed to the idea. "I may have had ulterior motives."

"Shock me."

The concrete bit into his knee, hard and cold, as he bent and scooped Beckett's foot. A startled sound shot out of Beckett and he braced a hand against the streetlight.

Zane set Beckett's surprisingly warm socked foot on his knee as he pulled back the tongue of the loafer. "I kinda thought by coming to her rescue . . . ."

Beckett frowned. "She'd fall in love with you?"

"Prince Charming coming to the rescue." Zane pulled the leather laces, tied them, and slotted a finger under the tongue to check he hadn't done it too tightly.

Beckett cleared his throat and planted both feet on the ground. "Let's get home."

Zane shoved to his feet. "Follow me."

"Not likely." Warmth wrapped around his fingers and Beckett tugged him in the opposite direction. He gave an incredulous shake of his head. "Scared of a spider, but you throw yourself in the middle of an altercation with an enraged bastard."

"It's quite simple, Becky. The enraged bastard . . . didn't have eight legs."

Beckett side-eyed Zane, tugging out a deep smile.

"Where were we, then?" Beckett said. "That's right, Natasha and Pierre—"

"No more talk on Tolstoy. Please." Zane playfully wriggled his fingers in Beckett's firm grip, and Beckett abruptly let go.

"How about the brilliance of James Joyce?"

Zane stole Beckett's hand back. Cold, deft fingers slid over his large clumsy ones. Startling energy had Zane's hand twitching.

"Zane?" Beckett's voice sounded quiet, uncertain.

"Bromance, Becky."

"Feels an awful lot like romance to me."

"The two are related."

Beckett's step faltered. "What precisely is the difference?"

"We're platonic."

Beckett stared at their joined hands, and Zane tightened his grip. "Platonic."

"It means we don't have sex."

His explanation was met with a blank stare. "Did you read that on wikiHow, too?"

Beckett shook his head. He continued walking with a gentle tug on Zane's hand. "Just so you know, it's probably not a good idea to hold hands like this."

"Yet you're not pulling away."

"It's cold, and your hand is surprisingly hot."

Zane winked at him. "Why, thank you."

The professor lifted a brow at him. "So, James Joyce?"

"How about Beckett." Zane squeezed Beckett's hand. "I want to know more about him."

A subtle quirk of Beckett's lips.

"Samuel Beckett. Irish writer, born in—"

Zane groaned.

We were together. I forgot the rest.

—Walt Whitman

Chapter Six

B linking off sleep, Zane stared up at the pointy ceiling and decided he liked this. Not the pointiness, and not the narrow room or the bed—the bedsprings creaked and groaned with the barest shift of his body and the mattress sagged in the middle—but the homely taste in the air. The whiff of overdone toast in a faraway room. The dusty sunshine coming in through the window and warming his face.

It felt like a home. Like lots of nice memories had been made in the house. Like lots more were still to come.

It was a feeling he gravitated toward. A feeling he hadn't experienced since he was fifteen and Jacob was still living at home. He could remember Jacob bounding into the room with a loaded giant soaker, asking him to help devise a plan to piss their other brothers off.

He should think of a plan to convince Beckett he should stay.

His phone dinged, and he lurched upright to grab it.

Not an email from Rocco about his illustrations.

He slicked a hand through his knotted bed hair. He figured

that Rocco hadn't mailed on the weekend, but he hoped he'd give him feedback today.

The message was an auto-reminder that his visa ran out in twenty-nine days. *So beginneth the countdown.*

He threw back the sheets and stubbed his toe on the toothy bear head of his rug. He hopped up and down with a pained laugh.

Plan. Tomorrow's mission would be convincing Beckett to let him stay. Today's mission was finding a potential soul mate —at the very least scoring a Meet Cute date.

But before any of that could happen with reasonable chance of success?

He needed coffee.

After scrubbing up, he tugged on a hoodie and rocked into the kitchen. No one was there but a ginger cat who jumped onto his heel, clawing his nice jeans—and that charming blister. "You know I'm not a real fish, right?"

He fed Leo and made coffee.

Five minutes later, he set his mug in the sink and slunk to Beckett's room. While the rest of the house spoke of careful organization, Beckett's bedroom reminded Zane that no one was perfect.

Creams and aftershave bottles cluttered the dresser. A blazer was casually tossed over an armchair, and sheets were wantonly draped over a large bed.

Beckett was sitting at the end of the bed, unbuttoned blazer over a crisp white shirt, tying polished brown leather shoes. A leather shoulder bag lay open on the bed next to him, thick wads of paper stretching the inside. Student essays?

Zane leaned against the doorjamb and crossed his ankle. "Either you are right, or pretentiousness is catching."

Beckett leaped off the bed with a startled yet impressively elegant twist of his heel. "Come again?"

"The coffee," Zane said, walking into the room. He

strapped the hefty leather bag over his shoulder. "I took one sip and . . . ."

A smug twinkle hit Beckett's eye. "I was right."

"We're heading back to King's."

THE FRESHLY ROASTED SCENT OF COFFEE MADE HIM SALIVATE.

The same barista as yesterday set two coffees onto the shiny wooden counter. Zane adjusted the strap of Beckett's bag and pulled out his wallet.

Beckett whipped his out too.

Zane batted his wallet away, grinning. "I'll pay."

Beckett eyed him like he was nuts. "You got it last time."

"Yeah, but you're letting me stay with you."

"You paid for the groceries yesterday. I think I can shell out for our coffee."

"But—" Narrowed eyes cut Zane off. The barista's amused gaze ping-ponged between them. Zane bent, catching the faint musk of Beckett's aftershave, and spoke at his ear. "How stubborn is a Taurus?"

Beckett twitched, rocked an inch away, and rubbed his ear. His glance at Zane was fleeting. "Do you like your coffee cold?"

Zane stuffed the wallet back into his pocket and said animatedly, "Why haven't you paid already?"

The barista laughed. "Guys, guys," he said, a smirk eating his face. "Today they're on me."

They thanked him and took their coffees to go.

Beckett stopped at the street corner and Zane bowled into him. A splash of coffee lurched out, thankfully landing on the cup and not Beckett's sleeve. "Sorry. I was literally on a different planet."

"Literally, were you?"

"Yeah. The pitfalls of being a dreamer."

Beckett smirked and gestured to his leather bag. "I'm heading the other way."

Zane held on to the strap. "Past that string of restaurants I saw yesterday?"

"Yes."

"Is it a pretty walk to work?"

"Charming. Now if you'd give—"

"Any nice after-dinner kissy spots I could take a date if I'm lucky enough to get one tonight?"

Beckett sighed. "Keep my bag and follow me."

They walked side by side, giant hoodie and tight blazer. Beckett led them over a historic cobblestone bridge, past an antique bandstand in the park, to a wild alley of weeping willows.

"You're certainly dedicated to making a good impression," Beckett said behind a sip of coffee.

Zane breathed in the fresh spring air. The morning walk had stirred electrifying shivers through him and they were compounding. "The after-dinner walk-and-talk is a prime romantic gesture. I have to perfect it. Has to be memorable."

Beckett stumbled over a tree root and Zane cuffed his arm, steadying him. Beckett brushed himself off, even though he hadn't spilled coffee. "Memorable. I suppose this walk—"

"—is better than the cemetery?"

Was there dirt on Beckett's thighs? He was crunching his coffee cup as he scrubbed at himself. "On the other hand . . . if your date can handle a grave after-dinner walk, chances are high she'll stick around for good."

"You're dead right."

Beckett stopped with the imaginary dirt. His lips jumped in rhythm to Zane's step.

Zane took their empty cups and tossed them into a trashcan marking the edge of campus.

"Mondays I work until eight," Beckett said quickly. "I've no doubt you'll find a date. Enjoy it, and I'll see you tomorrow."

"Tomorrow? I like that you think I'll find a date, but I'm not Casanova enough to have sex on the first date. Not even the third date." Zane preferred to know a person. Preferred to share at least one good laugh before he hit the sheets. "Prepare to find me curled up on that fat armchair in your living room."

At the sound of distant chiming bells, Beckett hurried his step to a Victorian auditorium, and Zane kept pace.

He shoved his hands into his hoodie pocket, staring long-ingly at pompous pillars and brass-on-brick accents. It smelled of old wood, and books, and an insatiable urge to learn.

All very Beckett.

"So this is where you pontificate." It could become a favorite word. Sounded awesomely rude.

"Would you like to come and watch?"

Zane choked on a cough. Images of a naked Beckett lounging on a chaise cupping his hard cock sent an unfamiliar jolt to his gut.

"Zane?"

Zane shelved the image. "More lectures on Tolstoy? As exciting as the offer is——"

"This is a *creative* writing class."

Creative? Like, learning how to write his own stories? Zane rocked on the balls of his feet.

Behind Beckett, a slew of students filed into the audito-rium. All youthful vigor. Brains bursting with quotes. Fingers itching to write the next great American novel.

"I *draw*, Becky."

Beckett observed him with a musing look. He stepped closer, the tail end of his breath flickering against Zane's chin. Those cautious blue eyes soaked Zane in, making him fidget with the strap across his chest. A warm palm landed at his heart and skated up under the strap. "I *teach*, Zane." He lifted the strap of the bag, and Zane ducked out of it. "If you want, you could draw *and* write."

Zane could hear Jacob urging him to take it. To make progress on creating his own comic.

Beckett slung the bag over his shoulder and backed toward his lecture hall. "Think about it."

Zane rubbed at the ghost of the bag strap. He couldn't bring himself to hold Beckett's gaze and stared at his leather shoes until the archway swallowed him.

Draw *and* write.

Zane wavered. He didn't want to leave.

Just didn't know how to convince himself to enter.

Optimism his middle name, Zane chased after a date *and landed one.*

Erin made a great online impression and suggested meeting after yoga class for drinks across the city. It messed with his after-date walk-and-talk plans, but if she wanted to meet at her end of the woods, he was game.

He left the jandals at home in favor of tidy black Oxfords with mint trimming. Once his Uber spat him on the curb outside Franny's, he silenced and pocketed his phone.

Erin sat at the bar in tight jeans and a turquoise shirt reminiscent of his boots, her yoga bag draped on the bar to identify her. Not that she needed it. Her bright red hair would have done the trick.

He moved over a sticky floor to the bar stools. "Erin?"

She smiled and dragged a lazy eye down his length. "Yeah, nice. What's your poison?"

Certainly not alcohol. He planned to remember his Meet Cute. "Ginger tea."

Her ponytail swished as she stopped waving down the

bartender and looked at him. Her mouth twisted into a seductive smile that had Zane backing up an inch. "You like ginger, do you? I've got a lot of that you can try at home."

Before he could protest, she dragged him outside into the cool evening. She tiptoed fingers between his shirt buttons and he blinked, mind scrambling to find the best way to turn her down without—

Her finger hit the bottom of his chin. "How about a little taste now?"

She captured his face and kissed him.

Despite an entire beef and broccoli bowl, Zane *still* couldn't kill the aftertaste of his terrible date. Not even Darla's colorful company had picked him up.

He slouched back to Beckett's and to the attic, veered around the bear head, and strapped on his earphones. Public Service Broadcasting's "Progress" pumped in his ears and he plopped onto his squeaky bed and stared at the trunk base where his bloody boots stood on display.

He drummed his fingers over his stomach.

He fell off the horse? He'd get back on. His next date would be better.

Had to be.

At his phone's vibration, he checked out the photo of Cassie that Jacob had sent. Poor girl had Jacob's nose. He smiled, a tiny needy ache pulling in his stomach.

Zane: When can I see you guys?

No response. Jacob was probably busy with the baby.

An email notification popped up and Zane scrambled into a sitting position. Rocco, regarding his work on the last *Scarlet*

Sentinel vs. Fire Falcon panels. With clammy fingers, he shut off his music and pulled the headphones to his neck. A nervous smile stretched his lips.

> *Got the latest draft. The panels are fine. But you don't draw what I ask you to. You've added too much emotion to Fire Falcon. What I like about working with you is that you follow the script to the letter and never add your own flair to my stories. The last two serials you've gotten a little ahead of yourself. I'd appreciate if you'd just stick to what you're good at: color not concept.*
>
> *I'm sure you understand my point. You draw well.*
> *Thanks for delivering on time.*

Zane scooped his fingers through his hair. "Right."

He slunk into the blue-tiled bathroom and flung open the cabinet under the sink. *It doesn't matter.* Rollo didn't like his panel. No point in dwelling on it.

Among a collection of abandoned household items, he found a dusty purple bottle that looked promising, squirted some into the claw-footed tub, and filled it with warm water.

The bath foamed with bubbles, its lavender scent strong. His eyes stung. He sniffed.

What he needed was to be kind to himself. He ducked back to the cabinet and pulled out a dozen tealight candles. One trip to the kitchen and back, and he had matches to light them.

He stripped out of his T-shirt and yanked off his pants. The floor tile coldly bit the soles of his feet. He twisted toward the bath and paused at his reflection in the mirror.

Large, square shoulders, a tapering torso, gently defined muscle. Blond hair at his chest, darker tufts under his arms and at the base of his uncut cock. Legs, long and corded.

Disappointed brown eyes returned his stare. He turned away, shut off the main light, and submerged himself in the hot water.

Maybe what Luke had said at Equestrian Mode was right. At least he had good looks going for him.

Footsteps sounded, a muffled thump outside in the hall, and the bathroom door burst open. Beckett strode inside, the top buttons of his shirt loose, fingers prying the buttons at his pants. His gaze landed on the bath, and he and his fingers froze.

Beckett scanned the flame-studded bath. "This is the twenty-first century. I pay the bills on time. We have electricity."

"I'm romancing myself."

"Having a light on would have stopped me from charging in here. Locking the door also would have helped."

"I have a weird tic about locking bathroom doors. What if I slip in the bath and no one can help me?"

"You'd be less likely to slip if you could see what you were doing."

"Candles are so pretty, though. Don't you use them?"

"They're emergency candles in case the power goes out." Beckett glanced at the toilet. "How long were you planning on luxuriating?"

"You can pee in front of me, I don't care."

Beckett chewed his bottom lip as he inched toward the porcelain bowl.

"By the way," Zane said, "there's beef and broccoli and some rice on the stove for you."

Beckett hesitated at the toilet, his back mostly to Zane. "My favorite." Did Zane detect a splash of shyness in Beckett? How sweet.

"Thank Darla. She was nice enough to tell me what you liked and found me a recipe."

"Did I have beef in the freezer?"

"Nah." Zane grabbed Beckett's shampoo, sniffed the gentle scent, and liberally applied it. "Nipped to the store. We were out of toilet paper, too, so I grabbed some while I was at it."

Beckett lifted the seat and his shoulders seemed to bunch.

"Would it help if I close my eyes?" Zane asked.

Beckett shook his head and snorted. "Just give me a second. You're kind of distracting."

He hadn't finished washing his hair, but he could step out of the bathroom and give Beckett privacy. Water sloshed as he heaved to his feet. Beckett glanced over his shoulder and did a double take. "Whatever you're doing, it's not helpful."

"I thought—"

"Submerge all that muscle under the cover of bubbles this instant."

Zane laughed and did as he was told.

Beckett cursed under his breath. The heavy tinkle of pee hit water, followed by a breathy chuckle. "Word-of-the-day toilet paper?"

Zane scrubbed his hair. "Thought I'd need it to keep up."

"You are something else." Beckett's tone mellowed. "How was your date?"

"It was not love at first sight."

"I never suspected it would be."

"It wasn't even *like* at first sight."

The toilet flushed. Beckett fixed himself and turned to the sink. Washing his hands, he studied Zane through the reflection in the mirror. "Will you go out with her again?"

"No!"

Beckett stared down at his hands he was still rinsing. "Want to talk about it?"

"She said I was an underwhelming kisser."

Beckett turned off the tap, grabbed a hand towel, and faced Zane. "That was a polite offer. You were supposed to decline."

"In my defense, I didn't even want to kiss. She lunged at me. Then had the bones to say I suck at mouth-to-mouth."

Beckett dried his hands. "I wasn't on her side, Zane."

"You're on my side?"

"I can't be sure." Beckett surveyed the door. "But if you call it mouth-to-mouth . . . ."

Zane sank deep into the water, bubbles tickling his lips. "Oh man, what if I *am* a terrible kisser?"

"That beef and broccoli smells delicious." Beckett inched toward the door, clutching a hand towel.

"Wait."

Beckett pivoted, gaze fixed somewhere above Zane's head.

"I'll need that towel."

Beckett frowned and shook out the tiny towel. "This? It wouldn't cover one cheek."

"Then I'll leave the bathroom covered only in bubbles, or you'll bring me your biggest, fluffiest towel?" Their gazes caught, and Zane flashed his pearly whites.

Beckett's eyes darted from the clothes puddled on the floor to the bath. "Didn't think all this through, did you?"

"Story of my life," Zane said with an upbeat laugh.

Beckett shrewdly read it, the amused curve of his lips faltering. "Are you . . . ? Is this . . . ?" He gestured to the bubbles and candles. "Are you having a bad day?"

Zane shrugged. "I have shoulders wide enough to carry the heaviness of the Earth, but some days they are barely enough to hold the hollowness of my head."

Beckett's soft intake of breath reached Zane, right to his bubble-laced toes. "Zane . . . ."

Zane ducked his hair under the water and washed out the shampoo. "Nothing a little daydreaming and a lot of drawing won't mend."

Beckett dropped his hand towel in the sink, picked up one

of the candles, and perched on the tiled rim of the bath. He played his fingers over the flame and it flickered between them.

"Would you show me some of your work?"

The light of the flame threw shadows over Beckett's face, making his eyes appear soft.

If he had a pencil nearby, Zane would have a hard time not drawing this frame right here. Yet, it'd be a challenge to sketch the right emotion; to elicit the same little shivers in the viewer that raced through him now.

"Do you really want to check out my work or are you saying that to be nice?"

"I'm saying it because I want to be mean and cruel and make you cry." Beckett reached into the tub and flicked bubbles in his face. Zane blew them off with a laugh, and their gazes melded. "I want to see all your stuff."

Becky, you just made my day. "Then as soon as I'm ready, I'll stuff you."

Love sought is good, but given unsought is better.

—Shakespeare

Chapter Seven

Starting the morning at King's was becoming tradition.

Today their cappuccinos stood at a high table overlooking a quaint, oak-lined street. Soft air breezed inside, mixing with the delicious aroma of roasting coffee.

Armed with his laptop, Zane was ready to jump back into the dating trenches. Beckett had a late start and was reading the newspaper across from him with the same intensity he'd used to study Zane's illustrations last night. Concentrated and curious.

Bright pink hearts bubbled up on his screen and a sensual female voice erupted from his speakers. "*Looking for love? Look no further.*"

Zane pounded on the keys, desperate to mute the volume. Beckett gave a wry grin. Zane couldn't see Beckett's eyes tracking any lines and kicked him under the table.

Beckett peered over the paper at him. "Another day searching for the one?"

"That, and convincing you we should bunk together when your sister comes."

Beckett's newspaper flopped over his hand and he struggled to set it upright.

"In fact, I will convince you to let me stay until I marry or am kicked out of the country."

"Zane, you and me in bed together——"

"Look, I'll understand if you don't want me to stay. I'm determined we'll survive me moving somewhere else. But . . . I need to convince you to keep me."

Beckett's cell phone alarm dinged. He slipped off his chair and looped his bulging bag over his shoulder. "I've got to go. If I don't drum in the importance of Oscar Wilde, none of my students will——"

"Care?"

"Pass their paper."

Beckett's fake scathing glare tickled Zane.

Zane kissed his fingers and blew him a kiss. They both hesitated and Zane felt a curious flush at the base of his neck, but . . . bromantic, right?

He charged on, getting louder as a frowning Beckett headed out the door. "I'll convince you, Becky. I'll twist your arm. I'll literally hook you."

ZANE MADE GOOD ON HIS PROMISE LATER IN THE AFTERNOON, refusing to slip out from Beckett's fingers. The man had him for good, and Zane had the perfect idea how to make him realize that all on his own.

In jeans, jandals, and a jacket—Beckett was clearly having an influence on him—he took himself to the specialty wine store next to the secondhand store where he'd bought his bear rug.

He entered the oak-scented store and meandered through tight aisles of fancy labeled wine.

He gnawed his lip. Did he choose the red wine from California? What about a South African one? Definitely not award-winning Australian. He glared at a skipping kangaroo on one label.

Beckett needed Kiwi wine.

"Can I help you?"

Zane twisted to a sales clerk wearing a black "Stop Whining and Start Wining" T-shirt. She smiled and righted a bottle on the shelf.

"I'm looking for a good New Zealand wine?"

"We have a whole section, just this way."

He followed her around the corner to a wall of Kiwi wines. His eye caught on a Marlborough pinot noir, and he was thrown back to the first time he'd traveled the South Island. Jacob had organized it the year he'd left home. They'd taken Jacob's van and toured for three weeks. On the ferry heading back, Jacob had told him he was leaving for the States.

He still ached remembering the shock. The hollow sense of loss and abandonment.

Zane swallowed the lump in his throat and stared at the wine. "What's a wine that says, 'Don't throw me out'?"

"Oh, need to get on her good side, huh?"

"His. Yes." A delicate cursive design caught his eye. He picked up the bottle. "Would this charm him?"

"That has tones of chocolate. Do you know what he likes?"

"Nuts. We're two peas in a pod."

She smirked. "What kind of budget did you have in mind?"

"What does a good wine go for? Something around the hundred mark?"

She scanned the shelves. "What's his birth date?"

"Can you pick his favorite wine by his zodiac?"

She grinned. "Not currently one of our methods. But we may have a bottle from his birth year."

Right. Cool. "His birthday is May 11 . . . ." Wait. What

year? "Just a minute." He called Beckett, who picked up with a distracted hum. "Quick question. What year were you born? Like, 1980?"

The line crackled, followed by a moment of silence. "Zane?"

"Yeah?"

"How old do you think I am?"

"Late thirties?"

"Late——" Beckett made an indignant sound. "Good God. I *just* turned thirty. 1988."

Zane angled the phone and told the clerk Beckett's birth year. He smirked as he resumed chatting with Beckett. "Close. The eighties. What were they like?"

"Wild. I was a raging fan of Mommy. Screamed for her every four minutes."

Zane could picture it. He probably enunciated every holler. "Do you still call her Mommy?"

"Why are you calling?"

"It's nearly five, are you still at work?"

"I have papers to grade. I'm heading home to continue there."

"Do you always grade at home?"

"Most of the time. Especially today."

Did Zane detect frustration? "Are you good, Becky?"

"Delightful. Dandy."

"Dishonest?"

Beckett sighed. "Why are you calling?"

"Why else? To charm your pants off."

ZANE BOUGHT WINE AND ANOTHER GIFT FROM THE SECONDHAND store and raced back to Beckett's, determined to find out about Beckett's day.

He entered quietly, hoping not to distract Beckett. He slipped around the corner and halted. Standing in front of the hall mirror, thumbs hitched into a pair of Calvin Kleins, the professor was eyeing his physique.

Beckett had seemed flawless clothed, but practically naked, tight muscles flexing, Beckett was perfection. Sloped shoulders, gracefully lean body, gentle tan of smooth skin. Smooth everywhere.

Zane gripped his fabric bag of bribes. God, how many times had he wished for such a body for himself growing up.

"Late thirties!" Beckett muttered to himself.

"When I said I want to charm your pants off," Zane said, startling Beckett into a hop, "I didn't mean it quite so literally."

Beckett planted hands on hips, fingers half splayed on skin, half on boxer-briefs. "Should I be disgruntled at your wildly incorrect assumption of my age or impressed you used 'literally' correctly."

"You seem good at multitasking. I'm sure you can be both." Zane's gaze was drawn to Beckett's drumming fingers and the soft way the light in the hall touched his side, chest . . . . When he got to Beckett's face, he found the man watching him thoughtfully.

"Had enough ogling?"

Zane stepped toward the taut, smooth slopes of Beckett's body, pausing a foot away. Close enough to feel a surprising lick of heat run through him. "Not really. You're hot." Zane winked and pivoted into the living room. "It's almost enough to make me slide up a notch on the Kingly Scale."

Beckett followed, strained voice hitting the back of Zane's neck. "The what?"

"The Kingly Scale. It's a sliding scale that identifies how straight or gay or bi you are. Really, Becky. You should know this." Zane rounded the kitchen island and set his bag of bribes on the counter.

"Kingly Scale?" Beckett asked, voice hopping like the corners of his lips. Zane eyed him, and Beckett cleared his throat. "Sure it's not called . . . something else? Kinsey, perhaps?"

Beckett didn't like being wrong, did he? "Pretty sure it's the Kingly Scale," Zane said, adding a kind smile.

Beckett stepped behind the table in a shaft of window light that did hypnotic things to his profile. He hadn't lost his smile, but Zane didn't trust it—although any type of smile beat the frustration he'd detected on the phone. "Why are you smirking like that?"

Beckett's eyebrows arched. "Like what?"

"I said *almost* slide up a notch. You're stunning, and I like admiring. But I'm pretty sure anyone would."

"That's not why I'm smiling. Well, not the only reason." Before Zane could follow up, Beckett grabbed his jeans off a pile of clothes slung over a chair. He turned his back to Zane and shoved them on. He turned around again to slip on his shirt. He pointed at Zane's bag. "What did you buy?"

Living with you, I hope.

"A little education, among other things." He pulled out a postcard of a world map. "Come here."

With languid grace, Beckett pushed off the windowsill— still buttoning his shirt—and moved to the other side of the counter. "Closer."

Beckett raised a brow.

"It's a tiny postcard."

Beckett rounded the counter, keeping a notable few feet between them.

Zane pushed the postcard under his nose and moved closer until he felt the pleasant thrum of energy radiating between their arms.

"Careful there, Zane. Any closer and I'll need a whole new scale."

Zane laughed and passed him a pen. Beckett was funny. "Circle New Zealand on this map."

Beckett scowled.

"I'll give you a clue. It's an island."

Beckett snatched the pen, clicked it, and watched Zane while circling Australia.

Zane laughed out a groan. He took it back. Beckett wasn't funny at all. "Let's try again: national animal?"

"Kangaroo."

He was doing this on purpose. Had to be. "Okay, for real now. Clue, it's a bird."

"Emu."

Zane growled into Beckett's ear. "I could literally jump you for that."

Beckett gulped. "Must take after your national animal. What else is in the bag?"

Tossing out a laugh, Zane drew out the bottle of Kiwi wine and planted it before him. Beckett snatched it up, eyes lighting as he murmured wine jargon. Zane rested a hip against the counter and admired the enthusiasm.

Much better than the hint of frustration he'd heard earlier. Still, he didn't want to ignore the pain he'd heard.

Beckett's tongue darted over his bottom lip. "What?"

"How was your day?" Zane asked.

Beckett's lips twisted down, and he pulled out two wine-glasses. "It was picking up."

"What happened at work?"

"You know, I should clean up the rest of my clothes." Beckett swiveled toward the table and Zane cuffed his upper arm, gently tugging him back around.

"Come on, Becky."

"This wine must have cost a fortune."

"Fortune favors the bold." Zane absently stroked his fingers up and down Beckett's upper arm. "I want to continue living with you. What happened today?"

Beckett scrubbed a hand over his jaw. "Luke was offered a job in my department as an assistant professor."

"Your *ex-husband*, Luke."

"Thank you for that necessary reminder."

Zane winced in sympathy. "No freestanding bookshelves to sink behind?"

"He walked into my shared office with the same smile that won me over and asked if there would be any hard feelings if he took the job."

"How is he a professor? He's a complete idiot! Tell me you told him that."

Beckett cast his eyes toward the postcard, blinking rapidly. "Remember when I said people are complicated?"

"Oh, no . . . ." Zane didn't like where this was heading, but he understood.

Beckett nodded. "I gave him my most carefree smile and said I look forward to working with him."

"Oh, Becky."

"It gets worse," Beckett said, pain etched in the depths of his eyes despite a stoic expression.

Zane knew the emotion intimately. He pulled Beckett against his chest.

Beckett stiffened in his hold.

"Bromance," Zane whispered into his dark locks.

Beckett sank against his chest and dropped his forehead against Zane's shoulder. Beckett's warmth radiated through his soft shirt under Zane's palms as he rubbed Beckett's lower back.

He felt a strange connection holding Beckett like this. He was slender and strong and bursting with intelligence Zane only dreamed of. There were a million combinations of words to offer such a smart man, but Zane only found one.

It fell stupidly from his tongue. "There, there."

Warm breath puffed over his collar to the base of his neck. "He officially starts in August but has been invited to the staff dinner at Chiffon next week."

Zane clamped his palms against Beckett's hips. "The one you've been looking forward to? The one you bought clothes for?"

"Did I show you? I opted for the blazer in platitudinous tan."

"*Bookish* tan, Becky."

"The worst part?"

There was more? Zane squeezed Beckett closer.

"The head wants him to take over my beloved creative classes and wants me to focus on historical lit."

"The *Toy Story*s of the world?"

Beckett pulled back, thumbs stroking Zane's nape, and he smiled with fond amusement. Zane might not find the words Beckett needed, but maybe he could draw them for him.

Beckett dropped his arms, twisted to the counter, and opened a drawer. He cleared his throat. "I have the feeling this is a bad idea. A terrible idea. And I'm going to do it anyway."

"Do what?"

Beckett uncorked the wine and poured a small serving into each glass. He picked up both glasses and handed one to Zane.

Zane pinched the stem and felt the vibration as Beckett clinked their glasses together. "You can stay."

"Your home is my home? Thursday we bunk?"

Beckett swallowed, Adam's apple jutting. He murmured into another sip of wine, "An ill-advised idea, indeed."

And when one of them meets with his other half, the actual half of himself, whether he be a lover of youth or a lover of another sort, the pair are lost in an amazement of love and friendship and intimacy.

—Plato

Chapter Eight

Z ane raced up to the attic, giving Beckett time and space to grade his papers. He emptied his bag of bribes: two Viking-style blowing horns, a small brown belt, a large nose ring, and the strongest glue he could purchase.

He gathered up the bear rug and settled it on the bed. "If I'm keeping you," he murmured. "You need a makeover."

He listened to music as he worked. Beckett's ghost, light and tingly, wrapped around him.

At the finishing touch, his phone dinged. Jacob?

He pried apart his fingers and peeled off a fine layer of gum. He snuck downstairs and washed his hands thoroughly, barely drying them before checking his phone.

Not a cute picture of his niece but another email from Rocco.

He slumped onto the closed toilet seat as acid swished in his stomach.

As Scarlet Sentinel vs. Fire Falcon *is ending, I've started drafting a new project. I wanted to know if you'll commit to illustrating it? I've attached an outline of the idea. If you're interested, I'll prepare a contract. I hope you understand the reason for my candor in my last mail. I like your style, but I am the one with complete creative control.*

He bounced his phone over his knee, wishing he felt thrilled to be asked. To be told he was any good.

Instead, his stomach sank to his feet. Jeez, this was awesome. His favorite activity in the world was to draw, and now he could barely muster a flutter of excitement.

It was a job, though. It didn't pay much but it gave him routine, and it felt good to say he worked rather than admit he mostly lived off his inheritance.

Women wanted to know he was self-sufficient and could provide for a family.

Without his inheritance, he couldn't.

He squeezed his phone and his eye caught on the word-of-the-day toilet paper.

Metamorphosis

Noun.
A complete change in appearance, personality, circumstances, etc.

What about brains?

If he were smarter, would he be able to create his own stories? Find a way to live off his work? If he had his own graphic art serial, would he have more luck finding love?

Zane stood, slipped his phone into his pocket, and splashed water over his face. Could he get that smart? Or should he take up Rocco on his job offer?

He needed a little more of that wine. And a lot more help from Beckett.

ZANE NERVOUSLY SIPPED HIS WINE.

Beckett sat in a professor-like poise at the dining table, noting in the margins of the paper before him. His blazer lay slung on the adjacent chair, and he'd swapped out his wine for what looked like ginger tea in a heart-themed mug.

The lights were on and the open curtains meant the windows reflected everything.

Zane took another sip and set his glass on the table with a clatter. He gripped the knobs at either side of the dining chair. Wood dug into his clammy hands.

He let go and grabbed his glass again.

Beckett's red pen paused and then continued. Without looking up, he spoke. "What do you want?"

Oh, just the whole metamorphosis of self from stupid to smart. "Nothing."

"You're pacing in front of me. You keep opening and shutting your mouth like a fish."

"Like Pisces."

"What do you want?"

Zane gestured to the red pen and the piles of papers. "You're busy grading stories."

"Tends to come with the job."

"Yeah. Makes sense. You grade good. I mean, you look good grading. I mean, you know. It's good that you do it."

Beckett turned those intense blue eyes on him. How anyone in his class could concentrate with Beckett looking at them, he had no idea. Maybe they got used to the little jumps in their chest every time their gazes connected?

"Zane?"

Zane's shoulders deflated, and he dragged out the chair and slumped into it, blazer soft against his back. "Jacob thinks I should—" Zane stopped and tried again. "*I* would like to write a graphic novel serial. I wondered if you'd help?"

Beckett's brow bunched with mild confusion. "I thought you did this for your job?"

"It's not the illustrations I have a problem with. It's the story."

"Right."

"Yeah."

"What do you need help with?"

"The plot and the character arcs. The concept. Also, theme. And anything else I've forgotten."

"You want me to help you write the entire story?"

"Such a generous offer."

Beckett leaned back and tapped his pen to his mouth. Did he know he was tapping the wrong end of it? Little red marks blotted the underside of his lip. "Are you doing this because Luke might take my creative writing classes, or do you really want to write your own story? Because yesterday I offered for you to attend my lecture and you didn't seem interested."

"Yesterday I was stupid. Today, I'm metamorphing. Meta-morphosizing?"

"Metamorphosing."

"I've a ways to go." He tossed out a grin. "I really want to write my own story, and if you could help—if you *want* to—"

"I want to."

Zane almost choked on his "Thank you."

A cunning look hit him as if Beckett was about to add something. "*If . . . .*"

There it was. Zane leaned forward and eased the pen from Beckett's lips before he started looking like a vampire. "What do you want?"

"You." Beckett blinked at his confiscated pen. "You *reading.*"

"Me reading?"

Beckett gestured to the shelves in the living area. "You have your choice of book." He frowned as Zane dragged his chair closer, legs grating over the wooden floor. "To be clear: I won't write your story for you. I'll guide you through the process step-by-step."

"Could you also guide me through the book word-by-word?"

If Beckett didn't have time for that, maybe Zane could choose a book that had been made into a movie. Something he could study on his laptop in bed.

Amusement hit Beckett's gaze. "No."

"You won't guide me through the book?"

"No, you can't just watch the movie."

Read minds, could he? "What am I thinking now, Professor?"

Beckett cocked his head. The shift made the red ink on his bottom lip and chin more prominent. Beckett's tongue slid over his lip, just shy of the blots. His mouth pushed together as he spoke wistfully. "Probably not what I hope you're thinking about."

Zane lifted his gaze. "Yeah, no lingering analysis of *War and Peace* happening here."

Beckett tucked a lock behind his ear and it shifted back. "What were you thinking?"

Zane slid Beckett's barely touched tea over and dipped his index finger into the lukewarm liquid. Commence the look of bafflement.

Zane smothered a chuckle. A drop of liquid hit a student essay as he reached over the short corner space between them.

Beckett's voice jumped to a whisper. "What are you doing?"

"Your lips are so red." Zane slid his wet finger over Beckett's soft bottom lip.

Beckett's hitching breath trickled over his wet finger to the base where it met his middle finger.

"Is this . . . you being bromantic?"

Zane ran his fingertip back and forth over the splotches,

lifting his eyes to Beckett's wary-yet-curious ones. "Sorry, should I stop?"

Beckett gave the barest shake of his head as Zane's finger grazed Beckett's top lip.

Zane dipped his clean middle finger into Beckett's tea and reached out to continue removing the ink.

Beckett snatched his hand and stared at the red ink staining his index finger. He shut his eyes briefly. "Of course."

Zane smiled. "Don't be so hard on yourself. I do it all the time."

Beckett scrubbed his face with a pitiful laugh.

"About reading that book," Zane said.

Beckett followed his glance to the shelf in the kitchen.

"Can't be a cookbook, either."

Fair enough. "Can it be romantic, at least? With a good hook and an awesome Meet Cute?"

"*Pride and Prejudice,* Jane Austen."

Zane jumped out of his chair and stopped before the wall of books. "Are these in any particular order?"

"Alphabetical, starting at the top left."

Under *P* for *Pride and Prejudice*? Or *J* for Jane? How dumb would he sound if he asked?

He scanned the lower shelves. "How, um, fat is this book?"

Chair legs squealed, and Beckett strolled over and plucked a book from the top shelf. "Under *A* for Austen," he murmured, planting the book against his chest.

Zane grabbed it, locking Beckett's hand under his. He looked at Beckett, who kept his eyes focused on the book.

"I flunked out of school," he said quietly. "What if I don't understand all of it?"

"You can ask me any question you like."

"But . . . ." Zane shifted awkwardly.

Beckett weaseled his hand free. "What's the matter?"

Zane laughed. "Sorry, you'll have to deal with my stupid questions."

"The only stupid question is an unasked question."

A stray, sob-like lump jumped into his throat, and he swallowed it. "I was supposed to be charming your pants off. Yet you're literally charming off mine."

Beckett dropped a smile toward Zane's jeans. "Should we start with a quick lesson on literal language versus figurative?"

Zane set the book down and ducked into the kitchen. "Okay, but I'll need a snack. Maybe some cut-up fruit in case I have to heckle you for being a bad teacher."

Beckett scoffed, returned to the table, and picked up his mug.

"Can I get you anything?" Zane asked. "Hotter tea?"

Beckett stared into the cup. "I'm . . . happy with this one."

Zane grabbed a bag of pecans and ripped into them on his way back to Beckett.

"I'm literally dying for you to teach me," he said with a cheeky wink. He wasn't 100 percent sure of literal and figurative differences, but he could guess.

Beckett took a long sip of tea. "Literal descriptions are stating facts—saying something as it is. For example, your eyes are brown." A flickered glance hit Zane's gaze and returned to the tea. "Figurative language describes something by comparing it to something different, often using metaphor, simile, personification, hyperbole, or symbolism."

Zane swallowed his pecan and leaned forward. "Can you give an example?"

"Metaphor." Beckett gestured to the stack of papers to his left. "I'm drowning in work."

"No, Becky. Use my eyes as an example. That's more bromantic."

"You're killing me."

"Metaphor, right?"

"Hyperbole—deep exaggeration—although in this case . . . ." He shifted on his seat, lips curving into a crooked smile.

Zane leaned forward. "Hyperbole my eyes, Professor."

Beckett's brilliant blue eyes met his. Clear and bright with a touch of vulnerability. "They knock me off my feet."

The ground figuratively lurched under Zane, throwing him off balance. He couldn't ignore the warmth in his chest, spreading through his body—or his smile that didn't feel big enough.

Zane's phone burst into song and they both startled, falling back in their seats.

"Hyperbole? I don't know," Zane mused, leaving the table. "Sounds like a cliché to me."

He answered Jacob's call.

Beckett's voice trailed into the hall after him. "Sounds like you should give yourself more credit."

Zane lay on the squeaky bed in the attic, mattress laughing with Jacob at retold misadventures with his new daughter.

"I know they say having a kid is hard," Jacob said. "But it is *hard*."

Joy filled his brother's voice.

"Anyway, that was more of an apology why I didn't get back to you sooner. We would love it if you could visit Saturday? You'd have to bus, though. I don't want to leave either of my girls."

"I'm there."

Zane heard Jacob smiling through his voice. "I can't wait for you to meet her. Oh, hey, here's an idea. You could catch a ride with the professor if it's on a weekend he visits home. His family home is, like, literally the one that backs ours."

"Literally, literally? Or was that hyperbole?"

Look at him. Getting smarter already.

Jacob laughed. "We're separated by a creek. Anne says to tell Beckett to come see her and the baby too."

"His sister is coming Thursday, so I'm not sure. Will Luke be there?" Because in that case, he wouldn't even suggest poor Beckett come. In fact, Zane wasn't thrilled with the idea of seeing him either.

"Nope. We asked, but he and his boyfriend are at a wedding."

Phew.

They chatted until Cassie started making a fuss in the background and Jacob abruptly ended the call. Zane loved that his brother was there for his girls just like he had been there for him.

Infinite reasons to get smart: he'd stop making a fool of himself. Be luckier in the heart department. Make Jacob proud when he finished a story completely his own.

Make him clever enough to keep up with Beckett.

With that thought, Zane forced himself through the first pages of *Pride and Prejudice*. Was he meant to laugh or not? It sounded pretentious and funny. Reading it and imagining Beckett's voice as narrator made it better.

After a chapter, he tore a page out of his sketchbook and marked the page. With no side table, he rested it atop his suitcase and lay back in bed with his hands hooked under his head.

The made-over bear rug filled his side vision. No longer a bear rug, it now had Viking horns and a nose ring. It was a spirited bull. Sort of, close enough.

He was a visual person, and he liked symbolizing his goals.

Example one: the boots that stood on the trunk. He was

determined to put them to good use. They might rub his heels and look ridiculous on him—right now—but if he scored the right clothes, he could pull them off. They were too damn hot not to wear.

Example two: his all-time favorite comics lined up at the base of the wall like miniature posters. He wanted to create illustrations and stories as incredible as these artists had.

Example three: the calendar tacked above his bed, bright red crosses marking off the days before his flight home; his return ticket tucked into a fold at the back. He would put his heart out there to get trampled a hundred times if he had to.

Enter the bull.

Zane had been in Beckett's home four days and already knew two things: Beckett had a beautiful laugh, and he should be sharing it with a boyfriend who'd laugh back.

I think . . . if it is true that there are as many minds
as there are heads, then there are as many kinds of
love as there are hearts.

—Leo Tolstoy

Chapter Nine

A sickening thump echoed through the duplex wall. Zane abandoned his online chat with part-time librarian Clara and pounded out of the house calling Darla's name. Fear lurched up his chest. He jumped the porch fence and banged on the door as he opened it. "Darla?"

At a distant groan, Zane shouldered into the house.

He found her on the living room floor, rubbing her ankle, wildly berating a broken chair.

"Holy crap, are you okay?" He slid to his knees before her and she looked at him, a pink flush creeping into her cheeks.

"The Krav Maga is a little rusty."

"A little rusty is right, but it's not the Krav Maga."

Darla was limber enough to manage smacking him on the back of the head, so things were looking up. They shared a grin. "Where's the pain?"

"I'm sure it will pass."

"Don't be a ninny. Tell me."

"You cheeky fish."

"Stubborn mule."

"Bumbling buffoon."

He laughed. "Please, darling. I want to help."

"It's true. Flattery gets you everywhere. My ankle is a little tender. But it'll go away on its own."

Yeah, well, he wasn't taking any chances. He scheduled an Uber, scooped Darla in his arms, and escorted her to the local clinic.

During the long wait to see the doctor, he asked if he could call anyone. "Not your grandson? Are you sure?"

"He'll worry, and it's nothing. Their surrogate is due any week."

Zane messaged Beckett, giving him a heads up in case he got home before them.

Becky: Hold on, I'm coming.

Zane: You don't have to. We'll Uber back. :-)

Becky: Fifteen minutes.

The nurse had just called Darla in when Beckett arrived, car keys clutched as he scoured the room. Zane waved him to his corner of the waiting room. A magazine rested on Zane's thigh, opened at an article on the astrological signs in love. Darla had pressed it into his hands and told him to read it.

Beckett took the seat adjacent to him. "How's she doing?"

"She didn't injure her tongue. I'm sorry if I made it seem like an emergency. I didn't mean for you to drop everything and come."

Beckett palmed Zane's knee. His grip was surprisingly firm, and the heat of his palm seeped through Zane's jeans. "It's what family does."

Zane swallowed thickly. Jacob would have thought so too. "You'd make good family, Becky."

Beckett removed his hand and dropped his gaze to the magazine on Zane's thigh.

"Would you like to read it?" Zane offered.

Beckett's nose wrinkled. "Horoscopes?"

"That's how I feel when you talk about *War and Peace*."

"Then I thoroughly apologize." Beckett searched through the magazines on the table.

Zane lifted his magazine and read. Every few sentences he peered over the top at Beckett, who'd picked up a *National Geographic*. "Wha'cha reading?"

He loved how Beckett seemed so aware of everything that he never needed to lift his eyes off whatever text he was reading to answer. "A fascinating article by a Professor Callaghan Glover on dinosaur mating rituals. Did you know their courtship resembles that of the modern bird?"

"Did you know that if seduction were an art, Taurus would be Cubism?"

Beckett's eyes stopped tracking the text of his article. "What does that even mean? That it's piecemeal? Lots of little tokens of romance and nothing big?"

Zane hadn't read it like that. "Or that you love from all angles. Not just physical but emotional, too." Beckett looked at him, and Zane slowly lifted his article up over a smile. "Or maybe, like Cubism, your love is unforgettable."

Magazine pages slapped together, and Zane peeked over the top of his.

Beckett hunched forward toward him. "What else does it say?"

"Your monthly horoscope suggests you open your heart and take a risk. Have you thought about getting back out there? Dating?"

Beckett flinched, leaned back in his seat, and folded his arms. "What does it say about Pisces? You'll fall in love by the month's end?"

"Thought you weren't interested in this?"

"I'm a professor. I should probably be more open-minded. Hand it over."

He passed it over with a smirk, then dragged *National Geographic* off Beckett's lap. "I should probably be more open-minded too."

Beckett delved into the astrological sign article.

Callaghan Glover's article was intense. Peppered with big words that made him eye Beckett, wondering if he could ask what they meant. Reading the article was intimidating, but alongside that, there was a spark of fascination.

The clever words had him frowning. "Do you think it's possible to fall in love with intelligence?"

Beckett looked up sharply, and it was Zane's turn to keep his eyes glued to the text. He hoped the magazine masked the heat rising in his face. "I mean, is it weird that . . . . Never mind."

"Go on. I'm listening."

He lifted the article higher so he couldn't see Beckett in his side vision. "It's ridiculous."

Chair legs scraped over the linoleum floor and Beckett pried the magazine away. "I am ridiculously curious."

Zane lowered his voice, glancing from side to side, making sure no one would overhear him. "I've been thinking about it. All the women I've been attracted to are really smart. Is it weird to get kinda hot when someone uses big words I don't know?"

Beckett straightened, fingers drumming over his knee. "Sesquipedalian prose turns you on?"

Zane jerked a finger at him. "Exactly what I'm talking about. Wait, what does that mean?"

"Sesquipedalian? Polysyllabic."

"Now you're just doing it on purpose."

Beckett rubbed his jaw, hiding his smile. "Long-winded words turn you on."

He was beginning to realize they did.

Which would make things harder for him. Women who used long-winded words weren't interested in anyone who didn't understand them. He groaned and flopped back into his chair.

Beckett bounced the rolled-up horoscope magazine on the inside of his knee. "There are no rules of attraction, Zane. Trying to impose rules might make you miss out."

"Yeah, you're right. I wouldn't want to stare into the face of love and never recognize it."

Beckett smiled, then looked sharply to the right, where Darla was being wheeled out, loudly complaining that she didn't need such attention.

Zane pushed to his feet. "We're up."

Beckett drove them home, and Zane carried Darla inside. For all her protesting about the wheelchair back at the clinic, she sure wasn't complaining that he'd scooped her up and carried her to her duplex. Beckett opened her door with his spare key.

Darla smiled. "Never thought I'd get twice lucky."

"Twice lucky?"

"Having a strapping young lad sweep me off my feet."

Zane barked out a laugh.

"Just need a kiss, sweetheart, and I'll die a happy woman."

Zane nipped her lips into a humorous kiss and waltzed past Beckett with a wink to the living room.

"That solves your dilemma," she said as he set her on the couch. "I'll marry you."

"While I like the thought, I think I'd prefer someone eighty decades younger."

Darla gave him an affronted glare. "How old do you think I am?"

Beckett sidled next to him and side-eyed Zane. "Don't take it personally, Darla. Sweetheart here is abysmal at estimating age."

~

ZANE AND BECKETT REHEATED SOME SOUP DARLA HAD ON THE stove, and each had a small portion. They stayed with her until she was comfortable in bed. Again, she didn't complain about Zane taking her there.

Out on her porch, he let out a long sigh.

Late evening settled over the street. Blueberry sky, plumes of streetlight shining over young leaves, and a warm Beckett at his side. He needed to release the tension coiled in his legs. Too much sitting. Too much unease twisting deep in his belly.

It hadn't helped that he hadn't jerked off today. The last time had been after his and Beckett's after-dinner walk the night before last. He'd shut himself in the bathroom and made quick work of getting some release. It wasn't enough.

He'd been aroused all day, and the discussion with Beckett at the clinic hadn't helped. Maybe he should test his attraction to intelligence theory and see if reading more *Pride and Prejudice* got him going?

He heeled a hand over his plumping cock, adjusting himself.

It wasn't the subtlest move, but then, he wasn't the subtlest person. Beckett shifted, the porch groaning underfoot. "Please tell me that didn't come from putting Darla to bed."

"That" clearly referred to his semi, and there was literally no hiding it. Zane grinned and snagged Beckett's hand, pulling him off the porch and up the path. "Are you hungry? Because I could eat."

"Eat what, exactly?"

Zane let go of his hand and slung an arm around his shoulders. "Anything you want. It's on me."

They walked to a park glittering in lights and stopped at a hot dog vendor for some good old sausage. A small bandstand sat at the side of a pond, and a cuddling couple walked away as they neared. Zane and Beckett took their place.

Zane swallowed the last of his mustard-covered sausage. "How was work today?"

"More sorting out of classes for next year. It's a mess; it should have been sorted months ago."

"Sorry."

"I should be on leave, instead I've accrued thirty days to this year's twenty-four."

"Why don't you take it?"

"Because I am something of a workaholic."

"If you did take it, what would you do?" A strange thought, imagining Beckett's life without him around. After mere days together, they'd already woven a routine. This was what he meant when he said their lives were meant to converge. Being around Beckett just felt right.

"Read, definitely, and probably split my time between here and the farm. Mom runs a horse-riding club, and I like to help out."

"Maybe you should add *Scarlet Sentinel vs. Fire Falcon* to your to-read pile?"

"Can't confess I'm too interested in the story."

Oh. Zane nodded and leaned against the bandstand pillar and stared at the lights glittering over the pond's smooth surface.

Beckett softly tugged Zane's middle finger. "Not your illustrations, Zane. Your art is mesmerizing."

Zane glanced at him. Beckett's expression was earnest.

"I'm just . . . reasonably upset at the way Rocco seems to be treating you. Or perhaps I'm upset at the way you let him treat you. Your illustrations are just as important as the story. It's a team effort."

"I did it freelance. Signed all the contracts. I'm not a co-author. He pays me for the rights."

"You've undersold yourself."

Maybe. He rested his head against the neighboring pillar. "I couldn't read until I was ten. I could barely write until I was twelve. Pictures were how I told stories."

"What are your stories, Zane? If you could tell any story, what would it be?"

"A happily ever after. The underdog wins the prize."

Zane felt the prickle of Beckett's gaze heating his throat, jaw, making the hairs behind his ear stand on end.

"Okay, this is what I want from you," Beckett said. "This time tomorrow night, I want you to give me a logline summarizing one of your stories."

"A what now?"

"A one-sentence summary of your story, including a protagonist, their goal, the obstacles, and the stakes."

Zane gestured for them to leave, and they bounced down the three stairs. "Sounds hard. Could you give me one of these logs as an example? Oh, make it fun and put me in it."

"You're a little vain, aren't you?"

Zane chuckled. "Just a bit. Now log me, Professor."

Beckett shook his head as they curved around the bandstand.

Bright red hair and a yoga-thin body jogged down the path in their direction. Zane froze. Oh God.

Monday's date.

Calm. It'd be okay. She wouldn't come over and yarn about their terrible date and how his kiss felt like cardboard.

But what if she did?

Heat whipped up his neck. He pulled Beckett behind a pillar and jammed them against the foot-wide length. The ground was soggy and slurped underfoot, sliding his front up against Beckett's.

Beckett looked up at him in confusion, fairy light glittering in his eyes. Zane pressed a finger to Beckett's lips, which were cooler than his warm body that simmered against Zane's.

He brought his mouth to Beckett's ear. The scent of his aftershave mingled with the smell of nearby lady-of-the-night blossoms and earlier spring rain. "Just pretend to be really into me so my Monday date leaves us alone."

"Press against me any more and there'll be zero pretending necessary."

He was feeling it too. The uneven ground shifted, and pressing against Beckett felt pleasant. "How long, post-Luke, has it been since you snagged yourself a man?"

Beckett's breath puffed against the underside of his jaw. "I haven't."

"Have you thought about it?"

A smile played at Beckett's lips and he turned his head toward the path, void of joggers. "Recently, more and more."

"You should go for it, Becky."

"I might be tempted, but I'm pretty sure it won't end well." Beckett planted his hands against Zane's chest. "Your bad date has gone. We can go."

"What about your log?"

A startled blink.

"I want it."

Beckett shifted abruptly and the brush of his jeans' button over Zane's cock stoked his arousal. Zane's breath hitched, and he pulled back.

Beckett set his gaze squarely ahead and they began their walk home. "Here's an example of a logline," Beckett said, voice gravelly. "An unapologetic romantic must navigate the shifting seas of his heart to find true love by the month's end or be cast back to his homeland, leaving behind his brother, the only unconditional love he knows."

Freakishly accurate. Maybe Darla was right and he was an easy read. But that last bit, about Jacob . . . about it being the truest form of love he knew . . . .

He cleared his throat. "Are the 'shifting seas of his heart' the, um, obstacles to my goal?"

"Yes."

"What does that mean?"

"Discovering what you truly want from love. Learning more about yourself. Maybe coming to other realizations."

"Oh." He rubbed his jaw. "Like how I'm attracted to intelligence."

Beckett nodded. "How you see others, yes, but also how you see yourself."

"So it's true. Everyone does have a book in them."

Beckett hummed. "Yours is a slow burn."

"Nah, it's insta-love, Becky. You'll see."

He dug his hands into his pockets, a mistake. Walking was uncomfortable. He made another oh-so-subtle adjustment and laughed. "I'm so glad you have everything I need to fix this."

A flicker of something deep hit Beckett's eyes. "I have everything you need?"

"Every classic long-winded book imaginable. Alphabetically organized."

Beckett cast his gaze upward and muttered toward the stars, "Slow burn."

Then I examined my own heart. And there you were. Never, I fear, to be removed.

—Jane Austen

Chapter Ten

Zane spent the day with Darla, working on his logline. It was harder than he thought. Beckett was a genius.

After assurances Darla would be okay the rest of the evening, he snuck back over the fence and spent a half hour sprucing up. He planned to make this date better than the last. Part-time librarian, here he came.

The front door closed, and Beckett's voice trailed down the hall.

Grinning, Zane met him at his room door. The professor spoke into his phone, knotting himself as he tried to remove his bag. No one needed a gym membership with that cloth boulder in their life. "Half an hour, I'll be there."

Zane untangled the strap and took Beckett's bursting bag.

Beckett mouthed, "Thanks," and spoke into the phone while looking at Zane. "I might bring company."

Zane lifted a questioning brow.

Beckett finished his call and entered his room. Zane followed him and dumped the bag onto the bed, and slung himself next to it. He lay on his side and propped his head up on a palm, eyeing Beckett as he slipped out of his blazer and unbuttoned his shirt.

"You got my message earlier, right?" Zane said.

Beckett's deft fingers never once fumbled with a button. The shirt parted, revealing smooth, tanned skin.

Beckett's fingers stilled on the last button and Zane glanced up to find Beckett watching him. Beckett undid the last one and elegantly slipped off the shirt.

"You have a date," Beckett said. "You wanted my opinion where to take her."

"Still want your opinion. I'm meeting her at the bandstand and thought we'd go from there."

"The bandstand." Beckett hauled in a breath and busied himself pulling a navy shirt from his closet. "Some colleagues and I are meeting at Chiffon," he said, slipping on the sleek shirt. He looked at Zane over his shoulder. "You could bring your date along."

"To Chiffon?"

"It's the most fun you'll ever have."

Zane screwed his face in exaggerated doubt. "The most fun? Really?"

"Synonym standoffs?"

"There goes any hope we're talking cinnamon standoffs."

Beckett leveled him a look that sparked with vigor and determination. "Synonym standoffs are the best. Superlative. Top."

"Yeah, standing on stage in front of a crowd waiting for you to screw up a word. Your date laughing at you. Fun."

"I find it relaxing. Good for de-stressing."

"Distressing, you mean."

Beckett's gaze hopped with a laugh. "There's also a great selection of wines, some of the best hors d'oeuvres around, and great company. Enough stimulation for hours."

Beckett's excited energy scuttled over Zane like electricity, infecting him with a laugh.

"Now what shoes to wear?" Beckett stared at the shelves of shoes in his closet.

Zane pushed aside Beckett's bag, blocking half of the view. "Huh, you have big feet for your size."

They weren't bigger than his, were they?

He scrambled off the bed and slipped behind Beckett. His chest hit Beckett's back and Beckett stiffened. "Hold still a sec," Zane said, strapping an arm under Beckett's and over his chest. He pressed his left foot on the outside of Beckett's.

They were the same size.

"Definitely big feet."

Beckett's heart raced under Zane's palm. "Or yours are small."

"Is it immature of me that I'm thinking of your dick size now?"

Beckett croaked, "Immature, yes. Among other things."

"Yeah. I guess I'm very immature then."

Beckett crouched, his back sliding down Zane's front, skimming over his crotch, which naturally took interest in the friction.

Zane stepped back, and Beckett shook his head as he pulled out a pair of forest-green casual sneakers. "Big shoes does not a big dick make."

Did that mean he was small, then? Or run-of-the-mill average like him?

He cast a rough hand through his hair. He seriously needed to get his mind off dicks. He had a date tonight—and he still had no clue where to take her. Chiffon wasn't happening. He wanted to have a chance, not scare Clara off.

Beckett tied his shoes and slipped his blazer back on.

Also, he wanted Clara focusing on him and not casting hopeful looks at Beckett all night.

"As much as I am impressed with your stamina," Zane said. "I couldn't keep up for hours. I couldn't keep up for three minutes."

Beckett set startled blue eyes on him. "Huh?"

"The stimulating synonym standoff?"

He nodded furiously. "Yes, of course."

"Are you driving?"

Beckett shook his head. "It's a fifteen-minute walk."

"Great, I'll go with you."

Soft fingers fluttered at his chin and steered his face once more to Beckett's. "On one condition."

"You lecture me on literature the entire way?"

"You stop looking at my . . . feet."

Zane dropped Beckett off at Chiffon. They lingered for a moment outside the classy establishment. Haughty laughter trickled outside. Festooned strings of tea lights glittered through the large glass windows and glinted off Beckett's hair.

"Well." Beckett smiled, planting his hands on his hips. "Have a good night."

A soft breeze washed over him, and a curiously light shiver zipped to Zane's toes. "I have a seventh sense that tonight will be a turning point."

"What's your sixth sense?"

"Oh, um, my sense-ual side?"

Zane took Beckett's laughter with him to the bandstand where he picked up Clara. He took her to a seafood restaurant he'd passed on the way there.

The semiformal restaurant had a romantic ambiance. Low lighting, exotic fish tanks, and battery-powered candles on the square tables.

With dark hair tumbling around her heart-shaped face, big

eyes, and an impressively slinky black dress, Clara was definitely attractive. Her heels added a good two inches, bringing her to Zane's height when she stood.

Their conversation started off slow and steady. When their main dishes arrived, Zane was eager to bring out the questions he'd tried on Beckett over their morning coffee at King's.

While Zane firmly believed in love at first connection, he knew not all relationships ignited the same way; and Beckett had made a great point about the importance of learning a person.

He wanted to avoid the standard date questions about school and his favorite books. One, it never painted him in the best light when he admitted to dropping out, and most people dismissed his love of comic books and manga as boyish immaturity. Two, and much like this delicious salmon, he wanted to keep things fresh.

Zane leaned forward, stabbing a fork toward his date with a grin. "Do you have an inkling how you will die?"

Clara choked on her bubbly, gaze leaping to his.

"Oh sorry. . . ." He laughed at himself and lowered the fork to his fish.

The question had gone over so much better with Beckett. He'd barely batted an eyelid and said he was pretty sure Zane would kill him before the month was over.

The dryness had pulled a laugh from Zane. Clara made him feel like he was a psycho. "That came out wrong," he said with a sheepish grin.

Clara reset and gave a saucy laugh. She lifted her bubbly. "Choking is clearly the way I'll go. Let's just hope I die choking on something I love."

He scooped a forkful of dill salmon into his mouth, wondering what it meant that Clara didn't ask him how he thought he'd go.

On the one hand, death was a bit morbid to discuss on a first date. On the other hand, Beckett had asked.

"What about you?"

"Heartbreak, definitely."

"You can't die from heartbreak."

"Yeah, you can. My grandma did when my granddad died. She was healthy, fit as a fiddle. When he passed, she lost the will to live. Six months later she was gone too. She loved so hard, losing her husband broke her. I hope I die like that too."

"You hope *to die like that?"*

"Having truly loved, *Becky. Having truly* been *loved."*

He shook out of the memory, forcing himself to concentrate on Clara, plucking an oyster off her plate.

"You're an artist?" she asked. "Do you ever draw still lifes?" Okay, benefit of the doubt. And this question Clara was asking? Definitely promising.

"Not as a rule. I draw for a graphic novel series."

"Oh, that kind of drawing." She nodded. Zane smiled despite the slight sting at the dismissal.

"What kind of art do you like?" he asked.

"Nude sketches. Do you like breaking rules?"

He laughed tightly and hurried to his next question. "What does your perfect day look like?"

"Good conversation and better sex." She bit her lip and looked at him. "Lots of it."

Well, this was moving fast. Was she nervously blurting this out? He knew how that happened.

"I love adventures," she continued, holding his gaze in a way that made him squirm uncomfortably in his chair. "Do you?"

"I am more the misadventure type," he said, cautiously. Talking about her death hadn't put her off. Maybe she was the psycho?

She slurped another oyster and licked her fingers seductively.

The women in this town had more balls than any guy he knew. All power to them, but . . . .

Had he bitten off more than he could chew?

A foot landed in his lap under the table and Zane jumped at the pinching weight. Her heel sneaked along his inseam and hit home.

He screeched his chair back with a nervous laugh and leaped to his feet. If he didn't put some space between them, she'd eat him alive. "Need the bathroom!"

He fled to the men's restroom and locked himself in the end cubicle in case she thought it was an invitation. Crap, how did he always end up in these situations?

He slumped on a closed toilet seat and sent out a pleading text message to Beckett.

Zane: Oh, God. Save me.

Zane had never been so relieved to see those three dots signaling a return message show up on his phone.

Becky: Save you?

Zane: Charge in here and accuse me of accosting your boyfriend or something. Make a scene that will put my date off.

Becky: What's the problem?

Zane: She's trying to make me come. In the middle of the restaurant.

Becky: Are you close?

Zane: Not even remotely. Her heel strangled one of my balls and I'm hiding in the bathroom.

Becky: I meant the restaurant. But thanks for the visual.

Zane: Save the thanks for later. After you've arrived at Soul Sea.

Beckett had received his last message but wasn't answering. Was he on his way? He prayed so.

He shifted on his seat. One ball ached where Clara had heeled him. He prodded himself through his jeans and wrote again to Beckett.

Zane: You'll need to inspect me at home. See if I'm still intact.

Becky: Good Lord. Can't you check yourself?

Zane: I'm too scared. Besides, I trust you to know your way around the boys.

Becky: . . .

Zane chuckled, fingers flying over his phone.

Zane: What does that mean?

Beckett hadn't read his message. There was radio silence for a good few minutes.

Zane should probably escape the cubicle and face his date. Ideally, he would man up and tell her he wasn't interested in quickies under the table.

Or he could suffer through it until Beckett saved him.

Linger in here a little longer?

Twice someone walked into the bathroom, and twice it wasn't Beckett.

Time seemed to slow, and he reluctantly exited the cubicle. He moved to the sinks and washed his hands. *Get out there. Go on.*

He turned away from the mirror and slumped against the sink counter. He truly sucked at manhood. He should have learned from the last three date fails. Should have made a point of saying he wasn't interested in NSA.

He messaged Beckett. If he was great at anything, it was procrastination.

Zane: Hello?

Becky: I'm close.

Zane: To the restaurant, or . . . ?

Ten seconds later the restroom door opened, and Beckett strode inside. "The *restaurant*, Zane."

Someone entered the restroom and passed Beckett, pushing him closer to the sinks. Zane grabbed his hands and pulled him close.

"Thanks for coming," he said.

Beckett studied him, concerned. "How are you?"

Zane breathed in the trace of Beckett's aftershave. His hands were warm, as if he'd jogged here. The thought had Zane tugging him another inch closer.

Beckett's brows lifted in query.

He snapped out of his thoughts. How was he? "Still intact, I think."

"I meant with the situation."

Right. That. Zane hung his head and stared at their feet.

Beckett lifted his chin with a purposely distracting smirk. "Eyes up here."

"Could you make her leave?"

"How about I tell her you have a boyfriend? A boyfriend who, although he claims he's okay with you dating others, really isn't, but doesn't know how to say that because you guys just met, and deep down he is so broken that he doesn't know if he can risk loving again. But regardless, this boyfriend is jealous as fuck that you have a date tonight or any night."

An unexpectedly nervous laugh left him. He'd never heard Beckett swear, nor sound so serious. Which was saying something because he had a naturally serious voice. "English professors. You sure know how to whip up some convincing backstory. You'd do that for me?"

Beckett pulled out of his grip and glanced toward the door. "Will you tell your date you're sorry but you'd rather go home with me?"

"Hell yes."

Beckett swept his hand outward. "Lead the way."

When they strode back to his table, they found it vacated, a pissed-looking waiter piling their plates on his arm.

"Maybe I put her off myself," Zane murmured.

"Spending twenty minutes in the toilet while on a first date might do that."

They shared a bemused look, and Zane paid for dinner with an extra-large tip.

They passed Chiffon on their walk back. Beckett shrugged off Zane's suggestion to rejoin his friends, and they continued to the duplex.

At the click of the door shutting behind them, Zane gasped. "It's Thursday!"

Beckett paused. "I need a job where I forget the day of the week."

"Your sister is arriving."

"Late." Beckett checked his phone. "I take it back, she'll be here in an hour."

He followed Beckett to the kitchen and nodded to Beckett's silent question of wine.

"I can't wait to meet her." In fact, he was nervous. He needed to make a good impression on her. Needed her to like him. Needed Beckett to see it.

Beckett stilled, expression tightening as if he'd just realized something objectionable.

"What's she like, then? You with boobs?"

That earned Zane a withering glare. "She's beautiful and full of life. She lives from moment to moment, and crazy is her middle name. You'll . . . you'll love her."

Poor Beckett paled. It had been a long evening.

"Curl up on that armchair with your wine and a book. When I return, I will make you smile."

"How will you do that?" He tipped his glass to his mouth.

"I'm going to give you my log."

Beckett spat wine over his nice navy shirt.

WHILE BECKETT RETREATED TO THE BATHROOM, PRESUMABLY to clean his shirt, Zane found fresh sheets, stripped and remade the bed for Leah, and arranged his things in Beckett's room.

What a difference to hang his clothes in a closet and not live out of a suitcase. He could get used to this.

He draped his bull-headed rug over the armchair, head facing into the room. He was quite attached to the thing now.

He zipped on his boots, and, after one quick run-through of his logline, sauntered to Beckett.

Beckett lowered his book to his lap, open to the page he'd paused on. His gaze rolled up Zane inch by inch. A giggly thrill swept through Zane's veins, and his voice shook. "I don't know how anyone in your classes gets anything done."

"Why do you need boots on to feed me your logline?"

Zane jammed his thumbs into his pockets. "In case you don't like it. I promised you a smile."

"Lay it on me."

The air tasted thick as Zane hauled in a breath. "A heartbroken professor must learn to trust love in order to heal his heart or risk never finding true companionship again."

Beckett tilted his head to the side, a flash of pain lighting his eyes, quickly schooled. He placed his book aside and stood. He walked up to Zane, holding his gaze, and cupped his cheek, trembling thumb brushing over his skin. "I'm working on it."

Beckett withdrew his hand and Zane caught his wrist, keeping the contact another moment. "Good. Your story needs a happy ending."

Beckett's voice cracked. "Tomorrow give me the line for the story you want to illustrate."

"As you wish, Professor."

The doorbell chimed, breaking them apart.

Beckett disappeared into the hall. Thirty seconds later, a woman with wild locks and an even wilder smile lit up the living room.

"This is Zane?" she asked, looking from him to her brother. "Is there a reason you didn't tell me he's a spitting image of a young Chris—"

"Let's put your luggage away," Beckett said, one hand clasping his sister's arm.

Zane bolted upright. "Were you about to say Hemsworth? Becky, was she about to say Hemsworth?"

Beckett rubbed his brow.

Oh God, she was.

"I am not Australian!"

Beckett side-eyed him with a shake of his head.

Zane gave them a meek smile. "I mean, how about I whip us up a pavlova and we start again?"

～

THE PAVLOVA SUNK IN THE MIDDLE, AND HE MAY HAVE MISTAKEN salt for sugar . . . .

Not a great impression he was making on Leah.

He blamed it on his nerves. It felt like meeting the parents for the first time. His hands were clammy, his boots were killing his heels, and he'd rung out an ill-timed laugh, which he was still inwardly cringing at.

Jet-lagged, Leah begged off to bed. Zane gathered the last of his energy to weasel more information on Leah out of her brother. If he found out a few key tidbits, he could win her over. Maybe then Beckett would relax and not study them so hard like he worried they'd clash.

"Your sister . . . ."

Beckett took off to his bedroom and Zane followed tight at his heel.

The light flickered on, and Beckett abruptly stilled. Zane hadn't counted on it and thumped into his back. He steadied himself, planting his hands on Beckett's hips.

"What is *that*?"

Beckett stared across his room to the armchair.

Zane slipped to Beckett's side, one hand curving from hip to the small of Beckett's back. With gentle pressure, he steered Beckett to the rug in question.

"Good Lord, do I dare ask?"

Zane dragged his fingertips up Beckett's spine and gently squeezed his nape. "Look at him, so alive and kicking."

"It's a rug."

"Figuratively, Professor."

"Why does it have horns?"

"Because he's a bull. He's your inner bull."

"If that's the way you see me, I'm surprised you haven't run away."

Zane dropped his hand from Beckett and perched on the large bed. The boots were juicing his feet. He unzipped them, swallowing a sigh. "I'm not running anywhere." He stared at his swollen feet. "Couldn't even if I wanted to."

Staring at the rug, Beckett slipped out of his blazer and began on his shirt. His cheek twitched in profile. "You're insane," he murmured.

There may have been some truth to that.

Beckett slithered his jeans down his legs.

"Now tell me more about your lovely sister," Zane said.

Beckett paused, then used his feet to stomp out of the remaining denim. Socks removed, he tossed his day clothes into a laundry hamper. "I've got to brush my teeth."

"Wait." Zane yanked off his T-shirt and made quicker work shedding his jeans. Satiny blue boxers clung to his goods, looser than the gray boxer-briefs Beckett wore.

From what Zane could tell, Beckett was packing. Jeez, the guy had been blessed in the body department.

Beckett pivoted away, and Zane jogged into the bathroom after him. He'd never seen anyone stuff a toothbrush in their mouth so fast. Zane brushed his teeth alongside him and they watched each other in the mirror. They spent torturously long minutes trying to out-brush one another. Zane could do this for hours.

Finally, Beckett increased his speed scrubbing, scowled at him, and spat.

Foam filled Zane's mouth to the brim.

"Come on, Zane," Beckett whispered, and Zane gulped the foam in his mouth. He slid out the toothbrush.

"Did you just swallow all that?"

"I hadn't intended to." Beckett had startled him with that

soft whisper of his name. "Tasted better than I thought it would."

Beckett's eyes flashed, and he bowled out of the bathroom.

Zane nestled his clean toothbrush next to Beckett's and returned to the bedroom. The professor had turned off the main light and switched on his bedside lamp. He had tucked himself on the farthest side of the bed, back propped up by pillows, heel of his hand grinding his forehead.

Zane flung himself onto his back like a starfish. His hand hit Beckett's covered hip and he felt the man shift under him. The large bed felt incredible and supportive. He humped his body against the bed. Didn't squeal, either.

"This isn't your nightly routine, is it?" Beckett asked dryly.

Zane scrambled underneath the fresh covers and sighed. "This bed," he groaned. He smoothed his palm along the dark wooden headboard. "Monogamy, right?"

Beckett scrubbed his jaw, hiding a smile. "My dream bed."

"I wanna marry it."

"You haven't been in it one night."

"Are you telling me you didn't know you wanted this bed from the moment you first lay on it?"

Beckett's gaze landed on his and then pulled away. "I was worried it might be too good to be true. My last bed almost broke my back after a while."

Zane squirreled deep into the bed, funneling air under the sheets over his skin. "This is a keeper."

He turned his head on his single pillow and watched Beckett pull a book off his side table.

"I really messed up that pavlova, huh?"

"Whatever point you were trying to prove, it—"

"—bit me in the ass, I know. What's your sister's favorite breakfast? Waffles? Pancakes? Bacon and toast?"

Beckett frowned into his book. "Why?"

"To make her the best breakfast."

A sigh. "Of course."

Zane nudged him. "So?"

"Pancakes."

"I'll make a much better impression in the morning, Becky. I'll make her love me, you'll see."

He closed his book. "I'm tired."

Zane, too.

Beckett turned off his light and the room drowned in darkness. Zane twisted onto his side. "Why are you so far on the other side of the bed? There's plenty of room with me in the middle."

Beckett turned his back to him. "Yeah, I'm good here."

Nothing to nag about tonight, but Zane needed to change that.

I have no notion of loving people by halves.

—Jane Austen

Chapter Eleven

Zane woke up before Beckett, slipped out of bed, and started making breakfast.

Leah floated down from the attic in a silky dressing gown and Snoopy pajamas. "Should I be nervous to try one of these?" She eyed him and then the stack of pancakes he'd set on a plate for her. "Because I'm not doing what my brother did —does?—and swallowing anything salty."

Beckett had stoically finished his one spoon of pavlova.

If he hadn't broved him before, he broved him after that feat. After everything Beckett had done for Zane yesterday.

"What's your brother's favorite breakfast?" he croaked.

"Why?"

"Because."

She raised a brow and shrugged. "Eggs, sunny-side up, toast, and freshly squeezed orange juice."

Fresh Beckett sauntered out just as he started cleaning the frying pan to make eggs. He'd made the juice though, and poured both siblings a glass.

Beckett took his with quiet thanks and sat at the table, journal in hand.

Leah had found an easy groove with him, and Zane had to admit, he was rocking the charm this morning. Every few minutes, he'd glance over at Beckett, hoping to catch him watching, but every time Beckett scribbled harder in his journal.

"What are your weekend plans?" Zane asked Leah.

Beckett slammed his journal shut and Zane glanced sharply over. The professor stared at the leather journal as he fiddled with his juice glass.

"No plans. Catch up on sleep. See some friends."

Zane abandoned the eggs he'd just cracked into the hot pan and pulled Leah aside where Beckett wouldn't hear them. "Did you have any big plans with your brother this weekend?"

"No, why?"

"I just—" Flame caught his attention in his side vision and he jumped. "Shit, the eggs are on fire."

He grabbed the pan and submerged it in the soapy sink water. There went the last eggs.

There went Beckett's favorite breakfast.

"You all right?" Leah asked.

He nodded, and Beckett finally lifted his eyes. So cautious this morning. So quiet.

"Becky, would you visit Jacob and Anne's baby with me?"

Beckett frowned as his gaze flashed from Zane to Leah. He hesitated. "My sister just arrived."

"And she'll be here for a while. Come with me."

Beckett sipped his juice. "Darla needs help."

"I took pancakes over to her half an hour ago, she's doing fine."

"She might be putting on a show for you."

"Then we'll take her with us. Please come."

"Why do you want me there?"

"Anne would be thrilled if you show up."

Beckett drew his journal to the edge of the table. "I should focus on—"

"What? Your laundry?" Had Beckett slept badly? Something was off. Or—Christ, he was stupid!

Zane wound around the counter and stopped behind Beckett. Planting hands on his shoulders, he rubbed. "Luke won't be there," he said softly.

He dug his thumbs into the knots between Beckett's shoulder blades. Jeez, he was tight.

Beckett rolled his head back and rested it against Zane's sternum, looking up. Beautiful, worry-edged eyes bored into him.

"Please?" Zane asked. Wait, he knew what would win the professor over. "Plentiful pleases, my pretty pontificating prince?" He bent down and nudged Beckett's nose with his. "I'll let you lecture me on literature the entire way there."

The professor's eye sparked. "On Joyce?"

"Maybe something more joyful. Like Beckett."

"Huh," came Leah's contribution from the kitchen. Zane glanced over to find her sharing secrets with her brother through her stare.

Zane explained on Beckett's behalf. "We're bromancing."

Beckett's muscles bunched under his hands.

"Right. Bromancing." Her gaze swung from him to Beckett with a smirk. "I think you should go. I can check on Darla, and we can hang out anytime when you return."

He scrolled his thumbs up Beckett's nape. "See, your sister gets it."

"Fine," Beckett said unevenly. "I'll go with you."

Zane gently tugged Beckett's soft hair. "Also, could maybe drive us?"

Beckett drove toward Jacob's farm, their overnight bags sliding around in the back seat. They hadn't discussed the details, but Zane assumed he'd crash at Jacob's and Beckett would head to his mum's.

Beckett had worked late on Friday and fallen asleep the moment he hit the bed. He had woken up looking refreshed, but despite how well Zane had been getting along with Leah, Beckett remained unusually silent.

That would change by the time they got to Jacob's.

Zane kicked off his jandals and pressed the soles of his feet against the warmed leather seat. Although it made him dizzy, he had to draw. He pulled out his supplies and made fleeting sketches of the farm as he remembered it. Anne and Jacob had bought her childhood farm from her parents, funding their retirement and around-the-world trip.

It was a nice place, but for all the acreage, the main house was . . . charmingly pokey.

"You haven't sprouted literature, Professor."

"Spouted."

That was a start.

"Could we talk about *Pride and Prejudice*? I notice there is a lot of marriage in it, and I can't help but think you suggested the book to warn me."

Beckett adjusted his grip on the wheel and kept his eyes on the road. "Not intentionally, though now that you mention it, your situation is not too dissimilar. You came into my life declaring the importance of marriage in your life. Perhaps, like in Austen's time, you see marriage as a way out. If you don't marry, you'll be forced to head back home, and in a sense, like Elizabeth, you risk losing the power to decide your own path in life."

Zane squirmed. "Did you minor in psychology?"

Beckett's lips subtly twitched. He still didn't look his way, though.

"Mr. Bennet warned Lizzy against a bad marriage," Zane said, hoping he'd read it right and wasn't talking nonsense. "Like when you told me not to fool myself that I'd find love. I suppose that makes you my dad in this example."

Beckett wrung the steering wheel and groaned. "This was a mistake." He leaned back in his seat. "However, like Mr. Bennet, I don't want you to lose respect for your life partner. I made that mistake, and I wouldn't wish it on you."

"Luke is clearly a Wickham. Oh, if I am Lizzy, I wonder who my Mr. Darcy is?"

"You know, I don't think I'm much like Mr. Bennet. I'm much better with finances. I own my side of the duplex and will most certainly have a legacy to pass on to any children I may have."

"I don't know," Zane teased. "Mr. Bennet is witty, really loves books, and Lizzy is his favorite."

Beckett's lips twisted gently as he glanced at Zane.

Much better.

"Though I suppose, under all the stubbornness," Zane relented, "Mr. Darcy is all those things too."

"Yes. Under all that bull-like stubbornness."

Zane smiled. It felt . . . refreshing to be talking like this. Empowering, even.

Beckett's phone rang.

Zane picked it up from the console. "Your sister. Can I put her on speaker for you?"

Beckett's smile faltered. He nodded tightly.

Leah's voice burst vibrantly around them, and Zane grinned. "Could you bring some of Mom's jam back with you? It's a hundred times better than whatever I just ate from your cupboard."

She chatted some more and updated them on Darla. "She's doing well. Wants the fish to know that it's okay if he doesn't have a clue what's happening with his love life. The planets are in some kind of chaos? She mentioned taking your best friend on a date—that it might help kick things into place."

Zane shook his head with a smirk. *So* Darla. "What did she say about the bull?"

"Just that no one understands better than a Taurus the phrase 'you can't rush love.' Oh, and to trust your instincts, even if you worry things will turn out badly."

Leah ended the call with an upbeat "Bye!" and Beckett sighed. "Even the stars back me on my no love at first sight stance."

Beckett had bull-like stubbornness, all right.

Zane drew a picture of their first coffee meet-up at King's, a disbelieving expression painted on Beckett's face as Zane mentioned love at first sight.

It was amazing how easily he could draw Beckett. He had a memorable face and a perfectly postured body.

"You're smiling," Beckett said, startling him out of his sketch.

Zane looked over at him. "You're not."

"Yeah."

"What's wrong, Becky? You've been acting off since . . . since . . . ."

"Since my sister arrived?" Beckett side-eyed him. "My single sister, who is your age? My single sister, who is your age, who you get along with?"

Zane dropped his feet to the floor. "Are you kidding me?"

Beckett turned into a gas station and parked the car at the pumps. Zane stuffed his feet into his shoes, and they both stepped out. Zane set the nozzle in the car, glaring at Beckett over the roof. "I don't even know what to say. I'm not . . . I haven't once even thought . . . ." Hold up. Did Beckett think he was not good enough for his sister?

His hand clenched the nozzle.

"Stop," Beckett said, making sure to hold his gaze. "Whatever you're thinking that is making your face fall like that, stop it."

Zane tore his gaze away and shrugged. "You're being a protective brother. I understand."

Beckett stepped around the car. The nozzle shut off, and Zane stared as Beckett put it away and capped the tank. "Zane—"

Zane turned and walked into the store. Stuck in line at the checkout, he busied himself with the tourist pamphlets lining the wall. He picked a few up and studied them hard when Beckett sidled next to him.

He might be acting dramatic. But it felt warranted.

Beckett's gaze prickled over him and Zane lifted the pamphlet like a shield.

Apparently they were close to Greenville, a town boasting a permanent circus. The charming historical town was also known for its antique bookstore, Silver Pines.

The customers before him left, and Zane moved to the counter and paid for their gas.

He turned to find Beckett chiding him.

"See you in the car," Zane said, and hoofed back to the passenger seat.

He picked up his sketchbook and drew, unsurprised to find the pencil lines creating Beckett's face. Not the subdued Beckett of the car ride but the Beckett from yesterday, when he'd trembled against him, voice almost breaking as he said he was working on trusting love again.

Zane caught his breath. Of course, Beckett would be worried about who fell for his sister. He'd been scarred in love and would be sensitive to anyone forming a bond with his younger sibling. He wouldn't want her enduring the same pain.

It was admirable how much Beckett cared.

Beckett slid into the car and tossed a small foil package at him. Zane caught it against his chest, pencil stabbing his chin.

"I'm sorry," Zane blurted at the same time Beckett spoke.

"If you like my sister—"

"You go," Zane said.

Beckett pulled his gaze from the windscreen to Zane. "You have nothing to apologize for. If you like my sister, she'd be the luckiest woman in the world to have your attention."

Zane couldn't handle the tenderness flowing from Beckett into him. He looked down at the package in his hand. *Roasted pecans.*

His body blasted with lightness that made him off-center and goofy.

He relaxed into his seat, grinning. "Thanks, Becky. That was very Mr. Bennet of you to say."

Shaking his head, Beckett laughed and started the car.

"By the way," Zane said, popping a pecan into his mouth. "And please don't get me wrong, because your sister seems like a nice person, but"—he winced—"I'm not interested in her that way."

Beckett frowned and slid his hands up and down his wheel. "You're, um, not?"

"Nope."

"Not even a little?"

"Along with intelligence, I think I'm attracted to those who are settled or want to be. Hey, maybe I'm making headway on the shifting seas of my heart."

Beckett kept his eyes squarely on the road and laughed.

BECKETT PARKED IN FRONT OF THE FARMHOUSE WITH A familiarity that had Zane catching his breath.

How many times had Beckett parked here to pick Luke up for a date? Or to drop in to see Anne?

There was a whole history that Zane hadn't been a part of,

yet it felt like he was bringing an important person in his life to meet his brother.

Jacob walked out to their car in a black-and-red-checkered cowboy shirt. Thick dark hair the complete opposite of Zane's, but the same smile. They embraced with their usual fond smack on the back of the head. "You're a dad."

"You're an uncle."

Zane pulled back and glanced at Beckett. "Becky, you know my brother."

"Jacob," he said, shaking his hand, tilting his head toward Zane. "Should have warned me."

Jacob laughed. "Come meet Anne and baby Cassie. We're on the back deck. The grill is ready."

Beckett pulled out his jacket from the back. The sunny day was pleasant, despite the small bite to the breeze. "Want your hoodie, Zane?"

He was a Kiwi. T-shirt and shorts were good. "Nah."

A scuttling wind raced over them. "Are you sure?"

Zane followed his brother, tossing over his shoulder, "I'll tough it out. Come on."

The door shut, and Beckett caught up to him, stuffing keys into his pocket. Zane didn't miss the pointed glance to his *slightly* goose-bumped arms.

They rounded the wood-paneled house and were met by Anne's glorious grin and outstretched arms. She grabbed both him and Beckett into a hug. Beckett's side bumped against Zane, and the warmth of him was a clue he probably should have listened to Beckett and brought out his hoodie.

Anne fussed and hugged them again, and Zane slung an arm around Beckett's waist. If he angled Beckett close the entire afternoon, he wouldn't have to worry about those nippy breezes. Problem solved.

Anne let go, and Beckett's eyes said he knew what Zane had been thinking.

Beckett lifted a brow and teased him, readjusting his jacket over his forearm.

Well, of course, Beckett wasn't cold. He was sensible. He'd worn a long-sleeved shirt, and earlier Zane had glimpsed an undershirt.

Anne steered them to a cradle where the tiniest baby slept, dwarfed by a thick, warm-looking blanket. Cassie had a wad of dark hair, clearly her mum's, but the rest resembled a bright red squished tomato. All Jacob.

From the grill, Jacob stood watching them with a grin.

Zane smiled hard at him, then turned and hugged Anne once more. His throat felt sore. "You have a family. It's . . . beautiful."

He moved to Jacob, glad to stand near the grill's heat. "How are you doing?"

"Never been happier. Never been more tired, either. What about you?"

"I'm working on my own story."

Jacob turned a sausage. "I'm happy to hear it."

Zane nodded. "It won't be done by the end of the month, but I'll have an idea for it."

Jacob pointed the tongs at him. "Anne and I thought we could host a goodbye party for you at the end of the month. You could tell us all about your idea then."

Goodbye party. That sucked the warmth out of him.

"Still a few weeks away." Still was a chance he'd fall in love, marry, and become a real, proper, present uncle. He would visit a couple of times a month and help out. Babysit when Jacob and Anne needed a night off.

He could teach Cassie to draw.

Maybe the goodbye party could be a *surprise, I'm staying* party.

He nodded to himself and pointed to two beautifully grilled sausages. "Can I take one of those to Becky?"

He took two sausages wrapped in bread and smothered in ketchup and handed one to Beckett, who was laughing with Anne. The sound of the front doorbell dinged through the house.

"That'll be Tiffany and Blaire."

"We'll watch over the baby," Zane said, gesturing Beckett to sit on the bench behind the cradle with him.

Beckett draped his jacket over the back of the bench, sat down, and ate.

Breezes funneled up Zane's T-shirt sleeve and he slid a few inches closer to Beckett. The food warmed his belly but didn't help his arms. Beckett leaned forward, causing more air to hit him.

Beckett's smirk suggested he'd done it on purpose.

Anne returned with her guests, who cooed and ogled the baby. Zane hoped Cassie would wake soon so he could pick her up. For a cuddle, not because he'd use that lovely warm blanket to cocoon her against his chest.

Beckett passed him his half-eaten sausage to hold and sprang to his feet and greeted the girls as though he knew them.

Zane waved, vaguely recognizing them from the wedding.

He rubbed his arms, eyed Beckett's jacket behind him, and slung it around his shoulders.

Beckett strode back to him. "Really toughing it out there, Zane."

Zane laughed and dropped Beckett's sausage. Ketchup landed on the jacket sleeve.

"My jacket!"

Zane winced. He set the sausage next to him on the bench and, with nothing to clean the sleeve, brought the material to his mouth. He sucked off the sauce.

Beckett stared at the wet patch.

"It's fine, see? Barely anything there."

Beckett sighed, and Zane—while sorry—found the flickering emotion over Beckett's face amusing. More than amusing, *educational.*

He stood and slung the jacket over Beckett's shoulders. He pulled the lapels, rocking him in closer. "Did that irritate you?"

"Yes."

"Huh. In a click of my fingers, I irritated you."

Beckett shrewdly narrowed his eyes. "There's something behind that 'huh.'"

Zane smoothed the material against Beckett's chest, swallowing a grin. "Tell me, if you saw a man on the street hit his dog, how would you feel?"

Beckett's jaw locked. "Seething mad."

"Would you say you'd hate such a person?"

Beckett gave a hesitant nod. "This is a trap, but yes, I would. You don't hurt animals."

"Such an extreme emotional reaction."

"I don't like the way your eyes are dancing right now."

Zane slid one hand to Beckett's pocket. He wriggled the tips of his fingers inside the tight confines, and Beckett's lurching breath shivered down his neck. "It's just," Zane said, hooking a finger around the car keys, "if it is possible to hate instantly, isn't it also possible to love instantly?"

Beckett stared at him, mouth parted, speechless for perhaps the first time.

"Don't worry, Becky. You're not wrong about anything else." He pulled out the keys with a jingle. "I really do need my hoodie."

ZANE RETURNED WITH A HOODIE AND SOCKS UNDER HIS jandals.

Anne laughed. "You and Jacob really know how to sex up your feet."

"Here," he said, handing over the present he'd also brought from the car. "Just a little something."

She sat on the bench—cleared of half-eaten sausage—and picked at the tape. Across the deck, Beckett was immersed in conversation with Jacob. They glanced over at him and continued chatting. Were they talking about him?

Zane's foot jiggled. He wanted to leap up and listen in.

"I'm glad you brought Beckett along," Anne said. "I'm not into crazy fate stuff, but maybe it means something?"

Zane forced himself to concentrate on Anne. "Of course it means something. It connected us."

Anne ripped out a sudden yawn and stopped peeling tape to cover her mouth. "Sorry. Got about two hours of sleep last night."

Zane rubbed her back. "You're doing amazing." He smiled at Cassie, still sleeping in her cradle.

Beckett's laugh pulled his attention across the deck. What were they talking about? Not an embarrassing story of Zane as a kid, surely. Jacob wouldn't tease him like that, right?

Why *wouldn't* he tease him like that?

Jacob loved ribbing Zane.

Would it put Beckett off him, knowing the depths of his stupidity?

Another laugh.

He glued his gaze to Anne's torturous unwrapping. "A snow globe," she gushed.

"Except, not snow, tiny silver ferns." The ferns fell on top of a kiwi. Cassie was lucky it got to her; he'd been sorely tempted to unpack it and shake things up between him and Beckett.

"Thank you, Zane. Cassie is such a lucky girl."

His smile faltered when he caught Beckett moving toward them.

He rolled his shoulders. He'd act casual. So what if Beckett knew about the time he'd demanded to be taken to the zoo because he wanted to see all the erotic animals?

Beckett bit his lip, barely holding back a grin.

Zane sat on his hands and poured everything he had into focusing on Anne. "When she grows up, she'll be the best of both of you."

"More of Jacob, I hope. He's the kindest, most generous —" Anne hid her next yawn. "God, who else would sign away his inheritance because you needed it more."

Zane stilled. "What?"

He jerked his head up—gaze drifting past Beckett, who halted—to Jacob chatting with Tiffany and Blaire.

Jacob had given him his share of their grandparents' estate? Because he needed it more?

Anne gazed lovingly at Cassie. "He is fair. He is kind."

And he'd just punched Zane in the heart.

Horrible burning shame inched through him. Whatever childhood story Beckett had heard from Jacob, it was nothing to what Anne had admitted.

His hands numbed under him and his chuckle hollowed him out. He didn't dare look at Beckett. "I, uh, forgot something in the car."

He leaped to his feet and crossed the deck. Beckett called out his name, catching up. Strong fingers clasped the crook of his neck and a forearm pressed heavily against his shoulder blades. Beckett's words trickled over the side of his throat. "Anne's tired, she didn't mean you couldn't support yourself without it. She meant Jacob is wealthy and needed it less."

They both knew the implication was that Zane wasn't qualified enough to earn a proper living.

"Nah, it's fine. She's right. I wish you hadn't heard it though."

"Me? Why?"

He didn't know. But he didn't like it. It made him feel inadequate.

He shrugged and then wished he hadn't because Beckett dropped his arm, and he liked it there.

"Becky?"

"Yes, Zane?"

"I'm going to publish my own kick-ass stories. In ten years, I'll be putting Jacob's part of the inheritance into Cassie's account."

Beckett stared at him with soft eyes and an even softer smile. "I'll help you with your stories."

Zane dipped his head and whispered in Beckett's ear, "I'm kinda counting on it, Professor."

"Well, this is a surprise," a familiar male voice said. Zane's stomach twisted, but it had to be nothing to what Beckett was feeling.

Luke, arms full of wrapped gifts, had rounded the house.

When it rains, it pours.

Zane instinctively stepped in front of Beckett. Beckett's very own personal freestanding clothes rail. "What are you doing here?"

Luke rolled his eyes and laughed, lifting his gifts as if to say *duh.* "I expect to see my ex-husband at work, not so much in my sister's home."

"He's with me."

Anne's voice cut over the porch. "Luke! I thought you were at a wedding."

Luke slipped on a smile for Anne. Zane would like to think it wasn't genuine, but for all Luke's faults, he loved his sister. "Hey, sis. The groom pulled out at the last minute, and well, here we are."

"Chris is here too?"

"Putting our bags in the spare room."

Beckett flinched, bumping Zane's arm. Probably the same spare room he had a hundred memories of.

A sour taste shot up Zane's throat, and he glared at Luke. He'd never disliked someone more in his life. He felt literally sick with it.

"The groom really left his bride at the altar?" Anne whispered.

Luke grimaced. "It was horrible for her."

Beckett stepped around Zane. "Much worse than leaving shortly afterward."

Luke's smiled tightened. "We had two hundred guests. I didn't want to humiliate you."

"How considerate."

Anne looked gray. "How about we all head back and have a drink, hmm? I have a nice merlot, Becky. Some cider, Luke."

Force an afternoon of pain on Beckett? Not happening. "Yeah, we're going to head off, Anne."

Beckett spoke to him. "You can stay here. I'll go home and pick you up tomorrow."

Zane looked at him, then at Anne. "You and Jacob have a beautiful baby. I look forward to spending a lot more time with her. Just not today."

He left with Beckett.

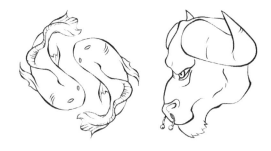

Love is blind.

—Geoffrey Chaucer

Chapter Twelve

"This day is turning out to be a bit of a roller coaster," Zane said as they backed down the long driveway onto the main street. "I feel like I'm fifteen all over again."

Beckett shifted gears and pressed on the gas.

"Can't get out of there fast enough, huh?"

Beckett didn't say anything.

Zane picked up his sketchbook, and the pamphlet he'd taken from the gas station dropped out of it. The sight of it sparked an idea, and he typed an address into Maps on his phone.

Zane gestured with his phone. "Turn right at the next fork."

"My place is left and around the corner."

"Your smile is 5.3 miles away, starting with this right turn."

Beckett leaned against the headrest and let out a soft chuckle. He turned right, and just over five miles later they pulled up at Greenville's antique bookstore, Silver Pines.

Zane gaped at the beautiful repurposed chapel.

"This is my favorite bookstore," Beckett said. "How did you know?"

Zane hadn't known it was Beckett's favorite, but since it was close to his childhood home, he figured he knew of the store. He held up the pamphlet. "Fancy script and the word *classic*. Let's go inside."

Beckett landed a palm on his upper thigh and squeezed. Zane stopped, breath stalling. Beckett looked away from the chapel to him. "You have the biggest heart I know."

"Take as much of it as you like."

"You don't know what you're offering."

"What, gonna take it all?" Zane joked.

Beckett didn't answer. He restarted the car.

"Hey, wait, aren't we going inside?"

Beckett removed his hand from Zane's thigh and drove three minutes through a network of streets, from boulevards to narrow cobblestone alleys. He parked again. "Now, let's go inside."

When Zane spotted a brightly colored comic book store, he ripped at his seatbelt and bounded toward the store.

"I could kiss you, Becky," he called out, gleefully yanking the door open.

Beckett's voice trailed behind him as the world of comics swallowed him whole. "Go for it."

BECKETT WAS THE ONE WHO WENT FOR IT.

After Zane showed him the issues of *Scarlet Sentinel vs. Fire Falcon*, he bought all of them—and was currently ordering what the store didn't have.

Zane overheard two guys gushing over a comic series he hadn't heard of. He snuck closer to peek over their shoulder and saw a half-page panel of two guys dueling. "Any good?" he asked.

The two swung around and grinned. They were good-looking with geeky T-shirts; one read *I like reading books on helium, it makes them hard to put down.*

He needed that shirt. Beckett would love it.

The dark-haired guy wearing a polo shirt stretched out the comic issue he held, and Zane took it. *Fence* by C.S. Pacat and Johanna the Mad. "Other comics are pointless."

"No offense, but I'm a big fan of many comics, so . . . ."

"Smart riposte!" Helium Shirt said, and the compliment fueled Zane. He flickered his gaze to Beckett standing at the counter and wondered if he'd overheard.

Beckett paid for his purchases, his voice carrying as he spoke to the clerk.

Zane concentrated on the comic he held and then watched Helium Shirt slide an arm around his—oh, they were dating?

Or bromancing like he and Beckett?

Now they were kissing. Boyfriends, then.

He shouldn't stare. Except, they looked adorably in love. And when had he ever turned away from love? He especially liked the way they smiled into their kiss.

PDA was so underrated.

He wanted that, too. Wanted to be so comfortable with someone he'd kiss them in the middle of a conversation with a stranger.

"Where do I start?" he asked, and he wasn't only talking about *Fence.*

TEN MINUTES LATER, HE HAD THE FIRST FEW ISSUES OF *FENCE* bagged on his lap as Beckett drove them to his childhood home.

They pulled into a long gravel drive toward a very *Anne with an E* farmhouse.

Zane climbed out of the car and imagined a young Beckett

hiking into the house after a shitty day at school. He leaned against the car and watched Beckett pull out their bags. The sun warmed his back, and the heat from the car toasted his front. The biting wind from Jacob's place had gone. Or maybe the house buffered it.

Beckett caught him staring and stopped, back door open, bags slung over his shoulder. "What?"

"I'd love to check out your bedroom."

Beckett started to smile and then stopped suddenly. He shoved the bags back into the car and shut the door. "You know what? It's lovely out. We should enjoy the afternoon."

"Do you not want me to see your room?"

Beckett fiddled with his keys. "You'll see it," he said, glancing across a green paddock toward a wooden barn. "But first, let's soak in the outdoors."

Zane pushed off the car, meeting Beckett at the hood where he was adjusting the hem of his ketchup-stained blazer. "Fine, we'll put off checking out young Beckett's room."

"Excellent."

"On one condition."

Beckett pressed his lips together. "Name it."

"Answer another question for me."

"If it's another question about how I'm going to die . . . ."

"No, we're beyond whats and hows."

Beckett lifted his head and eyed him. "Where are we, then?"

"At whys."

He cocked his head, curious and hesitant. "How did we get to whys so soon?" he mused. "It's been a week."

"Why did we get here so soon, you mean?" Zane knew why. Brove at first sight. "It feels like I've known you forever." He softened his voice. "Why did Luke leave?"

Beckett studied his shoes as he gave a raw laugh. "Why didn't I suspect that?"

"Why don't you tell me?"

Beckett hitched a thumb toward the barn. "Come. Stables are this way."

Zane walked alongside him. "If you don't want to tell me, I understand. But I'm dying to know."

"Can we ride first?"

"You bet." Beckett opened the barn doors, and Zane halted. "Wait. Ride?"

"You can take my horse. Wanda is a beauty."

Zane ran after him, eyeing the activity at the stables. "Just because I'm a Kiwi and we're all farmland and seventy million sheep, doesn't mean I can ride a horse."

"Of course not." Beckett reached for leather gear in deep shelves. "By that logic, you can ride a sheep."

Zane pinched Beckett on the ass, eliciting a startled hop. The equipment toppled against Beckett's face, muffling his laugh.

"There's more where that came from," Zane growled playfully.

"Not the disincentive you think it is, Zane."

"Ha! Because you're gay."

Beckett stared at him over the stitched edging of a brown boot. "No, not because I'm gay."

Zane rubbed his shoulder, stretching his neck. Not that it did anything to mask the heat climbing to his cheeks. "Um, right."

Beckett passed him a pair of boots. "Put these on. I've worn them in; they shouldn't blister your feet."

He held them up in a shaft of daylight streaming through the open barn door. "These are practically my boots. In brown."

Beckett's chuckle sounded from behind him. "And here they are in black. Zip 'em up."

Jandals kicked off and set on the shelf, Zane slid into the

boots, which he hated to admit felt better than his turquoise ones.

"Hey, these are—" He turned to Beckett. "Holy shit." He blinked at the tight black boots Beckett wore, snug on his calf and tight over his feet. "You *own* the style."

Beckett nonchalantly stood on tiptoe and plucked something off the shelf. Zane didn't know what, because Beckett's boots were absorbing his attention. "Intelligence. Security. And boots. I'm a boot man."

Just staring at the firm leather was sending signals to his dick.

"Zane?"

"Huh, what?"

He dragged his gaze up Beckett to a rather cocky smirk. "We wanted to ride?"

"Lead the way. But I'm not experienced, be patient with me."

"Trust me, I'm practiced. Let's get you on that horse." Beckett led him to a stall, where a silver-and-white horse whickered. She was a giant. At least six feet tall. Impressive and intimidating.

Over the gate, Beckett stroked her nose and rubbed under her mane. "Missed you, too."

"This is Wanda?" Zane asked. "Don't you have something smaller?"

"Like a pony?"

"How about a sheep?"

Beckett pinched his ass, and a pleasant zap shot through him, drawing out a laugh. Zane understood that anyone could enjoy that sensation regardless of orientation. The lingering tingles in combination with Beckett's boots wouldn't make it any easier to ride.

Fifteen minutes later, Beckett had prepared their horses

and guided Zane onto the back of Wanda using a stepping block.

The horse felt unfamiliar under him. A new experience, but not a bad one. He admired the grace Beckett displayed slinging himself on his chestnut stallion. Jasper apparently had a wild streak, but Beckett had him under control. He circled his horse and steered him next to Zane, facing him. If Zane fancied, he could reach out and pat Jasper on the neck.

But he felt comfortable death-gripping his reins. Very comfortable, in fact.

He delivered Beckett a crooked smile. "So. Luke."

Beckett nodded and pointed toward a sea of paddocks. "Let's head to the river. Sit straight, press your calves against her body, and move your pelvis forward at the same time—like you want to fuck—and she'll start walking. She'll follow my horse."

Their horses walked side by side through paddocks, a valley, a strip of forest, and onto a long stretch of gently sloping grass. By that time, Zane felt familiar enough with Wanda. Beckett was burning to ride faster, the energy practically bleeding from him.

"Go for it, Becky."

"No, it's fine—"

"I want to watch you."

"Wanda might want to follow, but she's well trained. Hold her back by slightly pulling the reins repeatedly."

Zane bit his lip. "I still want to watch you."

Beckett straightened in his seat and flipped his reins. "In that case . . . ." He winked, and in a bountiful burst, Jasper was cantering along the grassy stretch. Beckett bounced rhythmically in his saddle, sunlight striking golden threads in his hair, shining against his boots.

He rounded back. Such control of his posture. Forceful

thighs flexed with every step, and wind stung his cheeks a gentle shade of pink.

Zane murmured to Wanda. "I'm sorry you got stuck with me."

After another round, Beckett returned. He glowed with a light sheen of exertion.

"Is there anything you can't do?"

"Plenty, unfortunately." Beckett assessed Zane's posture, from his grip on the reins to how his legs hugged the horse.

"Am I doing it wrong?"

Beckett snapped his head up. "No, just, uh, checking." He turned his horse and called for Wanda to follow. Five minutes more, and they reached the river. Beckett led him to a large rock to dismount and took care of tying the horses to a post.

Zane adjusted his half-numb goods. His thighs would hurt tomorrow.

At the bank of the still arm of the river, he sifted for flat stones and skipped them across the river. Each one jumped five or six times. It wasn't riding a horse or knowing the intimate details of Tolstoy, but everyone enjoyed a good stone skipping.

Beckett was no exception. "You want me to teach you, don't you?" Zane said.

"Give me one of them."

Zane passed one over. Beckett angled incorrectly, and Zane wrapped an arm around his back and readjusted his elbow. Beckett side-eyed him.

"I know," Zane said, steering him into the throw. "The student becomes the teacher." He grinned. "Is this what it feels like?"

"What what feels like?"

"Being the smartest one in the room?" Or at the river, technically.

"Is it the most important thing?"

Zane dropped his arm and shifted back, feet sinking in the stones.

Beckett studied him, thumbing the flat stone. "What is it?"

"Nothing."

One eyebrow hitched.

"There's this stupid little memory." Zane shrugged. "It's ridiculous that it still upsets me."

"Tell me?"

Zane fiddled with the hoodie's drawcords and stared at the water. He'd never personally told this story. Usually it was his parents or his middle brothers who joked about it in front of girlfriends.

It slid off his tongue, thick with embarrassment. "Just before I quit school, I was in this play. I had a two-sentence role, and I stared out into the audience and couldn't remember a single word. I gaped like the fish I am until the rest of the cast just continued as if I'd said my bit. I was right in the center of the stage; my family kept flashing their cameras. My legs felt like lead and I couldn't seem to move myself off the stage. The drama teacher had to steer me off."

He pulled the drawcord so hard that he lost the other end in the hood.

"The family went to dinner after, and when I returned from the restroom, they were giggling about it. Jacob was the only one telling them to stop being asses. But the rest said to lighten up and grow a sense of humor. I just stood around the corner, Becky, cringing as my mum boasted that not everyone could be talented like my brothers."

With the press of his palm, Beckett stopped Zane from pulling his drawcord, pulled the thread still poking out from the hole on his hood, and tugged it. "That's a horrible memory."

"Yes, well. On the heels of that, my girlfriend dumped me because I was not 'future' material, and I messed up an English assignment. The teacher told me not to worry, not everyone was a natural wordsmith. Said at least I have talent in the art department and to pursue that. She meant well, I'm sure, but it was clear to me school wasn't my forte. I dropped out."

"How did your parents take that?"

"They had three kids make it to university. They were happy to have one kid take a different path, and not to worry, because between them they'd make sure I was covered." Zane shrugged. "I busied myself in what I was good at and offered out my services. Rocco found me, and I've been working with him for years. When my grandparents passed, I got"—he looked away from Beckett—"well, more than my fair share of inheritance apparently. After Jacob and Anne's wedding, I traveled, and when they said they were expecting, I just knew I had to stay here."

Not dwelling on the heavy twisting of his gut, Zane forced out a small laugh, gently shoving Beckett. "If only we'd met at the wedding, Becky. I'd have had you longer in my life."

Beckett moved in front of him, blocking his view of the river lapping the stones. "You are the most determined go-getter I know, Zane. I have full faith you can do anything you put your mind to."

The lump in his throat was difficult to swallow. "Thanks."

"I regret not attending Anne's wedding. More than I ever thought I would." Wind shuffled through Beckett's dark hair, and he shook his head, tossing a strand from his eyes. "The idea of being so close to Luke . . . at the time it was too painful to bear."

"What happened between you?"

"It was a living cliché."

"Doesn't mean it can't hurt."

Beckett nodded and gave a shaky smile. "I thought we had a good sex life. He was certainly getting enough. Turned out, not all of it was with me."

"I hate him. How could he do that to you?"

"He's younger than me by a few years. I was already settled, but he still wanted adventure."

Zane couldn't stop shaking his head. "I've been with you a week, and every minute with you feels like an adventure."

"It may feel like that at the beginning, but when the routine creeps into your bones, you might change your mind too."

"Sounds like Luke's problem was feeling entitled to the good times. Romance doesn't work like that. You don't fall in love and just keep falling. You fall, and when the ground catches up, you pull yourselves together, climb back to the top of the cliff, and fall again. You do that over and over until you die. I'm not saying hitting the ground doesn't hurt. Not saying that it's an easy climb to the top. I'm saying that it's worth it to jump again."

Beckett caught his breath and focused on his flat stone. "Speaking of jumping, how do I do this rock thing again?"

Zane steered Beckett into position, showed him how to angle his hand, then pulled back and watched.

His stone jumped three times and a surprised, elated streak shot through Beckett's expression. He doubled over and sifted through stones, finding the flat ones. He threw them, and Zane skipped his rocks alongside him until his phone rang.

He saw Jacob's name on the screen, turning toward Beckett as he answered. Beckett had shared something intimate and painful with him—there was no retreating from him in shame now.

"Jacob, hey."

Beckett freed himself from a stone and loosely knotted their fingers together. Zane absorbed the warm support.

Panicked, Jacob got right to the point. "I had so much money already, and Anne had the farm. It wasn't that I thought you needed it most, it was that I didn't need it, and you were at the start of your career. Mum and Dad funded the rest of our overseas experiences and I knew they were struggling financially to do the same for you. They sunk their share of the inheritance into repairing the house. I was trying to do the right thing. I love you, Zane. I want you to have the opportunities the rest of us had."

Zane rubbed his chest, Beckett's fingers staying with him, his knuckles bumping over his pec.

"Please, I hope you understand."

"I, ah, do. But Jacob, I'm putting that money into an account for Cassie."

"You don't have to."

"I have something to prove."

"Zane . . . ."

"I look up to you, Jacob, but sometimes I forget to look up to myself."

Beckett squeezed his fingers too hard, pride shining in his eyes.

"I want to stop by for a couple of hours tomorrow and cuddle my niece."

Jacob choked out a "Yes," then cleared his throat. "Luke is leaving after breakfast if Beckett wants to come too."

Zane smiled at Beckett. "I hope he comes with me, too."

Beckett winked, and Zane ended the call.

"You heard everything?" Zane asked him.

"Yes."

They walked back to their horses.

Beckett helped Zane mount Wanda and moved to Jasper. He peered up at Zane over his saddle. "I chose the wrong person to jump with."

"Don't worry. I'll help you choose the right person next time."

"You're only here another three weeks."

"You're forgetting I'm going to fall in love and marry before I have to go back. But if I'm not lucky, there's always long distance. I'll text. I'll video call you on an annoyingly frequent basis. I'll send you Kiwi care packages. You'll tell me all about who you're dating, and I'll tell you if they sound good enough."

"Can I do the same for you?"

"Tell me if my date is good enough?"

"And send you care packages."

"I'll be counting on it." Zane winked at him. "Now, maybe it's time you got back on the horse?"

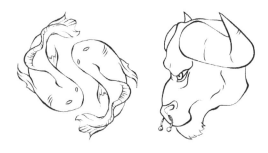

I like adventures, and I'm going to find some.

—Louisa May Alcott

Chapter Thirteen

Natalie Fisher may have been sentimental to name her son Beckett, but that was nothing to Beckett's childhood bedroom.

CDs, candles, and papier-mâché art clogged the bookshelves with a thousand memories.

Zane heard Beckett's footsteps clomping down the hall, and he hurried deeper into the room. He'd left Beckett chatting with his mum and used her helpful directions to navigate here before Beckett could stop him.

What didn't Beckett want him to see?

Zane snagged a book from the shelf next to the twin bed. He liked that not everything was a classic or college-required reading. At a glance, he couldn't spot Tolstoy at all.

He opened the book and flipped through the pages.

"I see you found my room."

Beckett stood framed in the doorway. "I also found your old yearbook." He stabbed a finger at Beckett's headshot. "Look at you."

Beckett sidled into the room and sat next to him on the bed. "Believe it or not, it's one of my better pictures."

"Gotta love the long hair." Zane absorbed the teenage face in Beckett's profile. Yep, he'd been born blessed. "Who were the guys you crushed on? This fella? Ran the chess club?"

"God, no."

"What? He looks hot."

A smile tilted Beckett's lips. "Does he? Huh. No, he never did it for me."

"I should have guessed you'd be more discerning than captain of the chess club. Who tickled you then? Your biology partner?" Zane leered at him. "Your English teacher?"

Beckett took the yearbook and flicked to the athletics section. "Back row, four from the left. Love of my teenage life. Harvey Finnegan."

"What was he? Some type of rugby player?"

"Rugby?"

"A less civilized version of football."

"Mmm, he was a linebacker, and he volunteered at the local soup kitchen with me. Danny McGill—class bully—sent a few nasty words my way and Finnegan made him *cower*."

"Nasty words? About you?"

"I had very long hair."

Zane studied this Finnegan. "You know, he and I resemble each other. Same build. Do you think I'm hot?"

"Depends, are we talking with or without the turquoise boots?"

Zane slipped the yearbook back on the shelf and lifted a honey-scented candle. *I think you're a romantic at heart, Becky.* "Are you still friendly with this Finnegan?"

"He's my closest friend. You met him at my get-together."

"You mean your *birthday party*."

"He works at Treble."

Oh. So he was smart as well as good-looking and sweet. Trifecta of perfection. "Sounds like you should have married him."

"He's straight."

"Do you still crush after him?"

"No, no. I might torture myself more than I should, but I usually know when to give up."

Zane froze. Finnegan was Books for Breakfast! The intimidating one who wanted to drag Beckett to Chiffon. "Are you *sure* Finnegan's straight?"

"Do you think I should try dating him?"

"No!" Zane lowered his voice. "I mean, he's straight. You should definitely forget about him."

Beckett angled a sneaky smile toward the floor as he walked to him. He leaned against the shelf, very close to Zane. Suspiciously close.

Zane tried to peer over his shoulder, and Beckett flattened his back against the shelf. He was hiding something. But what?

Beckett pretended like he wasn't blocking Zane. "You're probably famished. How about we head to the kitchen and find something to eat. After that, we can watch a movie."

"Can I choose the movie?"

"Yes. Anything you want."

Zane hummed. "Okay, sounds great." He made toward the door and held it open.

Beckett hesitantly pushed off from the shelf and hurried out. With a hearty laugh, Zane shut the door behind him and darted back to the shelf.

His minx-like chuckle faded.

Beckett returned, shaking his head.

"You didn't want me to see this?" Zane picked up a picture of Beckett and Luke in a shiny silver frame. Beckett's face had been captured mid-laugh.

Luke was smiling too, and Zane wanted to punch that cursory grin off his face.

"I didn't want you to have the wrong idea when you saw it."

"What idea? I don't have any idea. Why wouldn't you keep a picture of the man who broke your heart?"

Beckett took the photo and looked at it with a swallow. "Every time I come home, I want to lay it facedown, and every time I just can't."

"Are you still in love with that idiot?"

"Not even a little."

"Why don't you turn it facedown?"

"As a reminder not to fall in love again."

"As a reminder not to fall in love with *the wrong person* again? Then, I . . . I understand." Kind of. "Still don't like it."

Hesitantly, Beckett returned the photograph to the shelf.

Zane fought the urge to slap it down.

Beckett tangled their clammy fingers together. "Come," he said, drawing him out of the room. "Maybe it's time we did dinner and a movie."

"THAT IS WHAT I WANT TO WATCH," ZANE SAID AFTER EATING Ms. Fisher's home-cooked tomato, beef, and basil lasagna.

Warm reds and golds accented the living room, a lampshade in every corner. Two were illuminated, shedding soft light over porcelain ornaments and crocheted throw rugs and pillows. Zane sat with Beckett on a deep couch.

Beckett stared at the large screen, assessing Zane's choice of movie, and eyed him. "It doesn't free you from reading the book."

Zane glanced at Mrs. Fisher, who was curled up on an armchair fiddling with an incense stick. "What do you think?"

"The BBC version is long, but it is the best."

"You aren't too tired?" Beckett asked.

"Me, tired? I could go all night."

Beckett gave him a disbelieving look. "I've counted three yawns since we finished dinner."

"Nah, I'm good." Zane could manage watching *Pride and Prejudice.* "But you're right, you might not make it."

Beckett scoffed and started the six-part series, curling his legs up on his corner of the couch.

Zane had long since peeled his socks off. The tight weave of the couch fabric zipped over his heels as he stretched his legs out. He stuffed a pillow behind his back and made himself comfortable. The balls of his feet almost met Beckett's.

"How many times have you watched this?" Zane asked.

"Just a few."

"So many times you lost count, huh?"

"Well, I . . . I was very invested in the story growing up."

"Big Mr. Darcy fan?" Zane waggled his brows.

Beckett gently kicked his foot. "The biggest. I even rewrote the book in my first year at college."

Zane lurched upright. "Where is it? *That's* the version I want to read."

"It's a gay version. Set in modern-day Greenville."

"Give it to me now."

Beckett laughed.

Zane was serious. He swung off the bed to ransack Beckett's room, and Beckett laughed again, pulling him back to the couch. "I'd need to clean it up. But maybe one day . . . ."

"I'll hold you to it." Zane reclined, to his position on the couch.

Like that, they watched the first two parts. Halfway through part three, Mrs. Fisher retired for the night due to a four o'clock start the next morning.

The house grew quiet, and Zane was keenly aware of the sounds the two of them made shifting against the cushions, their laughter at something one of the Bennets said, and later, Beckett's rhythmic breathing. Were Beckett's eyelids drooping?

He wriggled down and nudged Beckett with the ball of his foot. On screen, Elizabeth and Mr. Darcy were exchanging glances.

The screen light made it difficult to read Beckett's expression, but his eyes were on his, if a bit unfocused.

"If you're not using that pillow on your lap," Zane asked, "can I have it?"

"What for?"

"'Cause."

"Because you're about to fall asleep."

Zane stifled a yawn. "Not before the end."

Beckett reluctantly passed him the pillow and hunched forward with determined concentration on the screen.

Zane plumped the pillow next to his and prodded Beckett again. When Beckett refused to look over, Zane gathered the last of his strength, sat up, and tugged Beckett lengthwise next to him on the couch. He jammed himself as far back into the couch as he could and strapped Beckett close. Beckett's back warmed his chest.

"What are you doing?" Beckett asked.

"Getting us into a position we will definitely not fall asleep in because, *of course*, we will both make it to the end."

A lock of hair tickled Zane's nose. He blew it away, and Beckett's chuckle morphed into a shiver that scuttled through to him.

He clutched Beckett tighter and nestled a leg between Beckett's parted ones. Elizabeth and Mr. Darcy verbally sparred, the tension so palpable Zane felt it thrumming through him as if it were his own.

"Get it together already, right?" he whispered, top lip skimming the hair at Beckett's nape.

Beckett groaned his agreement. "Except they both have issues they need to overcome. If they got together now, would it last?"

"We definitely need Lizzy and Mr. Darcy to last." Zane watched again. "Maybe if they just told each other what their problem was?"

"More than they already have? No, the true power of transformation comes in self-awareness." Beckett leaned against him and turned his head to look at him. "Until they understand their own thoughts, emotions, and actions, Elizabeth and Mr. Darcy aren't ready for commitment."

What Beckett said made sense. "Good thing they become more self-aware by the end."

"It wouldn't be such a powerful story without that growth."

"A good lesson for my own stories?"

Beckett returned to watching the screen. "Yes."

Zane drew down Beckett's shirt that had ridden up and flattened it over his hip. The added warmth of Beckett next to him made him sleepier. His thoughts spiraled around what Beckett had said.

He yawned. "Are you saying it's not enough to tell you to get out there and date? You need to realize that on your own?"

Beckett's chest expanded under Zane's hand with a large intake of air. "For example."

"Regardless, I think you should get out there and date again."

Beckett scrubbed his face and laughed tiredly. "Zane . . . ."

"What? I'm just nudging you along. But take your time getting there on your own."

"What if I like this bromance? What if I just want to enjoy you?"

Zane's breath got tangled with the butterflies that swamped his body. Sometimes it felt like he had so much brove he didn't know what to do with it.

He wanted to say something, acknowledge it somehow, but he couldn't. He pressed the tip of his nose against the back of Beckett's head and got a pleasant lungful of herbal shampoo.

They watched Pride and Prejudice until they succumbed to sleep. Zane drifted in and out of dreams, waking briefly when Mr. Darcy and Lizzy married and commenced their happily ever after.

He woke another time when Mrs. Fisher tiptoed into the room. Their gazes caught over Beckett's head. The bluish light of dawn slithered into the room, and Zane caught her concern.

Sometime in the night, Beckett had twisted. Their fronts were plastered together, and Beckett's legs draped over his thigh.

"Morning, Mrs. Fisher," he whispered.

"Natalie," she said, inching closer. The crease in her brow deepened. "It's been a long time since my son brought a friend home."

Zane wasn't sure, but it felt like the steady breath that puffed against his clavicle faltered.

"I'm so happy to be the one he has."

"Be good to him."

Zane nodded. "Always."

She left. He squeezed Beckett, and the gentle rise and fall of his back lulled him into sleep.

At some point, he shivered and groped for Beckett, only to have his hands land on vacant cushions.

No wonder Zane was cold. He rolled onto his feet, stretched his stiff limbs, and after a visit to the bathroom, tracked Beckett down.

The bedroom door was open, and Zane paused outside, looking in. Beckett sat curled on his bed, flicking through the comics Zane had illustrated in the car. His hair was wet from a recent shower.

In true Beckett style, he didn't lift his head. "Are you going to stand there staring or come in?"

Zane inched forward a step and halted.

The photo of Beckett and Luke.

It wasn't standing upright anymore.

It lay face down.

Beckett followed his gaze.

Zane's voice croaked from disuse. "Because I said I didn't like it?"

"Because I woke up this morning and needed to."

There is no remedy for love but to love more.

—Henry David Thoreau

Chapter Fourteen

A fter a day cuddling baby Cassie and bumming around the farm with Anne and Jacob, they drove back home to find Darla and Leah eating dinner on the front porch. With plenty of chicken casserole left, Beckett and Zane grabbed chairs and joined them.

Leah left them early to meet some girlfriends, promising she'd clean up tomorrow.

When they finished eating, Zane and Beckett entered a kitchen littered with a weekend's worth of dishes. The room smelled like spoiled banana. Beckett grumbled Leah's name, and Zane turned on the water.

Leah would have left this until tomorrow? "I'll wash, you dry?"

Beckett first took out the trash and opened the windows. Fresh air cleansed the room as they worked.

Zane daydreamed about the story he was outlining and startled when Beckett cried, "What are you doing?"

Zane looked into the sink. "Scrubbing this clean?"

"With a wire scrubbing brush? That's a very expensive nonstick pan."

He frowned. "And I want to clean it."

"Good Lord. Have you never washed dishes before?"

"I am literally doing what I've done every other night since moving in with you."

Beckett paled. "You've scrubbed this pan with that before?"

"What do you expect me to do? Lick it clean?"

"Use a dishcloth."

"Do you know how disgusting those are? Like, two hundred thousand times dirtier than the toilet seat."

Beckett paused, tone shifting. "Which is why you only use it for the dining table?"

"Exactly."

"Please use the dishcloth on my pan."

Zane dropped the metal scrubbing brush and thumped around passive-aggressively as he found a *clean* dishcloth.

Beckett nodded. "Thank you."

That little thank-you grated Zane the wrong way. He sullenly scrubbed the pan and put it on the drying rack. He plunked the next pot into the water, splashing bubbles onto his face, neck, and shirt.

He sighed. Served him right.

Beckett set down the plate he'd dried and turned Zane around. With his dish towel, he dabbed the bubbles off Zane's chin and neck.

Their eyes locked, and Zane felt the frustration bleed from him. "You missed a spot," he said and shifted Beckett's hands to Zane's shirt.

Beckett shook his head and dabbed him some more.

"Our first fight."

Beckett's hands stilled.

"It's a milestone, Becky. We have to celebrate."

"Celebrate fighting?"

"Celebrate making up."

"Will this be a thing every time we're annoyed with each other?"

Zane smirked. "I hope so. I'm sure some fights will take longer to get over, but that's cool. The celebration is always in proportion to the effort needed to make up."

Beckett resumed drying the dishes. "Two hundred thousand times dirtier?"

Zane nodded. Disgusting but true.

Beckett frowned. "Maybe just use your hand?"

"I don't know," Zane teased. "The things my hand does might make the pan *dirtier.*"

Beckett dropped his very nice, expensive pan. He caught it against his thighs and stowed it in the cupboard.

The ticklish glare Beckett sent him made the rest of the cleaning fly by.

When they were done, Zane threw himself on the armchair. "Now we celebrate."

Beckett tossed the dish towel into the laundry room. "How?"

"After you start that laundry, I'll let you talk about books, Becky."

Beckett's laughter trickled down the hall. A few minutes later, he returned with *Pride and Prejudice.* He cracked open the first page, and pacing before him, all grace and proper pronunciation, Beckett read aloud.

~

ZANE SMIRKED THROUGH THE ENTIRE CHAPTER BECKETT READ. At least three times, Beckett scowled at him over the page of the book and told him if he didn't stop smiling that he'd stop reading.

But Beckett obviously needed a lesson on follow-through.

Vibrations against his leg had Zane pushing off the

armchair and checking his phone. More pictures of cute baby Cassie, and an unread email from Rocco.

His stomach jerked at the thought of reading the message.

He stalked to the front door and Beckett tailed him.

"I need a walk."

Beckett lifted Zane's windbreaker off the coat stand and held it open for him. "I figured."

Zane slid his arm into the sleeves. The soft pressure of Beckett guiding it onto him disappeared. When Zane turned, Beckett was slipping into his shoes.

"You don't need to come with me."

"Is that right?"

"I have a charged phone this time."

Beckett finished tying his shoes. "I like turning on my radio and hearing nothing happened in the local news to make me mad."

Zane slipped on his sneakers. "You still listen to the radio?"

"You're missing the point."

Zane poked his tongue out. "What's gonna make you mad?"

"Hearing about your murder on Mulberry."

"I won't get murdered."

Beckett snagged his keys. "That's right."

With a smirk, Zane slid Beckett's blue scarf off the hook and stepped toe-to-toe to the man. "You think I need half a century of manly experience protecting me?"

Beckett cast him a withering glare, and Zane slung the scarf around Beckett's neck, wrapping the ends and tucking them in.

The tail end of a huff scuttled over Zane's neck. "You do need *thirty* years protecting you."

Zane glanced over Beckett's shoulder to the mirror. "I'm gonna find you checking yourself out later, aren't I?"

Opening the front door, Beckett waved Zane outside. "You don't have to ogle me next time."

They walked back to the bandstand in the park of lights. Maybe they would make a tradition of it?

"Busy week at work?" Zane asked.

"Chiffon, Wednesday night. Other than that, the usual routine."

"Oh, the staff dinner. I promise I won't SOS you in the middle of it."

"I'm hoping you won't, because I'm hoping you might come with me?"

Zane stilled. "I can't."

Beckett hugged his arms. "Do you have a date?"

"No." But he couldn't show up there. Too many smart men and women who had a hundred clever conversations up their sleeve.

Zane handed his phone to Beckett. "Read Rocco's email to me."

Beckett stared at his phone. "Phone's locked."

"It's Jacob's birthday. Date and month in that order and not the other way around like you do here."

Beckett typed it in and opened the dreaded email. "Hi, Zane. Disappointed, but I understand if you won't have the time. Good luck writing your own stories—uh, I'm not reading that part—ciao, Rocco."

"What part did you skip?"

"The part where the guy is frustrated that you won't drop what you are doing to accommodate him and his needs."

"Give it to me or read it."

Beckett sighed and read very fast. "Good luck writing your own stories. Judging from some of your emails, you'll need it."

Zane cringed. Exactly why he and Chiffon wouldn't mix. "Yeah, some of my emails were pretty bad."

They stared out at the glittering pond. Beckett ducked out

of the bandstand and returned with a spring up the steps. He grabbed Zane's hand and planted a smooth, flat stone in his palm. "Make the water dance?"

"Sounds romantic, Becky. I'm having an influence." The angle wouldn't work from the bandstand, so Zane moved to the pond's edge. Six times the stone jumped over the surface.

When all the ripples disappeared, Zane turned his attention to Beckett. "Why would it make you mad?"

"What are you talking about?"

"Sad, sure. But mad?"

"Some context would help drive this conversation onto a two-way street."

"Murder, Becky."

"Right. The purposeful killing of other people tends to elicit anger from me."

Zane frowned. "I meant my murder. Do you walk with me every night because you're afraid I'll get into trouble?"

"You haven't proven me wrong."

"My dying would make you mad?"

Beckett stepped up to him and clasped him around the neck. "I'm possessive. I don't like it when others take my things away. I don't like others even *looking* at my things the wrong way."

Beckett's clear, steady gaze made his toes curl with a flutter. "Am I your possession, Becky?"

A wavering moment, then Beckett steered them toward home. "Our bromance, yes. I'll hold on to that, thanks."

WEDNESDAY EVENING, ZANE STARED AT HIS PHONE, DATING APP open. He'd been staring at it for fifteen minutes.

Darla kept peeking at his screen from her spot next to him on the porch swing.

"You're looking ashen, love."

A boulder of unrest weighed his stomach down. This was the third day in a row he'd opened the app and couldn't bring himself to chat with anyone. It just . . . wasn't right.

He'd spoken to Darla about it yesterday, and she'd given him sage advice.

He needed to spend time pondering what he wanted from a marriage.

Maybe he should think about it while walking Beckett to Chiffon.

Beckett emerged from his side of the duplex after a shower, a shave, and a complete change of clothes.

Holy hell. Platitudinous tan had never been so . . . *fresh*.

His gaze drifted up Beckett's length to find blue eyes pegged on him.

Darla shooed him toward Beckett. One delightfully ungraceful hop over the fence, and he smacked into Beckett, grabbed the man before he fell, and dragged him to his bedroom.

"What?" Beckett said. "Do I not look—?"

Zane shoved him to the bed, dropped to his knees, and pulled Beckett's shoes off. He tossed them and pulled up Beckett's black socks under his jeans. "You could be heading toward the catwalk if I didn't know better. You should think about elbow patches, Professor." Zane sighed. "But since I know you won't . . . ."

He ducked to their closet and came back carrying his turquoise boots. "May as well go all the way."

"All the way," Beckett murmured.

Zane gingerly slipped the boots onto Beckett's feet and closed the inside zipper of each leg over skinny jeans.

One glance up, and Zane saw glazed eyes and Beckett biting his bottom lip. Beckett snapped out of his daydream and pressed one sole against Zane's chest with a wink. Zane rocked backward with the gentle force of it. "How do you like me now?"

Zane offered his hand, breath catching as Beckett took it. "I think I've gone up a half-notch on the Kingly Scale."

Beckett's eyes danced. "A whole half-notch, hmmm?"

"Maybe three quarters."

Beckett laughed and strutted around him. "Not looking too *ostentatious*?"

"Definitely three quarters." Zane narrowed his eyes. "You're having fun with this, aren't you?"

"Oh, Zane," Beckett said, leaving the room. "Let me count the ways."

Zane took a moment to adjust himself and scurried after Beckett. He grabbed the keys, shut the door, and caught up to him crossing the street.

"I think I should walk you," Zane said.

"I calculated as much. What I'm still figuring out is whether you'll join me."

Zane shook his head. "Two different worlds. Besides, look at you. Look at me."

Beckett eyed him. "I'm looking."

"Not exactly dressed for the occasion."

"You're perfect the way you are."

"A hoodie and yesterday's jeans?"

Beckett didn't respond. They walked to Chiffon, taking in the setting sun and tired tweets from the treetops.

Every time he glanced at Beckett, Zane's silent words formed like a scrambled thousand-piece puzzle with no guiding picture. He thought he understood the big picture, but he hadn't yet found all the edges.

Restaurant chatter and cheerful laughter grew louder as they moved down a line of eateries. They stopped outside Chiffon, and Zane remembered the last time he'd stood there with Beckett.

"Come with me," Beckett said. "Enjoy the night. Who knows, maybe you'll find love here."

Zane glanced at the smartly dressed people clustered around white-clothed tables outside and palmed the back of his neck with a laugh. Nobody wanted a fool bringing down the conversation. "I'm going back home."

"Then we'll go home together."

Zane couldn't conceal his bafflement. "You've been looking forward to this since before we met."

"You're only here another few weeks." Beckett stepped closer, a determined glint in his eye. "Your conversation is the one I care for most."

"But . . . but you dressed up like *that* for this."

"I can flaunt this at home."

"Please stay. I'd feel bad if you didn't have this night."

He stared at the man's flushed cheeks and mischievous blue eyes that were twinkling. "If I recall, Darla said you should take your best friend on a date to kick-start your luck in the love department. This could be that date?"

Beckett wasn't making the decision easier. Still, Zane had the same seesawing sensation in his feet that he had the day Beckett offered him to sit in on his lecture. "I don't . . . I'm not sure."

He wished he could.

Footsteps clacked on the footpath behind him, and Beckett's expression blanked. He gave a short nod, and Zane turned to see Luke closing in. Luke whispered to his boyfriend and opened the door.

The boyfriend scuttled into the restaurant. Luke's scrutiny darted from Zane to Beckett as he eyed their distinctively different clothes. "Are you coming in, Beckett?"

Why did Luke assume only Beckett was coming in? Why did Zane feel small?

If this was how *he* felt, how on earth was Beckett coping?

He couldn't leave Beckett here with that douche—sorry, Anne!—without support.

"We're both going in." He hooked Beckett's arm and they marched past Luke into Chiffon.

Beckett gracefully strode into the dimly lit restaurant, weaving through tables toward a private booth close to a platform stage. It felt like the moment he'd first met Becky, desperate to make a good impression despite being an outsider.

The patrons were dressed to impress, and there were too many pairs of thick-rimmed glasses to count. Dictionaries and thesauruses served as centerpieces for the tables marked *Synonym Standoffs*.

Elegance met wit, and here he was bouldering through the middle of it.

"You didn't have to," Beckett said.

"Yes, I did."

Beckett gave him a shaky smile that made his insides somersault. "We can leave at any time."

Light flashed onstage and a host spoke into a microphone. "Tonight's first standoff will begin in twenty minutes. Sign up for a spot if you haven't already. Three spots are still free."

"That's Puck, the merry wanderer of the night. Chiffon's best master of ceremonies."

"Do you stand off against him?" Zane asked, taking in the sprightly man with glitter in his hair.

"Nah, he's the word fairy. He chooses the words each pair plays with."

"You say play like it's fun."

A soft chuckle. "I'm sure Finnegan has booked us a slot."

"How can you be so nonchalant about performing onstage? Doesn't it feel like your stomach will drop out through your ass?"

"Quite the opposite. It's a thrill."

A strapping man with a wicked-cool grin waved them over,

calling Beckett's name. Zane recognized him by the sudden growl that leaped up his throat. Books for Breakfast. Finnegan. The love of Beckett's teenage life.

Yeah, he was jealous.

He wanted Beckett bromancing only with him—and it was clear from those laughing "heys" and backslaps that Finnegan was competition.

Okay, simple: Zane would make a good impression on Beckett's friends and colleagues while making it politely obvious that Beckett and he had an extra-special connection.

"Zane."

He snapped out of his thoughts. Finnegan was smiling warmly, extending a hand.

Zane squeezed it enough to leave a thumbprint. A fleeting frown hit Finnegan's brow. Zane grinned and slung an arm around Beckett's shoulders. "You and Becky have known each other a long time."

A surprised sound escaped Beckett's mouth, but Zane's gaze stayed rooted on Finnegan. "Yes, our entire lives. When did you meet him?"

Well, shit. "A week and a half ago. But I'm sure we knew each other in a former life."

More of Beckett's colleagues arrived, and with a gentle tug of his fingers, Beckett freed himself from Zane's arm and welcomed them.

Luke and his boyfriend returned from the bar with a tray of drinks and handed them out. Beer for Finnegan and an older-looking professor, and white wine for Beckett.

Luke offered it to Beckett with a smile, painting himself as the nice guy. But Beckett was a red wine drinker—anyone who had spent time with him knew that. Still, Beckett would look like a dick if he didn't accept.

Zane stole it off the tray. "You don't mind, do you, Becky? I'm kinda nervous meeting your friends."

Beckett snuck a sideways glance at him, lips twisting. "Be my guest."

Zane smiled tightly at Luke over the glass and drank deeply.

Beckett introduced him to Professor Lune and Senior Professor Annabeth Mable, who taught African-American literature and postcolonial theory, and who enjoyed discussing her views on contemporary Māori literature.

Zane almost dropped his wine.

Zane had no clue what to say even though he'd been read Māori myths and legends as a kid. For all his teasing that Beckett didn't know anything about New Zealand, he didn't know much himself.

Each colleague had an impressive title, and when they asked what he did, he fought a heavy blush and told them he drew pictures.

"He's an incredible artist with a fine eye for detail, and he has a clever way of seeping in subtext into his illustrations."

Zane couldn't blush any harder and excused himself to fetch another round of drinks.

Finnegan caught up with him at the bar as he searched Amazon for books on Māori literature.

He one-clicked a book and glanced at Finnegan. Zane coughed up a cardboard "Hey" and ordered drinks, including a New Zealand pinot noir.

"I saw what you did back there with the wine," Finnegan said. "For Beckett. Very nice of you."

He shrugged. "My brother-in-law was being a prick."

Finnegan tapped the bar top. "Help me out here, what did I do to deserve the flat looks you've been casting my way?"

Was it better to be frank? He sighed. "You're his best friend, right?"

"Yeah, we're pretty close."

"That's why it's hard to like you."

Finnegan grinned. "Are you and my boy . . . ?"

"See, you call him 'my boy' and I kinda want to punch something."

Hefty laughter shot out of him.

Zane scowled. "We're bromancing, and I kinda hate that he might be bromancing with you too."

"Bromancing?"

"I'm at a real disadvantage of being his favorite if you are. You've known Beckett forever. You have inside jokes I wouldn't understand. You do all that word-wittage stuff." Zane threw up his arms in despair. "You could probably finish each other's lectures."

"Bromancing?"

Zane shuffled back on his stool. "The fact you don't know what I'm talking about is kind of reassuring."

"Yeah, look, I don't get it, but . . . get out your phone."

Zane lifted a questioning brow but did as he was told.

"Open a new contact and put this number in."

Zane plugged in Finnegan's number and sent him a glaring emoji. "What's this for?"

"Beckett's friends are my friends. You need anything, give me a call."

"Are you always this nice? Because that's not making me like you any more."

Finnegan clasped a hand on Zane's shoulder. "Beckett has been the happiest I've ever seen him the last week. Keep doing whatever you're doing, including scowling at me all night if necessary." The bartender slid a tray of drinks across the bar and Finnegan picked it up on Zane's behalf. "Of course, I'd be happy if you didn't. Up to you."

He strode off with the drinks and Zane pulled himself together. Finnegan was a decent guy. The only person Zane should narrow his eyes at was the one who broke Beckett's heart.

He took a seat next to Beckett at the table, which still bubbled with conversation.

Beckett raised his glass of red with a thankful smile and took a sip. He weaseled out of a conversation and turned to him, holding up a small cracker with pesto. "These are delicious, if you want to try?"

Zane watched Beckett pop the cracker into his mouth. Beckett's throat worked with a swallow and he slid his tongue over his bottom lip, catching a stray crumb.

"Tell me more about your day, Zane. What did you do?"

"After the best coffee with you at King's, I spent the day with Darla." She and Leo had kept him company as he worked on his story outline. "Your sister still didn't come home, by the way."

"She messaged me. She took a spontaneous road trip with friends and might be back tonight. Or tomorrow. Or whenever she feels like it." Beckett fussed with the white tablecloth. "Did you scout for any more dates?"

He hadn't brought himself to do it. "I was *really* into my story outline."

"No dates on the horizon?"

Zane fondly flicked Beckett's nose. "I think you're forgetting this *is* a date."

"Excuse the interruption," Finnegan said, palming the backs of their chairs. He looked at Beckett. "We're on in less than a minute."

Beckett stood, catching Zane's worried glance around the table.

"Don't worry about leaving me here all alone," Zane said, scoring a snort from Beckett. He twisted his chair to face the stage and leaned back, folding his arms. "Wow me, Professor."

Challenge sparked in Beckett's eyes as he waltzed away with Finnegan.

Puck came onstage and explained the rules: They'd spend

one minute exchanging sentences using synonyms or idioms relating to the chosen topic. No more than two seconds could pass between turns. Veering off topic meant immediate disqualification. Wait too long to come back, game over. A bell dinged.

Puck dropped the topic "wood" and Finnegan, who had won the coin toss, began with an idiom. "I felt like a babe in the woods the first time I stood on this stage against you."

Beckett smoothly retorted, "You did an amazing job—keep in mind I get a lot of practice in my neck of the woods."

"Maybe I'll win this thing tonight, knock on wood."

"You're not out of the woods yet."

"Guess it's time to cut the deadwood out of my performance."

"See if you can get a wood butcher to help you."

Luke took Finnegan's chair across from Zane. "Beckett's good."

Zane kept his focus on Beckett. "The best."

Beckett nodded in appreciation of Finnegan's cleverness. Zane admired the small acknowledgment of respect.

It made his heart melt a little.

"You're kidding me," Luke whisper-shouted over the table. "Are you dating my ex?"

Zane reluctantly turned and looked at him. "What I am doing here has nothing to do with you."

Luke shook his head. "You're my brother-in-law. You're not supposed to—it's inappropriate, don't you think? Christ, I thought you were crashing with him, not fucking him."

Angry heat swamped Zane. He hated the way Luke spoke about Beckett. Luke had broken his heart, and he had no say in who helped Beckett pick up the pieces and patch them back together.

He pulled his focus back to where he wanted it. On Beckett.

"Whatever, you'll be gone at the end of the month," Luke muttered.

Zane leaned over the table and drilled Luke's gaze with a glare. "Our relationship doesn't revolve around screwing. It will last a lifetime."

"Are you telling me you two are *boyfriends?*"

"We're—"

"Just do me a favor and keep the touchy-feely stuff out of my sight. Because . . . weird."

Zane's jaw clenched.

Onstage, Beckett and Finnegan were tied, and Puck announced an alliteration tiebreaker. Because Finnegan had won the first coin toss, Beckett got to drop the first word. "Universities."

Finnegan added. "Unify."

"Unicycle."

"And ukulele."

"Users . . ."

What proceeded was a long, alliterated sentence, until Finnegan stumbled for a word.

The crowd cheered as the boys took a bow and trundled off stage.

"One of these days, someone will beat you," Finnegan said to Beckett as they approached the table.

"You made me sweat up there, Fin. Of all the days to do it, too."

Zane leaped to his feet and whipped Beckett into his arms. "You were amazing." He smacked a kiss on Beckett's parted lips, and Beckett froze.

Zane hugged him, breathing in his earthy scent and faint aftershave. He whispered in his ear, "Sorry, I kind of messed up down here with Luke, and it requires making you my boyfriend and fondling you in front of him."

Beckett's limbs relaxed, and he pulled back to look at him. "Boyfriend?" he mouthed.

Zane bit his lip and nodded.

Their gazes flickered toward their table and a bright red Luke.

"Fondling?" Beckett said, pressing his weight against Zane. Hands strolled firmly up and down the muscles of his back, and Zane hummed into the massage. He dropped his head and grazed his nose down Beckett's cheek, peppering three kisses at his jaw. He was freshly shaven, but a detectable prickle tickled Zane's lips.

Beckett's breath hitched and those deft fingers dipped under the waistband of Zane's jeans. One hand slid further, over the curve of his ass, bunching down his boxers.

His dick stirred to attention and he fought a moan. A blast of hot breath escaped over Beckett's ear. "That might feel a little too good, Becky. I want to make a point, not walk around with one."

Beckett chuckled and withdrew his hand. "Good Lord, I'm hungry."

"Shall we order dinner?"

"Only if I can pay for both of us."

Zane steered Beckett to his chair and pulled it out for him to sit.

Both Luke and Finnegan were staring at them, Finnegan while pounding on his phone.

Zane's pocket lit up.

Finnegan: BROMANCING?

Zane frowned and read the word three times before replying.

Zane: Yeah, he's mine.

After a delicious dinner and two more rounds of professors standing off on stage, Zane was starting to understand why Beckett liked coming here so much. It was pretentious but in a silly way. "Thank you for inviting me to this penis party," he said.

Beckett eyed him, something deep lurking in his eyes. "I'm afraid I might invite you to another one before the month's out."

"Don't be afraid. I was nervous, but you put me at ease. Invite me whenever you want."

Hand trembling, Beckett spilled wine on his plate.

Zane squeezed his elbow. "Are you okay?"

"Just having to show a lot of restraint." Beckett stroked Zane's face with a mere gaze. "It's taxing."

Zane looked down the table at Luke whispering to his boyfriend. "I hoped you were having a good night despite Luke."

"I daresay I'm having a *fantastic* night *because* of Luke." Zane frowned, and Beckett added, "You mightn't have come in otherwise."

"Oh, well I'm sorry for the taxing part." Zane grinned.

"Clearly sorry."

Zane chuckled.

Puck sauntered onstage and spoke into the microphone. "There is one space available. Do we have any brave takers?"

Beckett lifted his brow. "Would you like a turn up there? With me?"

"Never in a million years would I step onstage and wage a word war. Not with anyone, and especially not you."

"Especially not me?"

"Absolutely not with you. Pick on a brain your own size."

A snort had them both jerking their heads toward Luke, who had shuffled down the table closer to them. "Your own size and closer to your own age. Leave poor Zane. He wouldn't stand a chance against you or anyone here."

The words were true, but Zane hated them anyway. The good vibes that had been energizing him faded. He stared at the scrunched-up napkin on his plate.

Beckett stood and held a hand out to Zane. "My boyfriend and I are leaving to enjoy each other's company at home."

Zane took the cue, waved a hurried goodbye, and shuddered as he passed the stage on the way out of Chiffon.

Never in a million, trillion years.

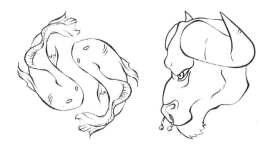

The very essence of romance is uncertainty.

—Oscar Wilde

Chapter Fifteen

"Don't get me wrong, I'm not at all upset," Beckett said. "But how did we end up boyfriends?"

They moved up the path, a few thankful steps from home. Zane was desperate to rid himself of the poisonous pessimism that was beginning to choke him. He needed a candlelit bath, pronto.

Darla's side of the duplex was dark. Her porch swing creaked in a gusty breeze. Zane opened the door and leaned against the cool wood to hold it open. Beckett was as perfectly put together as he had been when they had left.

"Luke jumped to the boyfriend conclusion on his own. I would have corrected him, but he made such a fuss about not touching you in front of him. Said it would be weird." Zane shrugged. "He wound me up the wrong way. I don't want him telling me how I can be or not be around you. That's our business, don't you think?"

Beckett leaned against the doorjamb. "How we are together—whether we touch, kiss, sleep naked, have sex or not —that is most definitely our business."

Zane swallowed, gaze lingering on Beckett's cool pose. "That's—" He cleared his throat. "That's what I thought."

Beckett pushed off the doorframe with the flat of his foot, and Zane's chest doubled in size.

Zane scored a hand through his hair. "Sometimes, I feel like . . . ."

"Like?" Beckett didn't move away nor move forward. He stayed still, patient as always.

"I need a bath."

Zane turned and fled into the house.

Flicking on the living room light was a mistake. Leah's scarf, leggings, and lacy underwear were strewn over the furniture as though she'd gotten lucky and hadn't bothered to clean up afterward.

Beckett stepped in behind him and cursed.

Zane had barely made it to the armchair when the sound of bedsprings groaning from the attic assaulted his ears. Jesus, that was loud.

Like really freaking loud.

Zane hadn't been the biggest fan of those squealing of bedsprings, but through the hollow ceiling, it was worse. Echoed.

Had Beckett heard him twisting and turning in bed—*had Beckett heard him jerking off?*

He glanced to Beckett, who caught Zane's panicked look, interpreted it, and calmly crossed the room toward him. Zane sidled behind the armchair as if it could protect him from the sheer mortification sweeping through him.

"Zane," Beckett said in a low, quiet voice.

Zane scrubbed his heated face and peeked at Beckett through his fingers. "The other night, when I was, er, getting into that long-winded book—"

Beckett's step faltered. "Oh, dear Lord—"

"You heard all that?"

Beckett slammed his eyes shut like, clearly not wanting to have this conversation.

Well, same here.

Slowly, Beckett reopened his eyes. "Yes, I heard you."

Zane groaned and ducked behind the armchair. He wasn't quite sure why he couldn't laugh this one off. He would have with anyone else. Hell, he would have with Beckett a few days ago.

The armchair shifted, and a chuckle floated from above him. Beckett teased the ends of Zane's hair and Zane reluctantly looked up. Beckett was peeking at him over the back of the chair with an amused expression. "Why have you gone shy?"

"I don't know."

Beckett's gaze flitted to his mouth and back to his eyes. "You know it's okay to do it, right?"

"Yeah. It's just . . . ." Something.

"Does it help to know I did it, too?"

"While . . . hearing me?"

"Will it be a problem if I say yes?"

Zane's breath caught, and his cock grew heavy. "I *really* need a bath."

"Not a cold shower?"

"I think you should take your sister's underwear off the lampshade and busy yourself in bed." At a small chuckle, Zane added, "With a *book*."

Beckett climbed off the armchair, giving him the space he needed. When the room was quiet, Zane crawled out from behind the chair and hopped into a shower.

Water cascaded over Zane's body, and he let it run. Skin wrinkled and scrubbed, he didn't retire for bed.

Not until he was sure Beckett was sleeping.

Not until, with painful clarity, he had figured out that puzzle.

❧

LIKE EVERY MORNING IN BECKETT'S BED, ZANE WOKE TO Beckett curled with his back to him.

Like every morning, Zane wanted to do something about it.

Unlike every morning, he had a better picture why.

Zane stretched, and his morning wood shifted against the sheets. He threw himself out of bed and into the bathroom. Leaning back against the tile, its coldness seeping through his threadbare T-shirt, he reached into his satin boxers and pulled at his dick. He trembled as he wrung out the most intense orgasm he'd ever had by his own hand.

Yes, he had the whys.

What he didn't have were the *hows*.

Nothing a good Google search wouldn't help with. But first: breakfast.

He cooked sunny-side up eggs and squeezed oranges for fresh juice. Beckett stepped out while he was setting their plates, damp from a shower, journal clasped in his hand. Their eyes met and Zane shook so badly one of the eggs dropped from his spatula and the yolk burst over toasted wholegrain bread.

Zane would have that one.

"Morning, Zane. You're up early."

"Yeah, I was, uh, restless. Thought I should get up and do something about it."

Beckett settled into his chair and cracked open his journal. He poised the end of his pen against his chin for a moment, bent over the blank page, and filled it with ink.

"Busy day at work?" Zane asked, sliding perfect eggs and a juice before Beckett.

"Usual Thursday with one evening class. Home at eight, all going smoothly."

A question shimmered in Beckett's eyes. A question Zane was working up the guts to answer.

He wasn't quite there yet.

He whipped back to the kitchen for his own plate and sank into the adjacent chair.

Beckett closed his journal and cut into his toast. He eyed the mess on Zane's plate, and that question seeped into a little twitch between his brows. "What are your plans for the day?"

"Doing some thorough research for my . . . story."

"I'll review what you've got and help you out where I can, if you like?"

Zane's throat constricted. "I think . . . I'm pretty sure . . . I would *really* like."

Once they'd finished breakfast, Zane trotted alongside Beckett to King's. He hoped that his nervous scuffing made up for his unusual quietness.

"I'll get our coffees!" he blurted, steering Beckett to the L-shaped couch from their first visit here.

When Zane returned with their drinks, he set the one with a heart before Beckett.

"Are you okay, Zane? You seem skittish this morning."

"Skittish?" He laughed so hard coffee sloshed over the side of his cup and onto his thigh.

Beckett lifted a brow, plucked his dry napkin, and palmed it against the curve of Zane's inner thigh. Zane jumped again and snatched the napkin, dabbing it himself. "I got it."

Beckett pulled back with a quiet nod and dipped his spoon into his coffee with a deepening frown. Well, great. Zane was doing a stellar job expressing himself here.

Life would be easier if he didn't have to find the words himself. If he could just open his mind and have Beckett pluck them out for him.

Imagine. It would make this moment far less confusing for Beckett.

All Zane had to do was think of them kissing.

Pressing their bodies close as their tongues tangled.

Naked.

Hard cocks rubbing against each other.

Whispering in Beckett's ear as Zane rocked deep inside—

"You've gone a surprising shade of red," Beckett said.

"Mind reading. Worst superpower ever."

Beckett sipped his coffee. "Is this to do with your story?"

In a sense. "Tell me, Professor, got a busy day at work?"

"You already asked me that."

"Oh. Right. Yeah, of course."

"Is there something else you want to talk about?" Beckett asked, words punctuated by his alarm buzzing.

Saved by the bell. Zane grabbed the professor's bag. "Later, Becky."

Beckett took a large gulp of coffee. "Don't I get to finish?"

Zane pried Beckett's almost-finished coffee away from him and urged him to his feet. He slung the bag strap over Beckett's head and untwisted it against his chest. Swallowing, he stood back for Beckett to pass. "If you don't drum in the importance of Tolstoy, none of your students will—"

"Care?"

"Land the perfect Meet Cute."

Beckett stared at him and there were too many shivers to cope with. "Go on. I'll talk with you later, Becky. I'll open up. I'll make it a night neither of us will forget."

Whatever our souls are made of, his and mine are the same.

—Emily Brontë

Chapter Sixteen

———————

L unch with Darla included ham and cheese sandwiches, the first of the season's strawberries, and a crazy bundle of nerves.

He'd blurted out his discovery to Darla to be met with an unsurprised nod.

"The planets have realigned, offering much-needed clarity. Good." Darla shuffled into the kitchen and made herself a cup of tea. "Interested? It takes the edge off."

"I'm good with water." He stretched back into his chair, dropping the phone he'd been ceaselessly surfing. "Though I may need help taking the edge off later. I don't know how to express myself."

She came back—barely a hobble now, as her leg had healed fine—and patted his hand over the table. "The stars suggest you may get a little help."

Zane hummed and scrolled through the open blog sites on his phone. "I want to surprise him somehow. Do something he'd never expect but would like."

"How about a treasure trail of naughty little notes for him

to follow, ending with you in the bathtub, two glasses of wine at the ready?" Darla said with a dreamy grin on her face.

"Something you did with your husband?"

"Or you could take him a packed lunch?"

"More appropriate. Except he's probably had lunch." Beckett did have a late lecture, though. What if Zane took him an early dinner?

He straightened. If he was quick, he could manage a couple of other errands, too.

An hour later he'd stolen Beckett's car, bought a nice wine, and was sitting at the gas station.

His phone awakened in his pocket and he answered with a grin.

"Zane, I hope I'm not interrupting anything."

"You're good."

"My sister rang in a panic. She thinks someone stole my car."

"Oh crap." So much for his gesture to gas up the car without Beckett knowing.

"Did you happen to take it?"

Now he looked like an inconsiderate jerk who didn't bother to ask before taking. He lifted the nozzle out of the gas tank.

"I'm sorry, I shouldn't have taken it like that."

Beckett cleared his throat. "It's insured. You can drive it. Maybe tell Leah? I've got a meeting with Mable."

"Wait, where is your—" Beckett was gone. "Office."

After returning the car with a full tank and a rushed apology to an amused Leah, Zane rocked up to Beckett's favorite Asian takeout. He requested a takeout container, and with the multicolored Sharpie pens he'd brought, he drew a picture of himself and Beckett. Blond hair and hoodie locking lips with dark locks and blazer. Clearly them, even if their faces weren't recognizable on account of *all the kissing*.

God, he hoped Beckett was on the same page as him. Hoped he wasn't about to make a mockery of himself.

Once he'd capped the last Sharpie, he ordered beef and broccoli stir-fry. Campus was a five-minute walk away but finding Beckett's office proved more difficult than he'd thought.

In fact, it required a call to Finnegan. "Don't tell him I'm coming. It's a surprise."

"This another bromance action?"

Romance, he hoped.

"Well, I couldn't tell him even if I wanted to since I'm out for the day. But here's where you need to go . . . ."

Professor Mable, who he met up with in the elevator, showed him to Beckett's office. She knocked and opened. "Looks like you're out of luck. He must have a class."

Late, of course. All these bursting bubbles of nerves were throwing him off his game. Who was he kidding? He'd never had game—but it'd never mattered, until now.

Professor Mable snuck into a wide wooden desk topped with a statue of a rearing horse and checked a freestanding calendar. She glanced at the clock on the wall. "He's running a class in Lincoln auditorium. You could meet him there after-ward. Or catch him before if you're quick."

"Thanks." No way he'd have a chance to eat. Maybe the world was telling him he had to find words, not rely on pictures like he had done his whole life.

With a sore laugh, he tossed the container in a trash bin. He thanked Professor Mable and took off quickly.

Fresh breezes stung his cheeks as he hopped his way across campus grounds. He could do this. He would do this.

At the sound of chiming bells, Zane hurried to the old Victorian auditorium. He hovered under the pillared archway and sank his hands into his hoodie pouch. He breathed in the scent of old wood and books and recent rain.

Squaring his shoulders, he entered the building and

followed the distant sound of Beckett's voice to a set of double doors. Beckett had once asked him to listen in on his lecture, and Zane was more than ready to take him up on the offer.

The door looked heavy, and he flung it open with a good dose of determination.

The wood swung on its hinges and smacked into the wall. Fifty heads swiveled toward him where he was frozen with mortification in the doorway. Beckett looked up startled.

Every inch of him wanted to flee. Instead, he grinned and fiddled with the door that had stuck itself on a latch. "Sorry I'm late, Professor."

A girl with daisy pins in her hair took pity on his struggle with the latch and helped him shut it. "Thanks," he whispered and peeked once more at Beckett, who was still staring.

He snapped out of it and cleared his throat. "Take a seat. We've just started."

Daisy Girl gestured to a free seat next to her, and he took it.

Suddenly he was back at high school. Everyone in class with paper and a pen, paying attention to every word the teacher said, while he lounged in the back marking his desk with a Sharpie.

He had Sharpie ink on him now, too.

Voice clear and steady, Beckett outlined what he would cover in the lesson. "For those of you already absorbed in the word of James Joyce, as well as for those hesitant to read him for fear the language is too obscure, rest assured, these next few lectures are intended to show you all the magic his stories offer. . . ."

Zane sat upright. Beckett was . . . good. Charming and easygoing. He infused his lecture with warmth and humor, and Zane had never experienced a teacher so in love with their subject.

Halfway, he couldn't bear it any longer. He needed to write notes too. He nudged Daisy Girl and motioned for a scrap of paper and a pen. She passed him one with a smile. Beckett faltered on a sentence, and Zane looked up to his gaze jumping away from him.

Zane scribbled notes, barely able to keep up with Beckett's flow of thought. Would Beckett review the material with him if he asked? Give him a one-on-one tutorial? His thoughts carried him to inappropriate places and he busied himself taking notes until the end of class.

While Beckett was packing his bag, a student snagged him into conversation.

Zane turned to Daisy Girl and returned her pen. "Thanks for this and the help with the door."

"Oh, um, yeah. Anytime. Are you new to this class? I don't remember seeing you, and I'm sure I'd remember." She blushed and dropped the pen.

Zane went to scoop it up for her. Their heads bashed together, and they sprang apart with a laugh. "Sorry," he said.

She grabbed the pen. "No worries. How's the head?"

"A few lost neurons. Nothing new."

"How about a coffee to make up for it?"

Zane stiffened. Oh. She was asking him out? Flattering, but he wasn't interested. Not in the slightest. He'd opened his mouth to ease her down when Beckett called out, "Evelyn, could I speak with you a moment?"

She jumped and nodded.

Zane shuffled back and let her pass. Evelyn and Beckett exchanged words while Beckett slipped the last paper into his bag. They parted smiling, and Evelyn left.

A new butterfly flapped in his chest with each student that exited the auditorium until he was a mass of flutters, staring into a cautious pair of blue eyes. "How did you like the lecture?"

Zane nodded. His voice sounded hoarse, "Can I walk you home, Professor?"

Love loves to love love.

—James Joyce

Chapter Seventeen

Zane coughed up countless words on their walk home, but none of them were the words he wanted to say.

Inside, Beckett headed to his room to ditch his bag, make a couple of calls, and freshen up, and Zane slunk to the kitchen for some pecans.

A bunch of dishes sat in the sink. Someone had made spaghetti and sauce. At least Leah had cleaned up the dishes she had used to bake those delicious-looking chocolate brownies. He helped himself to some pecans and then a brownie and started washing the dishes.

Good thing he was in a mood to procrastinate.

When he finished, the fading evening light inspired him to begin sketching. One sketch led to another, and once again he was staring at the graceful lines of Beckett's body. Stomach flipping, he distracted himself by eating another brownie, then squared his shoulders and went in search of the man himself. He found Beckett scrubbing his hands in the bathroom. "You took off your blazer. And changed your shirt."

"What are you eating?"

"Dessert." He moved in front of Beckett where he stood

drying his hands, broke a tiny piece of brownie off, and brought it to Beckett's lips.

"Before dinner?"

"My motto growing up in New Zealand."

"Your motto?"

"Never know when an earthquake could strike. I always ate dessert first, just in case."

Beckett shook his head and inched forward. He opened his mouth and sucked the piece from between Zane's fingers, their gazes catching.

This would be a good moment to say something. Or kiss him?

Zane broke another piece and fed Beckett more. Little shivers raced over Zane's skin.

"Chocolaty," Beckett murmured.

Zane lost his nerve and stuffed a big bite of brownie in his mouth.

Beckett sidled past him and out of the bathroom.

"Bring me another one?" Zane called through the open door as he started filling the bath. Because why not? He didn't have one yesterday.

He poured in the fruity liquid, and bubbles burst to life like blooming flowers. What on earth just happened? He blinked and snapped off the tap. Bubbles overflowed the porcelain rim of the bath, splashing onto the tiles. He found candles and set one per corner.

He should probably hop into the bath before lighting them this time. Last time he'd . . . he'd done something. Almost kicked one into the water, that's right. Jesus, that had been hilarious.

Imagine a lit candle plopping into the bath. Were bubbles flammable?

"What are you laughing at?" came Beckett's voice.

Zane twisted around, laughter making his eyes pinch with tears.

Beckett's face cocked to the side, eyes widening. So blue. So crazy blue. Wow, tears really sharpened Zane's vision. Beckett's eyes weren't just blue but streaked with teal, too.

"What did you put in those brownies?" Beckett asked, rubbing his elbow.

Reading Beckett had never been so easy. He was nervous. Did he anticipate Zane's kiss?

Zane stepped forward and slid his palms over the compact muscles of Beckett's shoulders. Beckett's shiver triggered one of his own. "Teal," Zane said, swooping toward that sensuous mouth.

Beckett sidestepped, and Zane toppled forward. A tight grip on his upper arm steadied him. "Have you ever made brownies? How much weed did you use? How many pieces did you eat?"

"I didn't bake." Zane smacked his tongue on the roof of his mouth. "If I did, I'd have used better chocolate. This American chocolate tastes weird. Wait, *weed?*" He shook his head defiantly and whisper-shouted, "Are you telling me I'm going to get high?"

"I'm telling you that you already are."

"No, no, no. I don't want to be high. My last flatmate was high all the time. Always ended up naked, fondling himself on the couch. Promise me I won't embarrass myself. Not that I'm not used to embarrassment, but not tonight. Tonight is our night, Becky. It's supposed to be full of—Jesus, how many bubbles are in this bathtub? I should probably get in before the water gets cold."

He tugged his hoodie over his head and nearly garroted himself on the knotted cord. He laughed into the swaths of material covering his nose and eyes. His elbows were stuck.

"Hold still a second," came a soothing voice, and Zane obeyed.

"Keep talking to me, Professor, your voice is a lullaby. And that's a *metaphor.*"

A soft laugh skated over his nape. His hoodie shifted, and he was free. Zane aimed for a sultry smile and lifted his arms. "Undress me."

Beckett balled Zane's hoodie in his arms. "That's probably not a great idea."

"It's the *best* idea."

"Excuse me while I go kill my sister."

Zane grinned, yanked off his T-shirt, and shoved down his pants. He almost fell trying to free them from his ankles, and his socks slipped off in the process. He plunked onto the side of the bathtub, and one candle fell into the bubbles. Just as well he hadn't lit them yet. Oh, he needed to light them. "Where are the matches?"

Beckett was banging his head against Zane's hoodie. "No matches."

"You're probably right." Zane pulled off his boxers and stepped into the bath. The water hugged his calves and bubbles tickled the backs of his knees. It felt incredible. Even his cock was taking notice of the sexy slide of water. "You shouldn't leave me in here alone."

"If I leave, you might die. If I stay, you'll definitely kill me."

"Are you, like, autocorrecting your mouth? 'Cause I think you mean kiss. Stay, and I'll definitely *kiss you.*"

"You have no idea what you're saying right now."

"Why won't you look at me? Does my hoodie smell really good?"

Beckett dropped the hoodie, glanced at him, and slammed his eyes shut.

Zane stared down. He was standing in the bathtub adjusting his semi. He laughed and sank back into the water that smelled deliciously fruity. "Maybe I'll taste good after this bath."

Beckett groaned.

"Maybe if I taste good, it won't matter if I kiss like cardboard."

Beckett's blue eyes were edged with wary curiosity. "What do you mean?"

Zane swiped the tea candles off the bathtub, scattering them across the bathroom floor. He patted the tile. "Sit next to me."

Reluctantly, Beckett inched closer but didn't sit. "Your date got to you, didn't she?"

"It's okay. It just gives me an excuse to kiss you ten thousand times."

"Ten thousand times?"

"At least. Mastery only happens after doing it that many times."

"My sister will die *a very slow* death." Beckett was standing close but not close enough. Zane shifted onto his knees, water sloshing over the sides. He balanced himself using Beckett's hips and looked up at those gently parted lips, feeling Beckett's battle to force more distance between them.

Zane locked his fingers more firmly on Beckett. His jeans were coarse under his hands—too much material between them. Zane's mouth felt hot and swollen, like he was bursting with a kiss. Like it might hurt if he didn't gift it.

His heart pulsed in time to the throbbing of his cock, pushing against the rim of the tub. "I'd like to pontificate." Such a deliciously dirty-sounding word. "Or watch you pontificate. Or maybe even pontificate together."

Beckett swept a hand through his hair, murmuring, "I have no idea what you're talking about."

Zane clasped him tightly, giggled, and pulled Beckett into the bath.

Water splashed as bubbles shot into the air. Beckett scrambled onto his knees, laughing so hard he was frowning. "Oh, for God's sake. We should have eaten dinner. I'm high now, too."

Beckett's soaked shirt was plastered against his chest and stomach. His weighted jeans sank low on his hips.

Zane drew a finger over a slip of skin at his lower stomach. Beckett captured his hand, stilling him. Zane felt the bulge under his palm and slid forward. One thigh meshed between Beckett's, and Zane's slippery hard-on pressed with bone-melting pressure against Beckett's hip.

Their breaths tangled, and Beckett shook his head. "I promised I wouldn't let you embarrass yourself."

"I could never be embarrassed kissing you."

"God, I wish you weren't high right now."

"This has nothing to do with being high. I've been navigating the shifting seas of my heart. Trying to overcome the obstacles of my insta-love story."

"Slow burn."

"Nope." Zane brushed a stray lock off Beckett's face. "I've become self-aware. And I'm ready to kiss you, touch you, have sex with you if you want."

"How many brownies did you eat?"

"I'm over the obstacles, Becky."

Beckett's hand trembled against Zane's, still locked on his lower stomach. "Not all of them."

"What?"

"You being high right now is one *major* obstacle."

"Why?"

"I can't know if you mean it."

"I mean it, Becky. I'll mean it tomorrow, too."

Beckett's eyes flickered with hopefulness and uncertainty. He studied Zane's lips and his eyelids shuttered. He leaned forward—and halted. With a tight groan, he lurched up and climbed out of the bath.

He grabbed a towel and groan-laughed into it. "I am a saint. Forever shall I be praised for this night."

"Whoa," Zane said. "You were here, and now, just like that, you're over there. It's like you teleported. Did you take my heart with you, Becky, 'cause I'm feeling kinda hollow over here."

"Get out of the bath or you'll catch a cold."

"I'm a fish. I'm sure I'll be fine."

"I'm a Fisher. If I have to, I'll reel you out."

"Not the threat you think it is, Becky. Oh my God, I totally just got what you meant about the ass pinch." Zane stood and swung a leg over the tub onto the mat. A towel hit his middle. "You liked *me* doing it. You want me to do it *again*."

"You are so high."

"High on you. Please let me play with your ass again. Even better, I'll do it while kissing you."

Beckett stalked out of the room. "LEAH!"

Zane hurried after Beckett, the room tilting with him as he rounded into the hall. Crazy. The walls were leaning. Fuck, there was a man watching him.

No wait, that was his reflection.

Laughter bubbled up his throat, and he leaned into the naked fellow. "We had a mission, what was it?"

Words on Beckett. Make him understand.

Where was the most princely man on the planet?

He floated into the living room where Beckett stood glaring at a plate of brownies, Leah shrugging across from him. "I didn't bake them. But I'll totally have—"

"They're trash-bound."

"Noooooooo!" Zane lunged for the plate, and Beckett swept them out of reach. "Are you crazy? That's, like, a kilo of chocolate right there."

"I thought American chocolate tasted weird?"

"Maybe I'll get used to it. Doesn't hurt to try."

"I beg to differ. It hurts a lot." Beckett's tone shift had Zane dropping his gaze to soaked jeans, bulging in the crotch.

"Does that erection mean we're on the same page?"

Tinkling laughter cropped up from Leah.

Zane pointed a finger at her and looked at Beckett. "She's high too."

"Oh shit," she said. "You'll have your hands full with that one."

Beckett grumbled. "If you didn't make these brownies, then—"

Zane slapped the counter. "Oh my God. I've had a brainstorm. I've had an epiphany."

"Going to share this sudden insight?"

Leah snorted. "Should I book you a spot at Chiffon, you word-warring willies?"

"Don't make me get onstage," Zane said, violently shaking his head. "I won't do it. Won't make a fool of myself."

"Yeah," Leah said, smirking. "Because you need a stage for that."

Beckett tossed the brownies into the trash.

"You are so lucky you are my future husband," Zane cried, dropping to his knees before the red can. He patted the side. "Rest in peace, lovelies."

He pressed his forehead to the cold metal. It massaged his head and—how had he never thought of doing this before? The ribbing on the metal felt fantastic.

Leah and Beckett spoke, their voices like crystal—and that was a *simile*. Gosh, living with Beckett really was making him smart.

"Husband?" Leah said. "Surely he knows you'll never marry again?"

Yes, he will! Maybe before the month was out.

Beckett's breath whistled. "He's high. He's not aware of what he's talking about."

I am. So aware it tickles my skin.

"He is into you, Becky."

Beckett shifted, wet sock churring against the kitchen tiles. "I know."

"You know? Does that mean you're reconsidering the whole *never marry again in my life* thing?"

"Of course not. Zane might be figuring out he is attracted to me, and I might be . . . weak enough to want his attention, but it can't go anywhere. He's too young. Anything we do together will simply be him testing waters."

"If you think that, why would you let him do anything?"

Beckett grew quiet and Zane shook his head, metal bumping along his hairline.

"Because you hope you're wrong," Leah said, hissing.

"I'm not," Beckett said, voice cracking. "He'll have a date with a girl before the week's end."

"Maybe he won't."

Why did his limbs weigh five hundred pounds? He couldn't move. Too heavy.

Needed to stand. Tell Beckett he was wrong.

"This isn't anything to do with Zane's age," Leah said. "You're still scared."

Ginger streaked past him, and Zane jumped to his feet. "Gremlin!"

Blue eyes clashed with his for a second before Beckett zipped across the room toward the hall. "Just Leo. He's probably heading back to Darla's."

"Darla. My epiphany." Zane hurried after the cat and yanked open the door.

"Wait," Beckett said close behind him. "Clothes."

Leah tossed a pair of athletic shorts. Zane jerked on the silky nylon and stuffed his feet into his jandals.

"Come, Becky. We're going to crack this case wide open." He halted on the threshold and looked over his shoulder. "Could you bring snacks? No. We'll eat after visiting our dear darling."

He hoofed down the path. One glance back and he found Beckett stuffing himself into a blazer.

Was it cold? Didn't feel it.

He stumbled out of the gate and approached Darla's. At the porch, Beckett was hopping the fence. Why hadn't he thought of that? He should have hopped the fence, too. Hey, he still could.

He pulled his leg up and stretched it over Darla's gate.

Damn it, the pickets were higher here.

He teetered on tiptoe, the blunt wooden stakes scraping his balls, throwing him back to his failed date at the fish restaurant.

Gosh, how perfect had it been, Beckett showing up like that?

"Are you coming?" Beckett called. "Or are you coming on that gate?"

Zane popped his other leg over and strode to Darla's door. The house was dark. "Maybe we shouldn't wake her?"

A snort came from beside them. They stepped off the porch and saw Darla in her nightgown leaning out of the window. "You're making enough ruckus to wake the entire street."

Zane folded his arms over his chill-hardened nipples and glared at her. "This is all your fault."

"You wanted something to take the edge off, Zane. I helped you out."

"I was thinking a nice cup of tea!"

"Brownies taste better."

Beckett exchanged an aghast look with him. "Oh Lord, my neighbor drinks weed."

"I have a condition," she said.

"Well, I don't," Zane countered.

"I beg to differ. I'm about to combust just watching you two." She smiled at them and started shutting the window. "Now get a room."

Beckett was already moving.

"Hey, wait up." Zane tripped and took Beckett facedown with him onto the lawn. A soft groan under him had Zane setting his weight on his arms, his front cloaked against Beckett's back. "Can you breathe?" he said in Beckett's ear.

"Just." Beckett pushed onto his elbows, and his ass pressed against Zane. His thoughts spiraled to immature places.

"Huh."

"What?"

"I have another reason you should buy elbow patches."

"And you've killed me," Beckett said, collapsing to the grass with a frustrated laugh.

Zane rolled off him with an apology. He helped Beckett up and they went back inside to raid the fridge. Classical music blasted through the house. Insanely intense.

Zane started shivering.

Beckett steered him into the bedroom and rifled through his drawers where Zane had stored his clothes. He pulled out a T-shirt and fitted it over Zane's head. Zane shivered violently. So cold.

He grabbed the bull rug off the armchair and wrapped it around himself. Beckett had long since changed into dry boxers and a T-shirt of his own. He tugged at Zane, urging him to the bed.

"Not without my bull." It wasn't the bull he wanted to be wrapped in, but the synthetic fur warmed his back.

"You can't sleep on the armchair, you'll wake up all kinds of stiff."

"Like I don't every morning."

Beckett's eyes flashed. "Come."

Zane relented, patting the bull and arranging him before sliding under the sheets next to Beckett.

He curled onto his side toward Beckett who was turning out the lamp.

"Becky?"

"Yeah?"

"I hate waking to you at the side of the bed. Will you stay close, like at your farmhouse?"

Beckett's breathing stuttered. Sheets shifted and warm limbs curled against his, one leg slipping between Zane's, a gentle pressure.

Zane groped in the darkness and found Beckett's hand. Their skin grazed as he slotted their fingers together.

"You put that photo of Luke facedown. There must be a part of you that wants me to mean it."

"Zane." Beckett's voice was an uneven warning.

"You're not pulling away, and this is more than platonic hand holding."

The back of Beckett's hand warmly rested against his chest, and he squeezed.

Beckett swallowed audibly. "I think you're still high."

Stay here, don't move. "Lecture me to sleep?"

"Definitely still high. Let me guess, you want to know all about Beckett?"

"Yes, but I want to be completely sober for him. How about more of that Joyce guy?"

In the faint light leaking in from the gaps in the curtains, Zane made out Beckett's smile. "It is a happy heart that re-Joyces."

Zane's beat wildly.

Love is composed of a single soul inhabiting two bodies.

—Aristotle

Chapter Eighteen

Z ane woke to an empty bed and hushed voices in the hallway. Beckett and Leah. His head spun and his throat was so dry it hurt, but he ignored the bottle of water Beckett must have placed for him on his side table, slipped out of bed, and pressed his ear up to the door.

His stomach lurched for sustenance and he hoped it wasn't loud enough to give him away.

Beckett had fallen asleep in his arms—smooth, slender limbs and warm breath—but this was the second time Zane had woken to his absence. There wouldn't be a third.

Clipped tones drifted through the door.

What were they talking about? Last night?

He needed to know what was running through Beckett's mind. Would he laugh off last night like it was nothing? Would he ignore it? Wait for Zane to bring it up?

"I've got to get to work, Leah."

"It's seven in the morning. You're running away."

"No, I'm calmly walking to campus to catch up on grading."

Hadn't Beckett said he liked to grade from home?

Zane swallowed a little growl. Beckett *was* running away.

"Get coffee and talk to him," Leah said.

"He was high. We say all kinds of things without thinking when we're high."

"Come on, you and I both know we mean what we say."

"It doesn't mean he was ready to say them. I'm not forcing this."

"Boys," Leah growled. "You're unbelievable."

"Goodbye, Leah."

Zane scowled. He understood where Beckett was coming from—to a point. Sure, he wanted to give Zane time and space to be sure about what he wanted. Great. Fantastic, in fact.

But skipping out before their daily visit to King's? Bad form.

Zane dressed, drank the entire bottle of water, and marked another depressing notch off his calendar.

Tomorrow, two weeks. He would be on a plane thousands of feet over the Pacific, crammed between two strangers, heading toward a beautiful country, warm parents, and an empty heart.

He'd thought it would ache from leaving his brother, but that ache had nothing on the one that was about to come.

As if the universe wanted to rub it in, Jacob called to arrange Zane's goodbye party.

Zane's stomach weighed a ton. The call ended, and he flopped back against the chair and stared at his bull. "Moping here won't bring me anything, I know, I know. Just feeling kinda . . . bullshit."

After a minute, he collected himself, his laptop, drawing tablet, and stylus, and made for King's.

The morning passed in the blink of an eye. He'd lost himself in music and his artwork as he drafted his story. He checked his outline three times. Deciding it was ready, he emailed it to Beckett.

Lunch with Darla was silent and involved a war of ever-narrowing glances. Dishes done, he kissed the old bag on the cheek and left for Beckett's last lecture of the day.

He snuck into the auditorium amidst a gaggle of students wearing thick-rimmed glasses. He slouched low in the seat next to Evelyn's. Beckett hadn't spotted him yet, and Zane wasn't sure how he felt about it.

He was still grumpy at him leaving like he did this morning.

Beckett burst into life at the front of the room, voice all flow and calculated pauses. Livelier than he'd been yesterday. Smiley, too. As if something had gone especially well in his day.

Or maybe literature did it for him.

Fifteen minutes in, his professor lost the thread of a sentence and Zane looked up from his notes and found Beckett blinking in his direction.

Zane snagged that surprised gaze and lifted an eyebrow. Hopefully it conveyed two things: his unhappiness about the abrupt disappearance this morning, and how eager he was to get him home.

Beckett continued with his lecture with notable distraction. He dropped his whiteboard marker, messed up slides, and caught himself repeating a fact he'd mentioned earlier in the lesson.

The lecture ended, and once more the room burst into chatter and shifting paper and groaning desks. Evelyn flashed him a small smile and stuffed her bag. She clucked and then smacked a palm to her head.

"You okay?" Zane asked.

"Yes, I'm a total ditz. I was contemplating whether to apologize for asking you out yesterday. Well, I'm sorry."

Zane frowned.

"You don't have to apologize."

She shrugged. "I didn't know you were taken."

"Yes, I am taken— Wait, how did you know that?"

"Professor Fisher kindly told me."

The professor did what now?

Zane sent her off with a tight wave. A few students straggled, buffering him from Beckett. Which might have been good, because Zane was fighting a sudden urge to bark. He breathed through the frustration and calmed himself enough to urge Beckett out onto campus.

"You were distracted in there today," Zane said.

"I can't imagine why."

"Maybe if you'd joined me at King's, you wouldn't have floundered seeing me in class."

"I'm about 100 percent sure I would have floundered regardless."

Keeping in stride with him, Beckett readjusted his leather bag on his hip and changed his grip on a bright yellow fabric bag.

Zane side-eyed him, waiting for an explanation about King's. About Evelyn.

None came, and he marched his boyfriend home in silence.

He shut the door behind them with enough oomph to make a point.

"Okay," Beckett said, setting down his bags and toeing off his shoes. "Am I missing something? Lay it on me."

Zane kicked off his sneakers. He didn't know where to begin. "You didn't give me a chance to say no to Evelyn. You're so careful not to nudge me—even when I'm being ridiculously clueless—because you believe in the power of self-awareness, and yet. Evelyn."

Okay, he did know where to begin.

And he wasn't finished. "You swept in there and meddled. You didn't trust me."

Beckett flinched. "Perhaps I assumed you were indifferent to her and I wanted to help her out."

"Oh my God, listen to yourself. You really *are* a Mr. Darcy."

Beckett raised his chin. "I didn't want to see you waylaid by a Wickham, *Lizzy*."

Zane stalked up to him, all burning frustration. "You know what?"

"What?" Blue eyes blazed, and there it was. Every secret and vulnerability, hope and fear bursting between them in a desperate second.

What a fool he'd been. He recognized that look. Every look they'd ever shared had the same magic.

He'd just been too breathless to comprehend it.

"Let's not forget how the story ends, Professor."

He tilted his head an inch, clasped Beckett's face, and kissed him. A firm press of their lips, fitting perfectly together. A gentle moan slipped out from Beckett, tickling Zane's lower lip as he pulled apart and kissed him again.

Arms wrapped around his neck, drawing him closer.

Zane slipped his hands to Beckett's waist and pulled him tight against his body. His chest fluttered, his body shivered, and his lips burned to taste more.

He teased Beckett's mouth with the tip of his tongue and parted his lips. Beckett gripped the back of Zane's neck and met the tentative brush of his tongue with demanding strokes of his own.

Zane was on fire. Their kissing grew frantic and he stumbled with Beckett down the hall and into their room. They fell onto the bed together, and Zane rolled off Beckett and onto his side, just far enough to get a good look at his boyfriend.

Beckett faced him, their legs hooked. "You kissed me."

Zane stroked the gentle jut of Beckett's jaw. Beckett's

mouth parted as if the small touch robbed him of breath. "You're trembling."

Beckett pushed forward a fraction and brushed their lips. "Restraint, remember?"

Zane believed it was a half-truth. "I want to be here with you, Becky."

"I know."

But Zane wasn't sure how much Beckett knew. "What are you thinking?" *What are you feeling?*

"I want you to touch me."

Zane gripped Beckett and rolled him on top of him. Beckett blinked down at him, his forearms braced against Zane's chest, the buttons of his blazer pressing into his stomach.

Zane tugged the back of the jacket. "Take it off?" he croaked.

Beckett pushed up until he was straddling Zane, his firm ass brushing his hard-on. He bit his lip at the shivers running through him.

Zane helped Beckett with his buttons. Their breathing was heavy, and Beckett's gaze darkened.

"Beautiful," Zane said.

Beckett paused, blazer half-shrugged off, and smiled.

Zane's fingers tracked over the shoulders of Beckett's shirt as he slid the blazer sleeves down his arms. "Inside and out."

Beckett leaned down and kissed him with a detectable shake in his breath.

Heart pounding, Zane worked at removing Beckett's shirt. Their tongues deepened their kisses, and they pulled at their clothes. Beckett steered him up to remove his hoodie and T-shirt, and Zane lost his mind when their naked chests slid together. A thousand volts of electricity surged through him, and he hugged Beckett close, his weight heavy, warm.

Zane clasped the back of Beckett's head, fingers fanning

through his soft hair, and he rubbed his cheek over Beckett's jaw and dropped open-mouthed kisses down his neck.

A stuttered gasp had him doing it again, arching into Beckett as he ground against his dick.

Beckett's tongue danced under Zane's ear, followed by the soft scratch of teeth. Like he wanted to bite him, suck a large hickey on his throat, and claim him.

Beckett returned to soft kisses down his throat.

"More," Zane murmured through a rush of shivers. *Go through with the hickey. I'm yours.*

"How much more, Zane?" Beckett asked against his collarbone.

Zane clasped Beckett's hips and thrust their dicks together. "There's too much material between us."

"We strip our pants, and then what do you want? You have to tell me how far you're willing to go."

Zane captured Beckett's mouth into a kiss and tugged his bottom lip. "I'll go anywhere you want to go. But . . . ."

"But?"

"I don't know what I'm doing."

Beckett donned a soft smile. He dropped a kiss on Zane's lips and snuck a hand between them to Zane's fly. The gentle pressure sent his dick from hard to aching.

He groaned and shoved at his jeans, arching to help Beckett peel them off his ass. His head dropped back against the mattress as his cock sprang free, and he clutched the sheets when Beckett's breath washed over his length as he tugged the jeans off him.

"Good Lord, you are insanely hot," Beckett said, standing up to yank off his own.

Zane pushed onto his elbows, looking past his heavy, upright dick to Beckett, who made quick work ditching his boxers.

Beckett's gaze raked Zane's body and he gripped his

straining dick, giving it a casual pump. His throat jutted with a swallow and he lowered his lashes. "I can stay here if you like."

"No," Zane said, sitting up, feet planting on the floor either side of Beckett's. "I would not like."

He braced his hands at Beckett's hips, slid them around the curve of his ass, and steered him tight into the space between his legs. He looked up into Beckett's heavy-lidded, cautious eyes. "Did you really jerk off while hearing me?"

Beckett nodded.

"That image hasn't left my mind, Becky. It makes me really, really hot."

"I've had to shower twice a day since you got here."

Zane groaned as erotic images filled his mind. His hand shook as he drifted it around Beckett's thigh and to the neatly trimmed base of his thick cock. He squeezed, discovering the weighty feeling of an unfamiliar hard dick in his hand.

Beckett gasped at the touch and Zane wanted to elicit more of those unabashed moans.

He stroked slowly, the soft skin over the cut dick tighter than his own. The head protruded, plum-like, and his slit glistened with precome. Zane swiped a thumb over it, checking with Beckett, who gave him an encouraging gasp.

Zane barely ever needed lube to rub one out, but he thought Beckett might.

Heat scrolled up his neck. He was insanely turned on and floundering in these new depths.

He let go of Beckett's cock, clasped his ass, and pressed his head against Beckett's stomach. He breathed in a faint trace of aftershave and the musk of sex. "How do I make you feel good?"

He massaged Beckett's cheeks and bit him lightly on the flat plane of his stomach, just left of his treasure trail. Beckett's stomach undulated and fingers drove through Zane's hair, gently pulling him back.

"Hearing your voice in the morning feels good. Laughing with you as you walk me to work, or over dinner, or while you're high feels good. Stop right now, and I'll feel amazing."

"Yes, so would I. I don't need sex. But Becky?"

"Zane?"

"I want to."

Blue eyes darkened, and Beckett pushed him back, ducked into his closet, and came back squeezing lube onto his fingers.

Zane swallowed, stroking his dick as he watched Beckett work the glistening liquid over his length. Shivers raced over his skin and Zane exploded in gooseflesh. The air felt sharper around his body as the tiniest shift of his hand stirred breezes against his hypersensitive skin.

Zane pushed his feet against the stitching in the blanket and propelled himself farther up the bed.

Beckett crawled up him. A shock of heat made Zane's cock jerk, and a nervous shake rolled through him.

Beckett's cock dragged against his thigh, hip. He braced against Zane's shoulder as he lowered himself over Zane.

Their rock-solid lengths meshed together. Heat and tension rolled off Beckett's body into his. Beckett inhaled against Zane's nipple, and the updraft of air had Zane squirming. "Promise me no big words, Professor. I won't last as it is."

"No sesquipedalian, polysyllabic prose?"

"Becky," Zane groaned.

Beckett laughed and stretched up, his cock sliding over his lower stomach. "I won't last long, either."

Zane lifted his head. Their noses bumped together, and their gazes danced a heady waltz.

A slow kiss turned into deep demanding ones as they gripped each other harder, arousal intensified. Zane rolled Beckett onto his back, his body frantically trying to move closer. Beckett arched into Zane, reached between them, and grabbed hold of their aching dicks, stroking them together between panting kisses. Their balls bounced together. Beckett murmured incoherently, fingers digging into Zane's shoulder blade.

Zane worked his hand back and forth, the squeeze of their cockheads sending a delicious rush through him that grew more intense with each stroke.

Beckett writhed under him. Elegant grace turned into trembling, jerking need, so raw and vulnerable that watching Beckett consumed him and made Zane's hand work faster and faster.

Oh God, he wanted to give more. He wanted to sink his cock deep inside Beckett's beautiful body and feel Beckett clench as he came over Zane's stomach. He wanted to have Beckett so deep in him that every pound stirred butterflies in his chest.

And . . . and . . . Zane wanted . . . .

Zane let go of their cocks to Beckett's confused moan. He slid down Beckett's body, palmed his hips, bringing his mouth an inch above Beckett's swollen cockhead. "Can I taste you?"

Beckett's breathing hitched, and he nodded. "You want to?"

Zane darted a tongue over him. Salty under the slight sweetness of lube. He tried again, suckling tentatively.

Beckett moaned like he'd just entered another realm of pleasure. If this made him feel that good, Zane wanted to give him everything.

He urged Beckett's legs apart, shifted between them, positioned so his cock rubbed against the blanket. He sucked Beckett into his mouth, the blunt end of him sliding over his tongue and pushing at the roof of his mouth. He adjusted his angle and sucked.

Beckett broke into a fit of dirty curses that had Zane on the brink of coming.

He squeezed the base of Beckett's cock and bobbed over

his hard length faster and deeper. His cock felt warm and heavy on his tongue. Making Beckett buck and shake and plead had him groaning.

Beckett bowed off the mattress. "Zane, I'm—"

Zane clasped his ass and took Beckett in as far as he could manage. Beckett gasped, and his cock pulsed in Zane's mouth, liquid hitting the back of his throat. Zane sucked him through his orgasm, just like he loved, and it wrung a cry out of him.

When he was sure Beckett was done, he pulled off.

Beckett's face flushed and his chest heaved as he caught his breath. Their gazes caught, and a flare of vulnerability shot through Beckett's expression before he swallowed and curled his finger. "Come up here, Zane."

Zane ignored his achingly hard dick, crawled up, and kissed his boyfriend. He wished Beckett knew how he felt. That he was here, 100 percent. That he could trust him.

Beckett looped his arms around his neck and smiled shakily. "Lie on me."

Zane did as he was told. His cock rubbed Beckett's thigh, and he hissed at the jolt of pleasure.

"That's right," Beckett said, cupping his cheek. "Rock against me."

"You've come already. I can sort this out in the bathroom if you like."

Beckett lifted his head and whispered in his ear. "I'd like you to rock against me."

Butterflies raced over his skin as he ground against Beckett.

Hands roamed over Zane's back and one finger reached around and skated over the crease of his ass. Zane lost his mind and rutted to a dizzying release. Come shot out of him and he slid through it as he continued to come over and over.

Beckett wrapped his arms around him and held him tight through it. Held him so tight, it was almost as if he feared Zane wasn't there to stay.

What comes from the heart, goes to the heart.

—Samuel Taylor Coleridge

Chapter Nineteen

Zane demanded Beckett not move from the bed and got a wet cloth.

When they were cleaned up, Beckett bounded off the bed, all grace and purposeful stride.

"Come back," Zane called out to him in the hall. "I haven't finished with you yet."

Beckett popped back into the room with his bright yellow bag and a quirked brow. "I admire your energy, Zane, but round two will have to wait."

Zane slung himself over to Beckett and yanked him in his arms. The bag banged against the back of his thigh. "No scathing remarks, but I like to cuddle afterward."

Beckett smiled into their gentle kiss.

Zane dragged him back onto the bed and they awkwardly kneeled in the middle. "What's with the bag?"

Beckett sat back on his heels and set the yellow cloth bag on his lap. "I have thought for a while you might find me attractive. That maybe you were a notch higher on the Kinsey Scale."

"Kingly Scale." Zane patted Beckett's shoulder. "Don't worry about it, Professor. Can't know everything."

Beckett rubbed his nose. "I wanted you to figure things out for yourself. I ran away this morning nervous you'd forgotten everything you said when you were high."

"The ten thousand kisses? Oh, I meant it." Zane leaned forward for another kiss and stole Beckett's bag. He looked inside and froze.

"I got to work this morning and found this."

"From the trash?" Zane said, fighting a twisting stomach and hot skin.

"No, it was sitting on my desk."

Had Professor Mable taken it out? "I hope you didn't eat the beef and broccoli."

"The food had been removed. The cook must have thought I'd want to keep this picture—and I do."

Zane rubbed his neck. "I thought you'd prefer words, Professor."

"When have I ever said that?" Beckett drew out the container with the picture of them kissing. "Staring at this made me very late to class."

"Was it also why you were so jubilant?"

"Until I spotted you and lost my mind, yes."

Zane set the container on the side table and steered Beckett lengthwise onto the bed. "I'm glad you liked it, Becky."

"Loved it," Beckett said, curling onto his side, back to Zane. He reached back and drew Zane's arm over his stomach. "Every time I look at it, I'll remember you."

Remember him.

There it was again. Beckett not believing this would last.

He could *tell* Beckett he was wrong, that he promised to be here from here on out. But Beckett had been right: self-realization held more power.

No, he couldn't tell Beckett. But he'd *show* him and let him come to the conclusion himself.

He curved his longer body around his prince like a city wall. He'd make Beckett trust that Zane was a fish a bull could rely on.

~

ZANE WOKE UP AND SMILED.

Beckett hadn't fled. Wasn't hugging the edge of his mattress. He was right where he was supposed to be, back pressed against Zane's chest.

Zane stretched his arm around that perfect body, hand lightly resting low on Beckett's stomach, a hard cock brushing against his forearm. His own erection was nestled hot and heavy between Beckett's thighs.

He breathed in their mingled morning scent and kissed Beckett's nape.

Beckett stirred.

"What do you want to do this weekend?" Zane whispered. "Name it, we'll do it."

"Tandem-read Tolstoy?"

"I take it back."

Beckett turned around in his arms. "We both have a crazy amount of laundry to do."

"And the weekly shopping. We're out of toilet paper."

"Already?"

"I might have gotten carried away reading it? Also, we need bubble bath and matches. Bin liners, and I'd love to make a Sunday roast, Kiwi style."

"Sounds great. I have some work to finish—sorry—and Finnegan wanted to go out for drinks tonight."

"Finnegan," Zane said, narrowing his eyes. Beckett laughed and Zane broke it with a kiss. "I don't mean it. I like the guy, you are good friends, and you should totally, absolutely take care of your friendships. Just so long as after all your pretentiousness . . ."

"I have the penis party with you?"

Zane nipped Beckett's lips. "Good plan. While you're out, I want to draft more of my main characters, anyway. Make sure they're perfect before I move forward with the story."

"I haven't had a chance to look at your outline yet."

"Take your time."

"It's just, I want to do it properly. Give it all my attention. I'll read it through this weekend, let it settle, then print it and write up my notes next week."

"I'm nervous about you reading it. You're probably used to outlines the likes of which Joyce might have written. Not ones from Muppets who got hold of a pen."

"Zane . . . ," Beckett said, tone admonishing.

"Pecans. We're also out of pecans."

Beckett rolled on top of him. "Speaking of nuts . . . ."

"Nice transition, Professor. Classy."

Laughter tickled Zane's chin. "Please," Beckett said. "Let me take care of you?"

A current of affection rolled through Zane, and Beckett dropped the softest kiss on his lips.

Zane lifted up and kissed back, massaging Beckett's hips, running a light finger over the small of his back the way he seemed to like it last night.

Beckett took Zane's hands and pinned them over his head against the soft pillow. He shook his head. "Just enjoy."

"Afterward, you."

Beckett shook his head.

"But——"

"Shhh." Beckett nibbled the side of his throat. Their erections slid together for a tantalizing second, and Zane exploded in shivers.

It was an unfamiliar feeling having someone wanting to take care of him. Unsettling, even. He was used to making sure his partner got what they needed.

"I want to suck you," Beckett whispered.

Hot breath fanned over the curve of his neck, followed by the slide of a tongue that had him catching his breath.

"Can I, um, tell you a secret, Becky?"

"Anything." Beckett dropped kisses on his chest, the hair tickling under his soft lips.

Zane bucked when Beckett captured his nipple and teased it between his teeth, tongue flicking against his pebbled skin. Surely Beckett heard the staccato rhythm of his heart?

He kissed his way to Zane's other pec, and thinking became a struggle. Zane tucked his hands under his head and watched Beckett, who shoved the blanket off them and returned to trailing kisses over his stomach. Beckett raked his fingers down Zane's sides, and Zane groaned.

"What did you want to tell me?" he murmured at his belly button.

"It's just . . . I've never . . . . No one has ever sucked me before."

Beckett froze. His fingers bit into Zane's hips. "What do you mean no one has ever?"

"I've had plenty of sex, just . . . no girl wanted to return that particular favor. It's fine. I don't need it. You don't have to either."

Beckett growled. "You're too goddamn giving in bed." He palmed Zane's stomach and shifted his head over Zane's erection. "And Zane?" He gripped Zane's base with the perfect squeeze.

"Yeah?"

"I want to. I really want to."

Arousal swept through him. Zane dropped his arms to his sides and scrunched the sheet between his fingers. He gasped in anticipation as Beckett lowered his mouth. His heart jack-hammered as Beckett's wet, hot mouth closed around the head of his dick.

Broken words ran off Zane's tongue, among them the promise he'd be coming hard—and soon.

Beckett worked his dick in and out of his mouth, all tongue and soft throat. If Zane thought his fingers were deft, well . . . .

He fought not to rise off the bed and piston into Beckett's perfect mouth. He threw his head back, hating that he couldn't see Beckett from this position, but the pleasure was insane, whipping heat through him.

His toes curled at every pump and suck Beckett gave him, and Zane was begging for release.

Beckett shifted, let go of the base of Zane's cock and clasped his ass from between his thighs. He pulled off and Zane moaned at the loss.

"Close?"

Garbled groan.

"Fuck my throat and come." Beckett drove his mouth down Zane's shaft and squeezed his ass, sending Zane orbiting in another world. Zane pumped fast into Beckett's mouth, and his orgasm blasted through him. Waves crushed every inch of his body and took him hostage.

Beckett inched off him, and Zane was too breathless to do more than curl a finger for him to come closer.

Beckett crawled up him.

Zane lazily traced his smug smile. "Your mouth is magic." He lifted his head and kissed him. "From the way you give words to the way you take them."

They kissed again, and Zane reached for Beckett's hard dick only to get batted away. "This moment is about you. I'm going to shower, and then we've got shopping to do."

Beckett climbed out and left Zane boneless in their monogamy bed.

~

The following week passed so fast, it felt like a montage.

They started the day at King's, worked, met up for lunch, worked some more, made dinner and ate with Darla, made their nightly walk to the bandstand, came back to read or draw, and made out like teenagers until they came down one another's throats. Then they'd fall to sleep a tangle of limbs and lectures and wake to do it all over again.

Zane loved it. Loved planning meals for the week, loved sitting in bed with music blasting and sketching panels, and loved listening to Beckett teach his classes.

They woke up late on Friday. Beckett kissed him as they rubbed their bodies together, his hand cuffing both their dicks. "We don't have much time."

The words were a panicked whisper against Zane's shoulder, and Beckett's strokes desperately quickened.

Zane forced himself to ignore his impending climax and meet Beckett's glistening gaze.

Zane kissed him and came two beats after Beckett. Never had an orgasm felt so intense and wrought with fear.

Beckett hadn't been talking about class, he'd been talking about Zane's visa. One week left.

A marriage proposal pounded in his chest, but no matter how much he believed they were meant to be, the next step had to be taken by Beckett.

All Zane could do was step up his game. He'd followed all the wikiHow instructions on cultivating trust—he asked questions, opened himself to any answer, gave the professor comfort and space to be with his friends—but it hadn't been enough.

He hadn't given Beckett a grand gesture.

Zane helped Beckett slip on his blazer. Dropping a kiss against Beckett's nape, he reached around to his front and buttoned him up. "I'd like to take you for dinner and a walk after class."

Their gazes met in the hallway mirror, and Beckett seemed to still in his arms like he knew this wouldn't just be dinner and a walk. A nervous blink was Beckett's response, and he scuttled out of Zane's arms toward the door.

"We'll be discussing Beckett in class today."

Zane smirked. "My favorite."

"*Samuel* Beckett."

"Definitely going to need dinner and a walk." But they both knew Zane was more than liking Beckett's literature lectures.

A small grin quirked Beckett's lips and he swung his bag over his shoulder and slipped out the door.

Despite heavy overcast clouds and a full day without Beckett, Zane floated to Darla's and sat with her on the front porch. She had nail polish out and one hand splayed over a magazine as she painted the nails on one hand.

"I like that shade of blue, darling."

She handed him the bottle and set her right hand on the magazine. "Thought you'd like it. Almost the exact shade of someone's bright eyes, hmmm?"

He dabbed a pearl of paint off the brush and brought it to her thumb. "I think you're a bit of a know-it-all."

"I don't know anything, Zane." She sighed. "I'm a Taurus, and my beloved husband was a Pisces. From the second I saw you, I saw him. I'm a meddling old bag who just wanted to relive falling in love again."

Zane picked up her hand, kissed the back, and returned to painting her nails. "It's a different type, but I fell in love with you, too."

"Too?" she said, wrinkles deepening with a smile as she gestured toward his side of the duplex.

"Him first."

"Does he know?"

"Not in so many words. But, tonight, Darla, I'll tell him. It'll be perfect."

The moment he said it, the clouds opened up and rain pounded the earth.

Darla grimaced. "Best not to read your daily horoscope, I think."

~

"Okay, this was not part of the plan."

"You Google-mapped our way to the cemetery, where we got mugged for cash. What part of that *was* the plan?"

Zane winced. So much for showing the professor he could trust him. "I thought . . . it was our first after-dinner walk. It was supposed to be romantic."

Beckett stopped pulling at his hair and sighed. A hand clasped Zane's jaw and a kiss followed. "At least he was a polite mugger. He gave me my wallet back."

"After stripping it of cash." Zane gritted his teeth in frustration. He hadn't even recognized they were being mugged until after it happened. He'd thought the guy just wanted directions. He'd smiled and everything.

What a great, protective boyfriend he made. Real winner.

"Hey," Beckett said, steering Zane's gaze to his. "Seventy dollars. Not the end of the world. We still have our phones."

"I'm sorry, Becky. This wasn't at all how this evening was supposed to go."

Beckett pressed him against the wrought iron gate, his warm weight slotting perfectly against Zane.

"If I can handle a grave after-dinner walk, I can handle anything, remember?"

This was his moment. He looked Beckett in the eye. "Beckett."

"Becky," Beckett corrected.

Zane's breath shook. "Beckett, I—"

Beckett's eyes flashed with apprehension rimmed with hope. Apprehension won out and he slapped a hand over Zane's mouth. "Don't."

"I'm not high," Zane said against his fingers. "I know what I'm saying and I want to say it."

Beckett looked away. "Look, these last three weeks have been intense. I've never been so attracted to a guy—never felt so at home with anyone. Being with you makes marrying Luke seem like the biggest mistake of my life. I f-feel stupid that I thought what he and I had was . . . . I didn't know a thing."

Zane smiled. These were his most favorite words Beckett had ever said—and he'd stuttered them. "Becky, Beckett, are you saying you love me?"

Becky dropped his chin and stared at the ground. "Your visa runs out next week."

"Let's marry."

Zane regretted it the moment he said it. He meant it, of course, but he'd promised that offer would come from Beckett when he was ready. When Beckett knew he could trust Zane. Not blurted breathlessly because he couldn't control the love sweeping through his veins.

Beckett tensed against him and Zane felt him pull away. "I . . . I . . . ." He slammed his eyes shut. "This can't work."

Zane's throat dried. He reached out and tried to lock their fingers together, but Beckett pulled away and stuffed his hands into his pockets. Zane had been left too many times not to know what was happening; still, he refused to believe it. "I only want you."

Beckett turned away and sauntered back the way they'd come. "Maybe you should take Darla up on her offer and score a green card through her."

Zane let him walk ahead, giving himself a moment to

compose himself. He'd brought Beckett here to lay his heart bare, but it may as well have been stolen along with Beckett's seventy dollars.

He had seen how broken the bull was tonight, and Zane didn't know how to fix him.

Through the bite of hurt, Zane rolled his shoulders. Odds stacked against him had never stopped him before, and he wouldn't fold now. Leaving a dozen feet between them, he followed Beckett through the woods.

Sticks crunched underfoot. His footsteps raised the strong smell of soil after the recent downpour. Their shoes squelched in mud, and the scent of rain hung in the air. Drops fell from overhanging branches when a gust of wind rolled through.

The path narrowed around a bend in the hill that overlooked a quaint cul-de-sac. Streetlights popped on, and if there weren't any awkward tension between them, they might have kissed where Beckett had paused at the edge of a short cliff.

Zane slowed and stopped a couple of yards to Beckett's side. They glanced sideways at the same time, and Zane held his breath, wondering how long Beckett would hold it before looking away. But he didn't look away.

Zane inched nearer and paused when Beckett mirrored him, stepping back.

"I told you from the beginning, I'm not looking for someone to MOC me."

"You want to marry within the week."

"I want to be married *a lifetime*."

"You're discovering your bisexuality," Beckett said. "You're curious and that's fine, but you can't want me forever."

"I do."

"You're young. There's so much you don't know."

If anyone knew that Zane had a lot to learn, it was himself. "I definitely should be lectured, and it'd be best done by someone who does it for a living."

Spontaneous laughter shot out of Beckett. "Oh, Zane, I've never laughed so much . . . ."

And Zane had never had such an intelligent man laugh with him.

"But I—" Beckett's reply cut off sharply as the precipice gave way under his feet. Beckett dropped to his ass, scrambling against sliding rock and dirt. Zane lunged for him, but Beckett dropped a few feet out of his reach with a sharp cry.

Zane's knees hit the ground hard and his heart thumped. It wasn't the longest drop, but it was big enough to hurt if Beckett fell. Zane couldn't reach him from where he'd grabbed a tree root and was hanging, facing the sliding wall of mud and stone.

"Becky, hold on. I'm coming." He eyed the drop. He was taller, bigger.

He wriggled off the edge that hadn't crumbled and jumped down. The jolt of the ground stung, but he landed without injury.

"I suddenly regret declining Finnegan's every invitation to hit the gym."

"Glad your humor is still intact, Professor." Zane positioned himself under Beckett, kicking the mound of freshly fallen earth to keep a steady stance. "Let go, I'll catch you."

"You know, this is probably good training for my arms."

Zane shook his head and, with gruff fondness, called back, "Just fall, Becky."

"I'm afraid I'll hurt myself." Beckett's fingers were slipping. He dropped an inch.

"I just realized something." Zane stared up at his dangling boyfriend.

"Mmm, what's that?" Beckett tried hard to sound composed, but Zane detected the strain.

No matter, Beckett would drop in three, two . . . "I've *literally* knocked you off your feet."

One.

Beckett fell with a snort and Zane caught him, snapping his arms around Beckett's waist and slowing his descent.

Zane hugged him, Beckett's dark hair tickling his chin, his warm chest heaving in Zane's arms. Beckett clutched his wrists and unlocked himself from his grip. An achy loss seized his heart and disappeared when Beckett turned in his arms and pressed close.

Zane read the confusion in Beckett's gaze. Felt him struggling and failing to hold back. Arms lifted around his neck and fingers speared through his hair.

"It can't work. It can't." Beckett kissed him.

"You're the smartest man I know," Zane said. "But this time you're wrong."

Beckett drove Zane away from the cliff wall, hands roaming and kisses deepening. "It can't work, but I can't stop."

Zane gripped his shoulders and searched Beckett's face. "What can I do?"

"Take me home," Beckett said.

AT HOME, THE NORMAL ROUTINE DEVIATED SLIGHTLY.

After Leah headed out for the night, they readied themselves for bed and slipped into their respective sides. Beckett's uncertainty and Zane's desperation could be heard in the snick of pages as they read side by side, could be felt in the shivers climbing through Zane, could be tasted in their toothpaste sighs.

"Are you actually reading?" Zane whispered.

"No," Beckett said. "But I'm pretending very hard."

"You say we won't work," Zane said, lifting his gaze to Beckett's, stuck in his book. "But what part of you will work better when I'm gone? Will you get out there and date? Find someone else who would walk to the ends of the earth for you?

Please promise me it won't be Finnegan, because he actually might, and that defeats the purpose of my point."

Beckett's throat jutted with a swallow. "I don't want to think about it."

"But it's your story. You have to keep writing it."

"Then you could say I have writer's block."

"Let me be your muse."

Beckett dropped his head back on the fluffed pillow and rested the book against his chest. He turned to look at Zane. "My muse?"

"Yes, I can be quite creative." To prove the point, Zane leaped out of bed and hauled the bull rug over him. It clung heavy to his naked back, scratching at his hips. He adjusted the head over his own and hunched forward. "I'll be as bullheaded as I must to convince you to keep me."

Beckett laughed. "Good Lord."

Zane climbed on the bed on all fours, peeking out at Beckett from under the bull's jaw. With one of the horns, Zane lightly butted his boyfriend's cheek. "You want me."

"Zane. You're twenty-three and—"

"Don't give me that bull. You need me."

Beckett scrubbed his face, muffling his exasperated laughter. "Whatever will I do with you?"

"You'll write to me when I go back home. You'll call me and send ridiculously expensive packages. You'll long-distance with me until I'm eligible to come back. You'll gaze lovingly at our food container picture or me on screen while we video call."

"Long distance?" Beckett looked tempted, hopeful.

Zane whispered conspiratorially, "Take the bull by the horns, Professor."

Beckett grabbed the rug head and pulled it off Zane. Arms yanked him forward against Beckett. The spine of Beckett's book dug into his chest, but he didn't care. He palmed Beckett's jaw, light stubble brushing his skin.

Beckett pressed his warm hands against Zane's shoulder blades. The crush of blankets separated their bodies, but underneath, Zane felt the ridge of Beckett's erection. "Tell me that didn't come from me wearing the bull, because—"

"I want to have sex," Beckett croaked. His chest rose, and the book burned his sternum. "I just . . . ."

Zane maneuvered the book from between them and repositioned himself against Beckett. He fingered the threadbare T-shirt he wore, the pads of his fingers sliding over Beckett's firm chest up to his soft neck. Beckett's pulse ticked.

"I do want it," Beckett whispered. "I want to feel you deep in me. Want to feel you around me, too, but with you leaving—"

Zane laid a finger over Beckett's mouth. "Shush." He brought the tip of his nose to Beckett's. "You never have to give me a reason not to have sex. I told you, I don't need it." He dropped a soft kiss on Beckett's rising explanation. "I'll never leave you for a lack of it."

Beckett's chest shuddered under him and he shut his eyes.

Zane brushed his lips over the corner of Beckett's. "This is all I need."

Beckett opened his eyes and Zane hooked his gaze and smiled down at him. "This is all I need."

Zane sank his fingers into Beckett's armpits and tickled him. Beckett bucked with a chuckle that grew into a deep laugh. He wrestled Zane off him, pushing him off and against the bed. Limber legs straddled him, and knees pinned Zane's arms.

Zane laughed so hard that he was practically crying, stomach undulating hard with each bout. He desperately caught his breath. "This is all I need."

He reached for *Pride and Prejudice* and handed it to Beckett. "And this is all I need."

Their gazes connected over the book. Beckett's arms and thighs were a shock of goose bumps, and Zane's skin fluttered, like all their butterflies had burst free to dance together.

Beckett lifted the book, squeezed his thighs around Zane, and read aloud. "'Elizabeth's spirits soon rising to playfulness again, she wanted Mr. Darcy to account for his having ever fallen in love with her.'"

Zane bit his lip. *This Lizzy wants his Mr. Darcy to account for it too. Perhaps admit it first.*

Beckett continued, "'How could you begin?' said she. 'I can comprehend your going on charmingly, when you had once made a beginning; but what could set you off in the first place?'"

What indeed?

Maybe, when he was ready, Beckett would share that with Zane, too.

Beckett cleared his throat. "'I cannot fix on the hour, or the spot, or the look, or the words, which laid the foundation. It is too long ago. I was in the middle before I knew that I had begun.'"

The flush in Beckett's cheek suggested otherwise. His Becky knew precisely the second, the spot, the look, and the words that laid the foundation.

Beckett stopped reading, set the book aside, and leaned forward. The kiss that came tingled. "It is impossible to read with you dreamily smiling like that."

Zane wrapped his arms around Beckett and held him close. "I guess we'll have to kiss ourselves to sleep, then."

Beckett's hair flopped forward, tickling Zane's forehead. Zane smoothed it back, only to have it flop again as Beckett kissed his cheek, the bridge of his nose, the space between his eyebrows. Soft lips hovered at his temple, and warm air trickled over his ear and down his jaw. He'd never had someone kiss him without it leading anywhere and it was the softest, most comforting feeling. There was something . . . unconditional about it, and it made his chest swell in all the best ways.

Another kiss drifted over his hairline, and another nibbled at the lobe of his ear.

"Let me kiss you back," Zane croaked, steering Beckett to his mouth.

Perfect.

No other word described this moment. Perfect. Perfect. Perfect.

Love is a smoke and is made with the fume of sighs.

—William Shakespeare

Chapter Twenty

"I'm going to get coffee and not daydream about you at all." Zane stole a kiss at the L-shaped sofa at King's. "Or maybe I'll just get coffee."

"Sit down, Zane," Beckett said in such a professor-like tone, Zane folded to the sofa. "I'm getting our coffee."

Zane blew him a kiss as he left. He wished it wasn't Monday already. The weekend had flown by with chores, an outing to a kite festival with Darla, and taking care of an ultra-drunk Leah when she stumbled home late Saturday night.

Ignoring the elephant in the room—Zane's upcoming departure—they flowed so well together. They shared an easy banter and always kissed in bed before Beckett turned to read and Zane to draw.

His main character had an uncanny likeness to Beckett. Different hair color, different clothes, but the same graceful lines to his body.

Zane stared starry-eyed at the professor's leather bag next to him. The flap was open, and like always, his bag was full. A bunch of papers with familiar words—his words—was peeking out.

His outline.

Zane nervously eased it out of Beckett's bag.

The amount of red ink blinded him. He blinked, his throat constricting as he read note after note. All constructive. All absolutely right.

All a pickax to his heart anyway.

There's a lot of energy to this story and it has every component of an action-packed and romantic story, but as the outline stands right now, it doesn't work.

Beckett had used three blank pages to detail why the main character's motivations weren't strong enough to hold a series, why the stakes needed to be higher, and where additional conflict could lift the story. He'd even written examples. The detail was appreciated yet excruciating.

Movement out of the corner of his eye had Zane glancing to the table where he'd once slapped a woman with her glove. Beckett sat with their coffees, watching him carefully. He must've seen that Zane had taken the outline and given him space to read through his comments.

Beckett offered him an apologetic smile that made Zane's chest sag to the pit of his stomach. He dropped his gaze back to the outline and rubbed his thumb over the staple holding it together.

More movement, and Zane shut his eyes as he felt Beckett approach. He felt the heat of him approach; the cushions shifted as he sat, and the scent of his soft aftershave hit the back of Zane's throat.

Zane drew up a smile that he hoped didn't wobble and peeled his eyes open. "Yeah, thanks for this."

Beckett set the outline on the table where their cold coffee now sat. "I wanted to go through it with you, after class."

"Speaking of class. Hadn't you better run, Professor?"

"Look at me."

Zane flickered his gaze to Beckett's and away again.

"Oh, Zane." Beckett pulled Zane to him, hands tugging at his shoulders. Zane slumped into the embrace, forehead pressing against the curve of Beckett's neck.

Fingers stroked his curved back as Zane fought to swallow.

"I'm on your side," Beckett murmured. "You've got a wonderful imagination. This will be a good story."

Zane wanted to believe him, but maybe he was saying that to make him feel better? Zane should be used to this. His entire school life, anything he'd written had come back to him bleeding red. The critiques shouldn't hurt this much, but they did.

He clutched Beckett and pressed a scared kiss against his pulse.

Beckett was a hundred-dollar merlot whereas Zane was box wine simply titled *red*.

Could he ever be smart enough?

Beckett steered Zane's head up and slotted their mouths together, warm and addictive.

A cell phone alarm went off, but their kiss didn't so much as hesitate. The café bustled while Beckett nibbled his lip and took kiss after kiss.

Zane needed this.

He had to make sure he was smart enough. *Would* make sure he was smart enough.

ZANE MADE A PLAN ON HIS WALK HOME AND IT INVOLVED Darla.

Precisely, it involved using Darla's library card.

After a day redrafting his outline at Darla's kitchen table, Leo purring on his papers, he whisked Darla to the library in Beckett's car.

The car Beckett had told him he could use anytime he pleased.

Darla had taken the opportunity to dress up and wore a sequin dress that matched her blue nails. Zane had talked her out of heels that looked like they hadn't been worn in decades, and she reluctantly wore flat slip-on shoes—and brought her cane.

Darling diva at his side, Zane stalked the nonfiction section of the public library.

"Crap. So many aisles. Where do I start?"

Darla snuck flirty glances at an elderly man reading a newspaper on one of the library's signature red sofas. "What do you want to know?"

"Everything."

"That's a little unrealistic now."

"Beckett knows everything. I need to, too."

Darla dragged her gaze away from Mr. Newspaper. "Our Beckett is a smart young man. But he cannot draw for the life of him. He hired someone to put the paintings on his walls. Got his Finnegan to set up his computer and home sound system. Gets his mom to help him with his taxes."

Zane plucked a book off the shelf. He could draw. Knew his way around computers and electronics pretty well. Taxes weren't a strong point, but he knew how to work basic tools.

Still, that wasn't enough.

He piled book after book on his arm and went with Darla to borrow them.

That evening, Zane sat across from Beckett at Darla's table, a beef and cheese lasagna in the oven. The house smelled of sautéed onion and garlic, and Zane hoped dinner would taste as good as it smelled.

The doorbell rang.

Darla pushed to her feet, grinning. She'd been anticipating this visit for the last hour while they played Cards Against Humanity. Her grandson and his husband were popping in for a short visit to show off the new additions to their family.

They listened to a ruckus of shrieks and adoration coming from the door, followed by the cry of a newborn.

Beckett looked over his cup of tea—ginger—and they shared a quiet smile. One that bordered on shy, like Beckett might be imagining coming home with his own babies. Zane's return smile elicited a small, somewhat nervous chuckle.

"Adorable," Darla said, leading two haggard but handsome guys into the living room.

The one who resembled Theo from Darla's photo flashed Zane and Beckett acknowledging dimples and set down a car seat with a moping baby.

"Jamie, how is it your little one stays quiet?"

"My calming presence," Jamie said, dryly. "Swap, and you'll see."

Theo shook his head, grinning. He peeked over at Zane and Beckett again, and Jamie shook hands with Beckett. "Beckett, nice to see you again."

Zane gave a small wave, and Jamie introduced himself. Probably would have been the right time to introduce himself back, but Zane just stared at the man's watch as they shook hands. Total brain-fart moment.

"You've been off work for a while," Beckett said to Jamie.

"And it'll be a little while longer, yet."

The baby cried harder, and Theo called out Jamie's name in panic. "Mine needs you."

Jamie gave them a secret smirk and backed over to the car seats.

Darla crouched between the two seats, cooing. Theo

stepped next to the quieter baby, and as if on cue, it started moping. "Oh Christ, it really is me."

Jamie lifted the first baby and patted its back while looking fondly at Theo. "It's not you. He's just grumpy"—the baby burped—"and had gas, apparently."

"Attic is so much calmer. He looks like you, too. Must be your stoic genes."

"Maybe," Jamie said, "it's because we haven't named this one yet."

Theo flopped onto the sofa. "I don't like any other name. Atticus is strong, and I love the nickname Attic. Other names don't sound special enough."

Darla kissed Attic and slowly pushed to her feet. "What names have you shortlisted?"

Zane pulled out his phone. He winked at Beckett and sent him a text.

Zane: What are your favorite baby names?

Beckett drew out his phone and read.
Ten seconds later, Zane's palm buzzed.

Beckett: I haven't thought about it.

Zane: Liar. Everyone has thought about it.

Beckett leaned back in his chair, typing.

Beckett: Don't laugh.

Zane: That immediately makes me want to laugh.

Beckett: Zane . . .

Zane: Okay, promise.

Beckett: Lyric for a girl. Sky for a boy.

Zane: OMG, you can't name our kids Lyric or Sky. They'll be beaten up.

Beckett: Fine. What are your favorites?

Zane: Boy, Xander—I'm a big Buffy fan.

Beckett: Let me guess, girl, Willow? (Praying it's Willow and not Buffy)

Zane snickered.

Zane: I was thinking Sydney.

Beckett: You like Sydney? You?

"It's a nice name," Zane said.

"Are you sure you're not Australian?"

Darla caught Zane's eye. "Maybe you have a few names these boys haven't thought of yet?"

Theo looked at them expectantly. "Yes . . . what's your name? Probably should have introduced myself when I came in, blame it on the brain fog. I only slept, like, six hours last night."

Jamie snorted, shaking his head. "You're on tonight, and six hours will be bliss."

Zane slipped off his chair and made proper introductions.

"Zane," Theo sounded his name. "Nice, but . . . ."

Jamie settled the now sleeping, nameless baby back into the

car seat. "Don't take it personally, no one's name has the right ring to it."

"Well I'd name him Jamie," Theo said. "But one of my boys already took it."

Jamie reclined into the couch and pressed a soft kiss against Theo's lips. Watching made Zane want to grab Beckett and kiss him in front of the world as well. Let everyone know he was his Mr. Darcy.

"Your who?" Theo said, straightening, staring at Zane.

He must have murmured that last part. "Darcy."

"I kinda like it." Theo swung his head to Jamie in elation. "Jamie, I like it!"

Zane glanced sideways to see Beckett looking over his phone at him while texting.

Beckett: Lizzy.

AFTER DINNER ALL TOGETHER, ZANE AND BECKETT WENT HOME to find Leah packing clean laundry from the basket into her suitcase in the living room.

"I'm off to Boston."

Beckett perched on the arm of his chair, seemingly unsurprised by Leah's sudden change of plan. "Who is he?"

"A musician. He's in a band called Hurry Me Home. He's really talented."

Zane spied the mess Leah had left in the kitchen and busied himself cleaning up.

"My house is always open for you if things don't work out and you need to come home."

Leah lunged at Beckett and hugged him. "It feels good to go where your heart takes you."

Zane looked away from Beckett's gaze lifting to him and smiled at the soapy water.

Before Leah left, she hugged Zane and whispered into his ear, "Invite me to the wedding."

Nice to know that one Fisher knew Beckett wouldn't get rid of Zane easily.

When she was gone and Beckett had excused himself to take a shower, Zane called Jacob. Since spending the evening with Darla and her family, he'd had a nagging feeling in his gut.

He lay in bed, a pillow propped behind him, and listened to Jacob recount his misadventures with Cassie. "Enough about us. How are you doing? Less than a week left. We're looking forward to that little goodbye party on Friday."

Zane let out a slow breath. "I wanted to talk about that."

"You sound nervous. Are you okay?"

Zane sighed. "I'm in love with Beckett."

The line crackled with Jacob's surprised breath. "You're in love with Beckett?"

"We're in love with each other, but we're working on admitting it."

A soft sound floated down the hallway, but no sign of Beckett.

Jacob's surprised voice filled the line. "Wow, I . . . . And you let me talk about poop for ten minutes. This is the conversation we should've been having."

"He's wonderful, Jacob. I know why he and Anne used to be so close. He is so clever and kind and warm and funny."

"I'm, uh, happy for you, Zane. But, you're leaving . . . ."

Yeah. That part sucked. "That's the other thing I wanted to talk about. It doesn't feel right to have a goodbye party anywhere else other than here. I know it's harder with a baby, but I was hoping you could come to us on Friday for the goodbye party."

Jacob croaked, "You bet. We'll make it work. I'll book a hotel tonight."

Zane's chest swelled. Nearly crying at all the love he was about to leave behind, Zane ended the call.

✑

So BEGAN A NEW NIGHTLY ROUTINE. AFTER DINNER AND A walk, they fell into bed. But instead of drawing on his tablet, Zane read books. Read and read and read.

The closer his departure, the harder he buried himself in books.

Two days before his flight, Beckett came into the bedroom from a shower, hair dripping onto his bare shoulders, towel slung low around his hips. Zane's cross on his calendar wobbled. He hurriedly snipped the lid on the pen and stuffed it in the mess on top of Beckett's dresser.

They looked at each other almost shyly, both rocking on the balls of their feet. They hadn't had sex since this time last week, and while it wasn't necessary, Beckett looked downright sexy and there was no way of hiding his response while wearing only satin boxers.

Beckett noticed the calendar and his expression shadowed.

The space between them was less than a few yards, but it may have been the distance to New Zealand.

"Video calls, remember?" Zane winked and bounded on the bed, scrambling to get under the covers. His erection wasn't waning, and grabbing his nightly reading wasn't helping.

New plan: Read for ten minutes, then slink away inconspicuously when Beckett was deep into a book of his own.

He lifted his book on queer history, shielding himself from Beckett's beautiful body. Soft footsteps padded around the room, drawers opened and shut, and blankets shifted. The bed dipped next to him and Beckett dropped something between them on the bed.

Zane refused to look anywhere but his text. He'd randomly opened to the middle of the book, and a graph was staring back at him.

He frowned at the image, reading the words "varying bisexual responses" under the horizontal axis, punctuated by numbers from zero to six.

He drew his gaze up to the text above the graph and slapped the book against his face with a groan.

"Zane?"

Zane shoved the book off him and wriggled under the blankets until he was submerged with his embarrassment and a very naked Beckett.

He groaned, and the groan grew louder when Beckett shuffled close, the solidness of his chest hot against his side. Beckett joined him under the covers. Light leaked in from the top where the blanket didn't quite close over their heads. Their cave warmed with Beckett's gentle laugh.

"What's the matter?"

What was the matter? Zane was an idiot, that's what. He consistently screwed things up.

He scrubbed his face and laughed. "I'm a bit cheeky. A big dreamer, and a bigger idiot."

"What brought this on?" Beckett said.

Zane peeked at him between his fingers. "It *is* Kinsey, not Kingly."

Amusement warmed Beckett with a smile. "The Kingly Scale warmed the cockles of my heart."

"Crap. Next you'll be telling me this isn't a monogamy bed!"

"Well, now that you brought it up . . . ."

Zane tried to roll away and Beckett climbed on top of him, the warm weight of his body pressing him into the mattress.

Zane's half-hard dick decided to make the situation more challenging and stiffened.

Beckett pried Zane's fingers from his face and smiled down at him. "It is a monogamy bed in the sense I only want to share it intimately with you."

"I thought it was one of those words that is spelled the same but with two different meanings?"

"Homonym?"

"You, merlot. Me, box."

"Come again?"

"What's the word I was looking for?"

"Mahogany."

"Right." Zane's sigh sifted between them, and it was the last one he'd allow himself. Idiot he might be, but he'd be an optimistic one. "It warmed the cockles of your heart?"

Beckett's chin dotted against his chin with a soft series of kisses. "Yes."

Zane palmed the back of Beckett's head and slid his tongue along that soft bottom lip. His voice grew husky. "Just, um, those cockles?"

Beckett answered by deepening his kiss. Through the thin satiny layer between them, Zane was left in no doubt of Beckett's arousal. It pressed solidly against Zane's.

"I hate that you're leaving. I hate it. Hate it."

The covers pumped as Beckett rocked, and air drifted between them. His kisses grew frantic.

"The thought of us being as close as we can get and then you leaving . . . . God, I've wanted to have you but . . . I've been hurt before, and I . . . ."

"It's okay, Becky. We can just hold each other."

Beckett's moan swept over the side of Zane's mouth to his ear. "I can't hold back a moment longer."

"What do you want?" Zane whispered.

"You inside me."

Zane gasped as Beckett reached between them and pumped him through his boxers.

Kisses scrolled down his neck. "I want you so deep inside of me, I can't *think*."

Oh, God. He wanted that too. "Are you sure?"

Beckett straddled him, blankets lifting and sliding down his back. The light of the room stung Zane's eyes. He blinked through it and found Beckett holding up a condom and a bottle of lube. "I was sure when I woke up this morning and you smiled at me. I was sure in the shower while I prepared myself. I was very sure the moment I overheard you on the phone with your brother."

Beckett had heard his declaration, then. However, it was one thing to overhear it, and another to say it face-to-face—Zane would make the moment memorable.

Hand wrapped around his erection, Beckett stroked himself. His rosy, plum-like head glistened with a smear of precome.

Beckett ground his ass against Zane's dick, and Zane clasped Beckett's flexing thighs against the rush of arousal pulsing through him.

Zane nodded, lost for words, grappling at Beckett to pull him into a kiss.

Beckett bent and penetrated Zane's mouth with his tongue. He worked his tongue in and out, slowly, and then faster. Zane cocked his hips in time to the deep kisses, eliciting needy groans. "Yeah, just like that."

"What do I do for you? To make it good?"

Beckett shifted down him and pulled at his boxers. "First we get rid of these."

The satin rushed over his dick, and he arched off the mattress, sucking in a breath. Beckett tossed them onto the towel on the floor and sat on Zane's thighs, hands gripping his hips. Zane's dick twitched in anticipation. Beckett curled a hand around him and stroked as he reached for the condom.

"What about preparing you?" Zane gasped.

"Did you notice how long I was in the bathroom before coming into the bedroom?"

Zane was about to come at the images rushing through his brain of Beckett fingering himself. His heart hammered as Beckett rolled the condom on him and stroked him with plenty of lube.

Beckett crawled up him, skimming the top of his dick, and pressed a slow kiss to his mouth. Zane pulled him back just enough to look him in the eyes. They were heavy with lust but also with emotion and a need that Zane felt too.

"You're beautiful, Becky."

Beckett smiled, poised himself, and inch by erotic inch, sank onto Zane's dick. His hair flopped forward as he dropped his chin to his chest, biting his bottom lip against a groan. He braced a hand against Zane's left pec, the pads of his fingers pressing hard. He squeezed his ass.

Zane nearly came, and he sucked in a breath, begging for a moment before Beckett started moving. When he caught himself, he glared at Beckett. "You should have warned me how freaking amazing you feel."

Beckett pinched Zane's nipple with a saucy smile, lifted off his cock, and sank back onto him. His channel gripped Zane perfectly. Tight, hot, and holy hell, Beckett was bouncing on him.

The sensation rushed through his chest to his scalp. Zane threw his head back on the pillow and planted his hands on the headboard behind him.

The bed groaned, or maybe it was him. Or both.

Beckett's dick slapped against Zane's lower stomach. The intensity of his mounting orgasm bordered on torture.

Their skin smacked, and Zane's hips rose off the bed,

meeting Beckett's rhythm. Zane clutched at Beckett's back and drew him down for a kiss. When Zane cuffed Beckett's cock and stroked him, their panting mingled.

Beckett slid his hands to Zane's shoulders and clutched him. Their gazes met, and Zane felt Beckett tremble. "Hate that you're leaving."

Zane hated it, too.

Beckett's jaw grazed his and he sucked the top of Zane's ear. "Fuck me so I'll still feel you when you're gone."

His whole body blasted with heat and need and frustration. He flipped them, Beckett on the mattress under him, digging his hands into Zane's ass as Zane plundered him. Hard and fast he moved, wishing it was deep enough to reach his heart.

A garbled moan sifted over his throat and come pulsed over Zane's stomach. Beckett's orgasm pulsed around Zane's dick, and in two more thrusts, he was coming so hard his vision short-circuited and he saw black with blotches of light.

Beckett squeezed Zane of every last drop until he collapsed. He caught his breath against Beckett's neck and couldn't stop groaning. Sex had always felt good, but this had been a whole other level of intimacy. It couldn't compare.

His orgasm had torn through him like a tornado, but it had left behind an unfamiliar ache. His chest felt heavy, his throat sore. He pushed up and looked at Beckett, lips raw, cheeks flushed, and eyes sad.

They cleaned up and then held each other. Beckett kissed the soft skin under his chin and reached for the book he was reading.

"Read to me, Zane?"

"This is a—what's it called when I do it, but you usually do it?"

"Reversal."

"Exactly."

"I love your voice."

"My Chris Hemsworth accent, you mean?"

Beckett drummed his fingers over Zane's chest. "Both insanely sexy."

"Where does that guy live?"

"Why?"

"Because we are never going there."

Wrapped in Zane's arms, Beckett soon fell asleep. Zane pressed a kiss against the top of his head and fought a sting behind his eyes.

How was it that tomorrow they'd already be saying goodbye?

A loving heart is the truest wisdom.

—Charles Dickens

Chapter Twenty-One

Zane followed The Stone Roses' "Ten Storey Love Song" to the living room, clutching a large rolled piece of paper. Walking through the duplex felt so familiar. It was strange that tomorrow he wouldn't come home to plum-colored walls and soft carpet, swollen bookshelves, and framed paintings of horses.

He paused in the doorway to the living room and breathed in the scent of the cinnamon and pecan muffins Beckett had made. They had been devoured over the last three hours, and Zane hated seeing the empty plate. Too much like a forecast of what was to come.

"My husband fell for that, hook, line, and sinker." Darla was chatting with Finnegan at the kitchen island holding a mug of questionable tea. She'd gone all-out, like every time they visited the library, wearing a bright yellow sundress and feathered earrings.

Finnegan caught Zane watching them and sent him a secret lift of his eyebrows. Zane nodded. It was time. He had been in cahoots with Books for Breakfast the last few days.

At the dining table, Anne cradled a sleeping Cassie, laughing with Jacob. Ever in love, and he knew the feeling.

He'd spent the first hour cuddling Cassie while sharing a tearful goodbye with Jacob.

The Cure's "Lovesong" came on—Zane had made a playlist with his favorite indie love songs, and this one had him swallowing. He rubbed his thumb over the rubber band holding together the rolled paper he held.

Casting an eye over the room, he found his Beckett, much like he had when he first laid eyes on him. Sitting on his over-stuffed armchair in front of the stone fireplace, locks dark against the light cushions. One leg slung over the arm, and a turquoise boot stretched snugly up his calf.

He could barely pull his gaze to Natalie Fisher chatting to her son at his side.

Beckett kept biting back a smile and sipping his wine, and Natalie patted his head, bent down, and kissed his cheek.

He wished he'd been closer to listen in on that conversation.

Natalie caught him watching and her smile blasted. She knew then that Zane was Beckett's boyfriend. Lover. Muse.

Beckett followed her smile to him and swung off the armchair, sitting upright. A shock of electricity had Zane tingling as he drifted to him.

As if everyone in the room felt the change in the air, they grew quiet and watched them.

God, Beckett was beautiful. The deep-blue eyes, the sharp cheekbones, the intelligence that simmered from him.

The navy blazer Zane had bought for him fit perfectly.

An ache curled up his throat. This time tomorrow, there'd be no Beckett sitting in front of him.

"I made you a little something," Zane said, and play-fully tapped the end of his rolled paper against Beckett's chest.

Beckett paused, emotion glowing in his eyes. He took the roll and opened it.

"It's Wanda and Jasper. I thought," Zane gestured to the paintings on the wall, "maybe you'd like one of my drawings up here, too."

Beckett's blue eyes brimmed with something overwhelmingly soft.

Their guests gathered around to admire the artwork, while Beckett continued to study him. "Thank you," he mouthed.

"You're welcome," Zane mouthed back. Then he cleared his voice and shot Finnegan a sneaky look. "And now it's time to get this show on the road."

Beckett gave a surprised frown. "We're going out?"

"We're exiting the duplex," Zane said with a wink. "We're departing for Chiffon."

ZANE HAD BEEN PREPARING FOR THIS MOMENT ALL WEEK. WHAT he hadn't prepared for was finding Luke at Chiffon's bar, cradling a cider.

Their party—minus Anne and Cassie, who'd retired to their hotel—followed Finnegan to their reserved table, unaware of the complication.

Beckett had lurched to a stop after spotting his ex-husband across the room at the same time.

"This was not how this evening was supposed to go," Zane murmured apologetically. "We can go somewhere else, I'll—"

Beckett steered Zane's chin around and looked him in the eye. Candlelight from the tables around them danced. "I don't care if this place is full of Lukes. This night is for us."

In the middle of the restaurant, Zane looped his arms around Beckett. He'd been saving this moment. Had devised the perfect plan to say these words, but to hell with it.

It felt too strong, too magical, and he couldn't wait a minute, a second longer. He planned on saying these words for a lifetime, and he wanted that lifetime to begin as soon as possible.

He leaned close and whispered in his boyfriend's ear, "I love you, Beckett."

Breathing in Beckett's scent, he drew back, grazing his lips on his jaw.

Beckett looked at him, tearful.

He opened his mouth, but Puck burst to life on stage, voice amplified through the speakers.

"Five minutes to our last synonym standoff, ladies and gentlemen. May I see our regular Beckett Fisher backstage."

Beckett startled and threw a frustrated look to Finnegan across the room. Finnegan jerked a thumb toward the stage.

"Looks like Finnegan booked us a slot. Let me race over and tell them I can't."

Zane glanced at the stage and back at Beckett. "But it's the most fun you'll ever have. The best. Superlative. Top."

"Yes, but not when you're looking at your boyfriend, sifting through a million words trying to find the best ones to tell him how much you love him, too."

Forget flying back to New Zealand. He'd just float there.

"Get up there and do your best, for me."

Beckett cupped his face and kissed him. "For you," he said and sauntered determinedly toward Puck.

Zane weaved around tables, elated and nervous. His mouth felt parched and he hurriedly rocked up to the bar for water. Luke glanced over at him and called down to him. "Wondered if you'd show up here tonight," he said. "Beckett sure loves this place."

Cold water slid across the bar, and Zane gripped the dewy glass. He reluctantly moved closer to Luke as he drank. "Why are you here?"

"Because Puck's working," he said. "He's the best MC this place has. Besides, I'm drowning myself in a little deserved misery."

"Where's your boyfriend?"

Luke raised his glass and drank. "That deserved misery would be because I no longer have a boyfriend."

"Well. Maybe you have to do some metamorphosing of your own."

Zane was about to leave Luke to his drink when Luke spoke again. "Anne visited earlier. Told me about your goodbye party."

"Are you surprised at not being invited?"

"No. I get it. Beckett had a big talk with me earlier this week. Told me you two are serious. That he and I should figure a way to be around each other."

Zane swallowed a tender, hopeful smile. "And will you?"

"I'll try." Luke took another sip as Puck spoke into the microphone.

Zane gulped down his water, stomach catapulting at the sight of Beckett poised on stage, casting a confused frown at Finnegan who hadn't followed him up there.

"Standing off against Beckett Fisher tonight, please make a warm welcome to a first-timer on this stage, Zane Penn."

Beckett's gaze swung around the room and locked onto him. Zane held it.

"You're going up there against *Beckett*?" Luke was flabbergasted.

Zane kept his eyes trained on his boyfriend and stepped around Luke's stool toward the stage.

"He's unbeaten," Luke said, stating facts. "He's a champion on that stage. You'll make a fool of yourself."

Zane stilled, then turned back to Luke. His chest shifted with a realization. Like the time in the clinic when he figured out he was attracted to intelligence. Or in the car with Beckett learning how important stability was for him. Or the night after his first visit to Chiffon where he figured out why he felt so strongly for Beckett.

He'd thought he'd overcome the shifting seas of his heart, but there was a large storm he'd been sailing through forever, and it was time for the sun to come out.

He spoke to Luke, but the words were for himself. "I might not be smart up here." He tapped his forehead. "But I am smart here." He dropped his fingers to his chest. "I will step on that stage because it's the most uncomfortable place I want to be. I'll stand in front of this crowd and likely make a joke of myself. I'll show Beckett that there is nothing in this world I wouldn't do for him."

Zane pointed to Jacob and Darla and Finnegan at their reserved table. "Take your cider, and enjoy the show."

Zane turned on his heel, gathered his guts, and jogged onstage.

"What are you doing?" Beckett murmured as Zane stood next to him.

"This was how I originally planned to say I love you. I jumped the gun. Got carried away."

Beckett chuckled. "Is this why I found a thesaurus under the bed this morning?"

Zane winked at him as Puck worked the crowd. He positioned them until they were facing each other, microphones pressed into their hands.

Zane gripped his with a clammy palm. It'd be over before he knew it.

Please don't be an obscure topic. If he could say at least one sentence, he'd be happy.

Puck's forehead shimmered with glitter. He smirked and spoke to the crowd again.

Zane's heart raced. Here it was. Beckett and Zane in a synonym standoff.

"Today's topic comes from a meddling neighbor and a close friend. Finnegan, Darla, stand up and take a bow. Beckett and Zane, blame those guys for any following cheesiness."

Zane jerked his head at the two grinning minxes. What had they done?

"Ready, guys?" Puck asked.

Beckett smiled at him, quirking one brow.

Zane remembered to breathe. "Yeah."

Puck did a coin toss and Zane called out tails. "Heads," Puck said. "That means Beckett starts. In the event you finish the minute without pause, we'll switch to an alliteration attack tiebreaker. Zane gets to drop the first word."

A tiebreaker. Like that would happen.

Zane bit his lip and looked Beckett in the eye. "Let's do this."

Puck hollered into the microphone. "Your topic: love."

Both Zane and Beckett glared toward their table, and then looked bashfully at one another.

Beckett spoke calmly. "Ours began with a bromance."

Zane's hand shook as he lifted his microphone. Personalizing this—making the topic about them—gave him butterflies. But loving Beckett? So easy, this might not be so hard after all. "You claimed my story was a slow burn."

Beckett inclined his head. "I resisted the idea of love at first sight."

Zane's voice dropped to a whisper that carried through the speakers. "For the love of God, we were both so clueless."

They continued dropping synonyms, idioms, and puns, and it was with surprise Puck called time. They were still going strong.

Beckett's gaze danced, making Zane forget what he was supposed to do.

Puck reminded him in his ear to drop a word and to start

the alliteration attack. They had a two-word phrase maximum —and it had to make sense.

Suddenly no words were left in his mind. He blurted the first thing that popped into his mind. "Pontificate!"

He hoped he wasn't blushing too hard.

Beckett smirked and continued, "the pleasure . . ."

"Of proudly . . ."

"Picking . . ."

Don't say penises, don't say penises. "Perfect . . ."

"Playful . . ."

"And perky . . ." Zane refrained from palming his forehead.

"Zane Penn."

Zane shoved his microphone at Puck and whisked Beckett into an embrace, his whisper catching in Beckett's microphone jammed between their chests. "You, prince."

Beckett held his gaze and kissed him.

Puck cheerfully announced Zane as the underdog who swept the champion off his feet, literally, and the restaurant erupted into a chorus of cheers.

Zane continued kissing the love of his life.

In vain I have struggled. It will not do. My feelings will not be repressed. You must allow me to tell you how ardently I admire and love you.

—Jane Austen

Chapter Twenty-Two

W hen they got back home, they kissed their way into the bedroom.

Beckett steered him to the edge of the bed and broke away. "You were amazing on that stage."

"Don't get used to it. Was a one-time thing."

"I don't even know where I'll start to write about this day."

Zane tried to grab Beckett, but he weaseled free. "Is that what you've been doing in that journal of yours? Writing our story?"

Beckett rifled through his leather bag. "I had to buy another journal to fit it all in."

"What are you doing, Professor? Because if you don't mind, I'd love to continue kissing you."

Their eyes met. "I have something for you, too," Beckett said.

Zane's stomach clenched. "Please don't give me a goodbye present. Please don't say goodbye at all."

From his bag, he pulled out Zane's second drafted outline and handed it to him.

Zane eyed his boyfriend warily. "You sure know how to kill the mood."

Beckett laughed. "It's so much better, Zane. You should be insanely proud of yourself."

"Really? It's good?"

"Really good."

Zane trembled as he looked over the outline. Red still marked the margins, but much less of it. And there was even a smiley face. "I'll send it to Jacob and work on a first draft impatiently while waiting to fly back here."

"I also have this."

A folded piece of paper flapped in front of him, and Zane eyed it. "What's that?"

"I pulled *a lot* of favors."

Zane tensed; something in Beckett's voice was making his belly flutter.

"Long story short, Professor Mable will take over my summer lit classes and Luke will cover my creative ones."

"What are you saying?" Zane unfolded the paper and his heart nearly burst.

"I'm coming with you for the summer."

Zane flew off the bed so fast, Beckett had no time to prepare and they stumbled back and fell into the armchair. The bull rug flopped onto the top of Beckett's head, a fiery gleam in its glassy eyes.

Legs snapped around his thighs, Zane kissed Beckett hard. "You're coming with me?"

"I'm coming with you. First class, because it was the only seat available, but I'm sure someone will swap with me."

Zane kissed him again. He couldn't even begin to . . . .

Another kiss. "Good. I promised myself to educate you on everything Kiwi. Wait, how do you know we're on the same flight?"

"I took your ticket from behind the calendar that's been ripping my heart out."

"You waited until the last minute to share this very important news with me? I'd be upset if I wasn't so over the moon."

Beckett drew a finger over Zane's nose to his lips and kissed him. "I didn't get the final okay until this morning. I booked the flight and printed it before your party. I wanted to make sure it would work out before getting your hopes up, and I wanted to tell you alone."

"You're *coming.*"

A smile broke Beckett's face. "Yes. And when you're eligible to come back?" Beckett spoke in his ear. "I'm marrying you."

Zane pulled back with twitching lips. "Is it immature that I'm a little gleeful your proposal came before the month's end?"

"It does sort of miss the point."

Zane pointedly looked at Beckett's feet and the bulges in their jeans. "Speaking of *points* . . . you've been in my boots all evening."

Beckett laughed. "I'm bracing for a lifetime of misadventure."

"Aren't they the best kind?"

"I suppose you're right. I might never have met you otherwise."

"We would have met. Fate. We are written in the stars."

"I don't believe in that stuff."

"You didn't believe in love at first sight either, and yet. Here we are."

"How did you know it was love at first sight for me?"

Zane hadn't. He'd hoped. "You protested too much."

Beckett shook his head with amusement.

"I'll give you something in return for telling me the precise second, spot, look, and words that 'laid the foundation.'"

"What will you give me?"

Zane danced his fingers up Beckett's blazer and smoothed the collar. "I always thought I wanted the holy grail of love at first sight, but I was wrong."

Beckett lifted a brow. "Wrong?"

"Love is intimate." Zane pressed a hand against Beckett's chest. "It takes time and experience to develop. Physical attraction isn't enough; it's about emotional fostering. About trust. That takes time and effort to nurture. I never want you to think I take it for granted." Zane playfully smacked their lips together. "Your turn."

Beckett cupped Zane's nape, fingers sliding into the base of his hair as their gazes met. "For all my arguing against love at first sight? For all my nervousness and fear?" Beckett leaned in, a welcoming wall of warmth at his front, and whispered in his ear. "You hooked me at *Toy Story*."

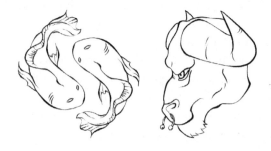

Reader, I married him.

—Charlotte Brontë

Acknowledgments

To my hubby: thank you, thank you, thank you. You are my rock and inspiration for romance.

Vir. My cheerleader. Thanks for all the motivational quotes and for listening to my incessant blabbering. You're one patient Aries.

Sunne. Always so sunny and ready to help. Thank God for your eye for detail and telling me how things are. I thought of you every step of the way with this one—you are such a Taurus, and I wanted this to be perfect for you.

Another crazy big thanks to Teresa Crawford, who, among other excellent edits, caught my love of the word pinch.

Cheers so much to Hot Tree Editing—Andrea, Bec, and Olivia—for working through a pre-beta and development edit with me.

Thanks to HJS Editing for copyediting—it's amazing how much you can cut and sharpen the narrative. You have magic fingers!

Awesome thanks to Posy at Labyrinth Bound Edits for your thorough proofreading.

Cheers to Natasha Snow for the cover art! Seriously, I love getting your covers in my inbox.

For beautiful chapter graphics of Pisces and Taurus, thanks go out to Maria Gandolfo.

Another thanks to Meags for sensitivity reading (love Australians xx), and to Andrew for helping me out with graphic art references.

And a final thanks to Vicki for being my final-eyes reader! <3

Anyta Sunday

HEART-STOPPING SLOW BURN

A bit about me: I'm a big, BIG fan of slow-burn romances. I love to read and write stories with characters who slowly fall in love.

Some of my favorite tropes to read and write are: Enemies to Lovers, Friends to Lovers, Clueless Guys, Bisexual, Pansexual, Demisexual, Oblivious MCs, Everyone (Else) Can See It, Slow Burn, Love Has No Boundaries.

I write a variety of stories, Contemporary MM Romances with a good dollop of angst, Contemporary lighthearted MM Romances, and even a splash of fantasy.
My books have been translated into German, Italian, French, Spanish, and Thai.

Contact: http://www.anytasunday.com/about-anyta/
Sign up for Anyta's newsletter and receive a free e-book:
http://www.anytasunday.com/newsletter-free-e-book/